Louise Cooper writes:

I first created Shar's world in my *Time Master* trilogy, and it has grown in my imagination ever since. But when I began Shar's story, I realised that although I had a 'feel' for her world, its landscape was still vague to me. I needed a reference, to make it more real.

It's lovely being married to an artist – especially one who draws beautiful maps! My husband, Cas, agreed to be 'Chart Master', and, feeling like intrepid travellers, we set out to explore this unknown territory. There were many new things to discover as the picture began to take form – and when the final map was complete, it was almost as if the world had taken on a life of its own.

Which perhaps, in a way, it has. Because I feel that I *know* Shar's land now, from its geography and history to its seasons and winds and tides. It helps me to believe that the worlds we invent *do* exist in a sense, and we can visit them in our minds, just as in the real world we take a holiday. So I hope you'll enjoy *your* holiday in Shar's world – and that you'll feel inspired to let your imagination roam, and make your own mark on its living, developing landscape.

THE DARK CALLER

LOUISE COOPER

Hodder Children's Books

a division of Hodder Headline

Copyright © 1997 Louise Cooper
Map Copyright © 1996 Clive Sandall

First published in Great Britain in 1997
by Hodder Children's Books

This Silver edition published in Great Britain in 2000
by Hodder Children's Books

The right of Louise Cooper to be identified as the Author
of the Work has been asserted by her in accordance with the
Copyright, Designs and Patents Act 1988.

10 9 8 7 6 5 4 3 2 1

A Catalogue record for this book is available from
the British Library

ISBN 0 340 77854 7

Typeset by Avon Dataset Ltd, Bidford-on-Avon, Warks

Printed and bound in Great Britain by
The Guernsey Press Co. Ltd, Channel Isles

Hodder Children's Books
A Division of Hodder Headline
338 Euston Road
London NW1 3BH

And speaking of cats . . . this is for white, deaf, sneezy Spike, who probably knows perfectly well that he's been used as a model in the story!

STAR PENINSULA

NORTHERN MOUNTAINS

FANAAN BAY

W. HIGH LAND PROVINCE

WESTERN SOUND

HAURIK

WESTER REACH

HAN PROVINCE

THE BRIG

CHAUN PROVINCE

CHAUN

NW NNW N NNE NE
WNW   ENE
W   E
WSW   ESE
SW SSW S SSE SE

S. CHAUN PROVINCE

SISTERHOOD COT

BYSSA

PROSPECT

C. A. SANDALL
© 15. X. '95 ©

KENNET HEAD

EMPTY PROVINCE

SKAROCK

HAVENING

EAST HAN PROVINCE

WHITE SHOALS

MELLEAN

WISHET PROVINCE

PORT SUMMER

SHU PROVINCE

SHU~RHADEK

This Map
Compiled
in the
183rd Year
of the
AGE of EQUILIBRIUM
by the
Chart Master
to the
High Margrave
SUMMER ISLE

L.T. SHIP

WHITE ISLE

PROLOGUE

In a world far beyond our Earth, though not beyond our imagination, a great and ancient castle of black stone stands on a pinnacle of rock at the edge of the wild northern coast. The castle is home to the Circle, a company of sorcerers whose duty is to keep the balance – and the peace – between the gods of Order and Chaos and their human worshippers.

For the Circle adepts, magic and the supernatural are part of everyday life. They hone and develop their psychic powers, explore the astral planes, and work with elementals and other creatures of the supernatural realms. Their leader, known as the High Initiate, is one of the three rulers of the world, and to train as an adept under his benevolent eye is a great honour and privilege.

It had always been Shar Tilmer's dearest ambition to become a Circle adept, and to follow in the footsteps of her dead parents. She had thought that her dream would never be fulfilled – until she made a terrifying discovery that led her to the castle, to a deadly plot, and to a breathtaking revelation about her own supernatural powers . . . a revelation in which the gods themselves took a hand.

The story of Shar's awakening has been told in *Daughter of Storms*. Now, her dream has come true, for she has been initiated into the Circle and begun a new life at the castle. She has made good friends, she has a promising future, and she is happy. The horrors of her experiences are behind her; there is no more danger either to her or to the people she loves.

Or so she believes. But evil, whether human or supernatural, is not easily conquered. Shar's deeds and special talents have made her the centre of great attention.

And in that may lie another kind of menace . . .

ONE

The woman was beckoning to her, and calling her name. Shar Tillmer knew she was dreaming, and the dream had recurred so many times that it was now horribly familiar. In the fog that shrouded them both – there was *always* fog – the woman was vague and ghost-like, and when Shar tried to run towards her, her feet became like stone. Every step was a terrible effort. Shar couldn't get any closer. Yet the mysterious, veiled figure kept calling urgently, 'Shar . . . come to me, Shar . . . come to me!'

Almost sobbing with frustration, Shar tried to call on the training that the Circle had instilled in her over the past few months. But she was only a first-rank initiate. She always knew when she was dreaming, but couldn't yet exert any willpower over the events or beings in her dreams. They simply carried her along, willy-nilly, and she couldn't control them. Yet this was no ordinary vision. It *meant* something.

Then, as it did each time, the fog started to become darker and denser. Shar could no longer see the woman, and could no longer hear her calling. Struggling with a throat and tongue that didn't want to obey her, she suddenly found her own voice.

'I know you, but I don't know *who* you are! Please, oh please, tell me your name!'

A cry echoed back to her through the fog, like the desolate call of a seabird. But there were no words. Everything was fading, fading . . .

With a jolt, Shar woke in her own bedroom in the castle of the Star Peninsula.

She sat up, shaking her head violently as the fragments of the dream shattered and vanished. Then, blinking, she opened her eyes. Morning light was coming in through her window as the sun rose above the castle's towering black walls. On the bedcover her ginger cat, Amber, mewed and stretched as her sudden movement disturbed his sleep.

'Amber . . .' Shar reached out and hugged the cat to her. She could feel her pulse racing, and there was perspiration on her forehead. 'Did you feel anything before I woke, Amber? *Did* you?'

Amber only yawned, suggesting that his telepathic senses had picked up nothing untoward, and Shar sighed with frustration. The same dream yet again, and still she was no closer to unravelling its mystery. Somehow, though, she felt that she knew the woman, and the feeling gave rise to an eerie intuition. She hardly dared acknowledge it. But at the same time she couldn't shake it off.

The dead could not come back, everyone knew that. Their souls were in the gods' keeping and never returned to the mortal world. Yet lodged within Shar – refusing to be ignored – was a powerful suspicion that the woman haunting her dream was her mother. Giria Tillmer Starnor had died fifteen years ago – or so everyone believed. Though her body had never been found . . .

Shar had been no more than a baby when Giria had supposedly jumped to her death from the towering rock stack on which the castle was built. She had no memories of her mother, and the only portrait she had ever seen was a sketch in the castle's library archives. Yet despite this, and the fact that the figure in her dream was always veiled, Shar knew instinctively that there was a connection.

She hadn't told her tutors. She was instructed to record all strange dreams and discuss them as part of her training. But in this case she had disobeyed. Her teachers would be sure to have another explanation, and deep down Shar wanted to believe that the mother she had never known *was* reaching out to her.

She sighed again, pushed her thoughts away and got out of bed. It must be nearly breakfast time, and Hestor and Kitto, her two closest friends in the castle, would be waiting for her in the dining-hall. Two daunting events lay in store for her today. One she greatly looked forward to; the other she dreaded, and could feel her cheeks prickling with embarrassment even as she thought about it. But it couldn't be avoided. Best, Shar told herself, to face it as cheerfully as she could.

She went to her wash-stand, poured water from the jug into the basin, and started to prepare for the day ahead.

The dining-hall was, in effect, the 'heart' of the castle. Huge and imposing with its vast fireplace, curtained musicians' gallery and rows of tall, arched windows, it was crowded when Shar arrived. Servants were already scurrying to take and serve breakfast orders.

Hestor and Kitto had found a table near the doors, and as Shar entered, Kitto beckoned eagerly. 'Where have you been? I'm starving!'

Kitto was always hungry; a result, Shar suspected, of the life he had led, before the momentous events of the early summer had brought them both to the castle. He had been raised by a band of brigands, whose leader might have been his father, and who had ill-treated him. Thin, ragged, and with the weals of frequent beatings on his back, he had grasped with both hands at the chance of a new life on meeting Hestor and Shar. Like Shar he had settled happily at the castle. He was even learning to read and write, and though he would never aspire to be a Circle initiate, a strong friendship had grown between him, Hestor and Shar.

Hestor Ennas moved over to make room on the bench for Shar, and Kitto greeted her with a grin adding, 'How's the heroine this morning?'

Shar groaned, and Hestor replied, 'Shut up, Kitto. She feels nervous enough already.'

'Well, I can't see why. All that attention – I'd revel in it! Anyway, there's nothing she can do to stop it.'

'I know,' Shar said ruefully, 'but that doesn't mean I have to like it. Honestly, it's *awful* being a heroine. Particularly when I haven't really done anything to deserve it.'

Hestor chuckled. 'If you think that, you must be the

only person in the castle who does. Probably in the world, for that matter.'

'Don't!' Shar grimaced. 'I already feel as if half the world's come here just to look at me.'

'They probably have. "The girl who stood up to a demonic attack, and saved the High Initiate's life into the bargain". You're a celebrity, Shar!'

'Well, I wish I wasn't.' Shar looked surreptitiously around the hall. There were a great many strangers here, visitors who had come for the autumn Quarter-Day celebrations, and they all seemed to be staring at her. Some of them smiled, and Shar blushed and looked quickly out of the nearest window. Outside, the courtyard was hectic with activity as the last touches were put to the decorations. The three-day festivities would begin tonight, with a great banquet attended by distinguished guests from all the ten provinces. Shar would be the focus of their attention, and to make matters worse she would be seated at the High Initiate's own table, in full view of everyone. This honour, admittedly, had nothing to do with her 'heroism' – she hated the word! – but it would still be acutely embarrassing.

A servant came to the table, and Hestor ordered breakfast for them all. When the woman had gone, he said, 'Never mind, Shar. You'll be wearing the grey sash by tonight, and then you can look down your nose at them all!'

He was referring to the other momentous event of the day – the reason why he and Shar were to be placed at the high table tonight. Traditionally, initiates who had completed a stage of their training were inducted into the next of the Circle's seven ranks on a quarter-day. Shar and Hestor had both passed their tests for second rank, and shortly before noon they were to join the other successful candidates in the eerie surroundings of the Marble Hall, deep under the castle's foundations. In the presence of the High Initiate, Neryon Voss, they would renew their Circle oaths and be formally welcomed, in the names of the fourteen gods, to their new rank.

Very few initiates reached second rank after only a few months' training. But there were good reasons why Shar had made such rapid progress in her magical studies. She was special. The Circle knew it, and she knew it too, though it still made her feel uncomfortable. Born under two rare signs: a supernatural Warp storm, and a double eclipse of the two moons. She was a Daughter of Storms, and a Dark-Caller – born with an intuitive link to the beings of the higher elemental planes, which owed no allegiance to anyone. Her powers were the reason for her fame – but their awakening had almost killed her, and she still felt the after-effects now, mostly in the form of hideous nightmares in which the monstrous forces of the Sixth Plane rose to menace her once more. The High Initiate believed that as her training continued she would learn to control and counter those nightmares. But the High Initiate didn't know about the other dream . . .

Kitto saw her sudden frown and said, 'Come on, Shar, cheer up! If I was famous, I'd enjoy every minute while I could! You know what people are like; the novelty will wear off soon enough, and then you'll just be a plain old junior initiate.'

'Laden down with work,' Hestor added, pulling a face. 'Everyone says second-rank studies are some of the hardest of all, so there won't be time to think about much else.'

For some reason, the thought of that broke Shar's dark mood. 'All right, I admit defeat!' She grinned. 'I'll cheer up. Promise!'

By mid-afternoon, Shar, along with everyone else in the castle, was in the thick of the revels.

The ceremony in the Marble Hall had been very low-key. She, Hestor and four others had solemnly made their pledges, then Neryon Voss, stern and splendid in his ceremonial robes, had placed the grey sashes over their shoulders. In the names of Lord Yandros of Chaos and Lord Aeoris of Order, he declared them Second-Rank Adepts of the Circle. There was no magical ritual, no calling up of power. It was simply a formality, and when it was done they all made their bows to the seven statues of the gods, then turned and filed out of the Hall, leaving its drifting pastel mists and its whispering echoes to return to the bright bustle of the outside world.

Shar felt strangely subdued when it was over, which was, perhaps, why she threw herself into the revels with a sudden burst of energy and enthusiasm. The weather was glorious, as early autumn often was here in the north, and banners, streamers and garlands festooned the castle's ancient black walls, giving the place a cheerful, festive air.

Music played, people mingled and talked and laughed, and outside on the greensward, between the castle gates and the rock bridge that joined the stack to the mainland, there were even some traders plying their wares to the wealthy visitors.

Kitto was helping the castle grooms to look after newly arrived horses, so Shar and Hestor explored the courtyard and the sward. But before long, Shar began to feel like a market sideshow herself. The whole world knew of her exploits, and to make matters worse they also knew her face. Drawings of her had been circulated through all ten provinces as her story spread. She was a celebrity, and she simply couldn't stay out of the limelight.

At first, people simply looked and pointed. But then they started to approach her, introducing themselves, paying her compliments and asking questions. Shar protested that she really didn't deserve all this attention, but it seemed that nothing could discourage her admirers, and at last, when no one else was in earshot, she turned to Hestor.

'I can't take much more of this!'

'Why don't you go to your room for a while?' Hestor suggested sympathetically. 'No one will disturb you there, and when Kitto finishes work we'll both come and find you.'

From the corner of her eye Shar saw yet another stranger coming towards them, a beaming smile on his face. 'Yes,' she said. 'I think I will.' She grinned faintly. 'Sorry, Hestor – you'll just have to enjoy the fun without me for a while!'

She hurried away, entered the castle through the double doors and crossed the entrance hall. On the main staircase she met several people coming down, but to her relief no one spoke to her – until, as she neared the top, a voice behind her said, 'Excuse me.'

Shar stopped and turned, to find herself looking into the brown eyes of a tall young man.

'Please pardon the intrusion,' he went on, 'but are you Shar Tillmer?'

Not another one, Shar thought, her spirits sinking. Reluctantly she replied, 'Yes, I am.'

To her surprise the young man didn't launch into a stream of compliments but only bowed rather formally, and said, 'My name is Reyni Trevire. I'm a musician.'

'Oh. Are you?' Shar looked blank, and Reyni laughed. 'Don't worry, you won't have heard of me,' he told her. 'I've just won my Mastership from the Musicians' Guild. I was a pupil of the composer who wrote the ballad in your honour.'

'Oh . . .' said Shar again.

'In fact,' Reyni went on, sounding just a little sheepish now, 'I'm to perform the song tonight, at the High Initiate's banquet.' He saw her expression and gave her a wry smile. 'I hope you don't mind *too* much!'

Shar realised he was teasing very gently, and her defences went down. She liked Reyni. He was natural and open and, quite simply, friendly. The fact that he was handsome, with his warm eyes and his dark, curling hair, hadn't escaped her either.

She laughed and said, 'Of course I don't mind. In fact I'm flattered.'

'You haven't heard my playing yet! But seriously, Shar – may I have your permission to call you Shar?'

'Of course.'

He nodded thanks. 'It was very impudent of me to approach you out of nowhere like this, but . . .' He hesitated, and in that moment a strange, queasy feeling of premonition lurched in Shar's stomach. She'd had such feelings before and knew better than to ignore them. Suddenly she was alert.

'The truth is,' Reyni continued, lowering his voice almost to a whisper, 'I had a reason for wanting to speak to you privately. I have a message for you.'

She frowned. 'A message?'

'Yes. I came by ship to Wester Reach, and while I was there, someone approached me. I don't know who she was, or how she knew I was coming to the castle, but she gave me a letter and asked me to deliver it directly into your hands.'

The queasiness tightened into a hard knot, and Shar felt her pulse quicken. 'What was her name?' she asked urgently. 'What did she look like?'

But Reyni shook his head. 'She didn't tell me her name, and I couldn't see her face clearly. She was wearing a veil.'

Shar's heart almost stopped beating. It couldn't be a coincidence. It *couldn't*.

'She would only tell me two things,' Reyni continued. 'One, that the letter is vitally important, and two, that I was to give it to you when no one else was around. So when I saw you just now, I thought—'

Before he could say any more, a voice below them called, 'Shar?' and, looking over the banisters, Shar saw Hestor staring at Reyni with a mixture of surprise and hostility.

Shar turned hastily to the musician. 'That's Hestor – he's a friend of mine.'

Hestor was starting to climb the stairs towards them. 'I'll try to find you later,' Reyni said in an undertone.

'Yes, this evening – perhaps at the banquet—' Shar was frustrated at having to delay. But, for reasons which she couldn't fathom, she did not want Hestor to know about this.

With a conspiratorial nod, Reyni hurried on up the stairs. Hestor reached Shar seconds later, and stared after the musician. 'Who was that?' he demanded.

His tone and manner oozed suspicion, making Shar feel irrationally resentful. 'His name's Reyni,' she replied. 'He's a musician.'

'Oh, is he?' Hestor said ominously. Then, 'What were you saying to him about the banquet tonight?'

Hestor was jealous, Shar realised, and she wanted to laugh. But she didn't. Instead, she retorted, 'If you really want to know, Hestor, he's to play my ballad at the entertainment.' She stared at him for a moment, then with a spark of sheer devilishness added, 'I'm greatly looking forward to hearing him.'

'I *see.*'

He didn't; in fact he had completely the wrong idea.

But Shar wanted to annoy him. She didn't know why, and it was quite out of character; but at this moment she didn't care.

'I'm going to my room,' she said airily. 'I'll see you later, Hestor. Maybe.'

She walked away up the stairs, leaving Hestor, baffled and angry, blinking after her.

TWO

The banquet was less of an ordeal than Shar had feared. The High Initiate, Neryon Voss, had never been a great one for formal ceremony, and the atmosphere in the dining-hall was relaxed and festive. Despite her misgivings, Shar soon began to enjoy herself.

To her relief, she had not been placed next to Hestor at the table. Their paths had crossed once or twice since the encounter on the stairs, but they hadn't spoken to each other. Shar knew that Hestor was still bristling about Reyni Trevire, but saw no reason why she should be the one to pour oil on troubled waters. If he chose to misinterpret what he had seen, she thought, that was his problem and not hers. Besides, she had other concerns. She couldn't stop thinking about the mysterious letter.

When the splendid meal ended, it was time for the entertainment to begin. Shar looked eagerly for Reyni, but as yet she couldn't see him. The first item was to be a performance by a choir from Wester Reach, the province capital. Shar was surprised and intrigued by their appearance. They wore extraordinary costumes – almost uniforms, for each one was identical – of dark blue linen emblazoned with white zig-zag patterns like lightning flashes. Both men and women alike had hair cut short to the ears, and narrow bands of gold fabric were tied around their brows.

'They call themselves the Keepers of Light,' a third-rank adept sitting near Shar told her. 'They're a religious sect devoted to the gods of Order – eccentric, but harmless. Apparently their choir is excellent and they're greatly in demand.'

That, as Shar soon heard for herself, was true. The applause at the end of each song the choir sang was tremendous, and when they finished, Neryon rose from his seat to thank them personally. The choir leader, a fair-haired man with kindly eyes and a gentle smile, bowed graciously. Then the whole troupe filed to the back of the hall, where they sat down in a neat row. Shar continued to watch them idly for a few moments, until the third-rank adept nudged her elbow, 'Look who's next, Shar,' he said. 'Your great moment's approaching!'

Shar blinked, and saw that Reyni Trevire had taken the place vacated by the choir. Her cheeks reddened as Reyni caught her eye and bowed slightly, and the adept chuckled at her reaction.

'You can't escape,' he told her. 'You'll just have to sit through it and be flattered!'

Further along the table Hestor, too, had seen Reyni bow to Shar, and scowled. Shar felt momentarily uncomfortable, but pushed the feeling away as Reyni settled his manzon – a long-necked, seven-stringed instrument – across his knee and struck a chord.

He began with a well-known ballad. He was a fine musician and had a very good voice, but Shar was by now too keyed-up to enjoy his singing. When the ballad ended Reyni sang another popular song, then as the applause died away he looked directly at Shar again.

'Thank you, ladies and gentlemen,' he said. 'And now I would like to sing a song composed by my own Guild teaching master, written to commemorate an act of heroism which will be recorded forever in our history. It is dedicated to a young lady who is present tonight—' he gestured courteously towards the high table '– and its title is "Dark into Light".'

Hot with embarrassment, Shar tried not to squirm on her chair as Reyni began to play. She had heard the song before, but never at a public recital. As it continued she wished she could slip under the table and hide until it was over.

When the song did finally end the applause seemed to go on for ever. People were smiling in Shar's direction, and to her horror some of the guests even began to call for her to take a bow. Reyni heard the calls, and suddenly he stood up and approached the table.

'Shar?' He extended a hand towards her, at the same time glancing at Neryon Voss for permission. Neryon grinned his approval, and Shar had no choice but to take Reyni's hand and step out. They bowed to the gathering together, and as they did so Reyni whispered from the corner of his mouth,

'I'm sorry I had to do this, Shar. But it was the only way I could think of.'

As he spoke, she felt him transfer something from his fingers into hers. It felt like a tightly folded piece of paper, and her pulse quickened.

'Hide it,' Reyni added. 'You can read it later, when you're alone.'

He released her hand, and hastily Shar pushed the paper into her sleeve. She walked back to her seat in a daze, oblivious to the attention being paid to her, oblivious to her dinner-companions' teasing jokes and to the resentful glare that Hestor was giving Reyni. The letter. She had the letter, and that was all that mattered.

Shar had no choice other than to stay in the hall, but as the evening went on her impatience grew, until she could have screamed. At long last, though, the entertainment was over and the first guests started to excuse themselves and leave. Snatching a chance, Shar made her excuses and fled, ignoring Hestor when he called after her. Out of the hall and up the main staircase she ran, heading for the privacy of her own room. Several cats saw her as she went. Since she'd been very small, cats had been attracted to her like bees to a flower; the castle's large colony was no exception, and by the time she reached her room she had a tail of five following her. They slipped in through her door before she slammed it behind her, and jumped onto the bed, where Amber was already sitting. Six whiskered faces watched intently as she fumbled to light a lamp, and she felt eager curiosity radiating from their telepathic minds.

For once, though, Shar took no notice. She was far too preoccupied, and her hands shook as she broke the seal on the letter and unfolded it. The writing was unfamiliar, and before reading so much as a single word she turned the paper over, looking for a signature.

It was then that she felt as if the ground had suddenly collapsed beneath her. For the name at the end of the letter was her mother's.

My beloved daughter, it began. I know it will come as a great shock to you to receive this, for you have always been led to believe that I was dead. That lie was the least of the evils done to our family by your father's brother – Thel Starnor, and because of his evil, it is only now that I am free to find you and tell you the whole truth.

You and the world now know that Thel murdered your father in order to gain control of you and the special powers that the gods have granted to you. Everyone believes that I took my own life after your father's death, but the truth is that Thel abducted me – perhaps even he could not stomach the idea of killing a woman – and for more years than I can bear to remember he kept me a prisoner in a remote district in Empty Province. With his downfall I was set free, but for a long time afterwards I was gravely ill. Only now, on my recovery, have I learned of what took place at the castle, and of your part in it.

Shar, my dearest child, you will wonder why I have not simply travelled to the Star Peninsula to find you. I cannot – in truth, I dare not. For you and I are both still in danger. The nature of that danger, and how I know of it, are matters which I dare not explain in this letter. All I can say is that the risk we would run by meeting at the castle is too great to be taken. But it is vital that we do meet, and quickly. Only then can I explain all, and help you to avert this new peril. Please, Shar, please trust me. This message is not a deception.

17

I am who I say I am, and can prove that to you if you will only give me the chance. You must come to Wester Reach. I have friends here who can ensure our safety, and if you go to the Bronze Bell Tavern, they will find you and bring you to me.

Please, please come. It may mean the difference between life and death for us both . . . something that, perhaps, your dreams have already told you. Tell no one of this letter, or of your plans — secrecy is vital. I shall wait eagerly.

With my enduring love, and my heartfelt prayers for your safe arrival,

Your mother, Giria Tillmer Starnor

The letter fluttered from Shar's hand to the floor and she stared blindly at the glowing lamp. She felt sick with shock. Could this *possibly* be genuine? Shar so desperately wanted to believe it was, yet she was horribly aware that someone could be trying to dupe her. Neryon Voss had cautioned her to be wary; one group of evil-doers had already tried to use her powers, and others might have similar ideas. Hestor's mother, Pellis, who was a fifth-rank adept, had also warned her against false friends. This message could easily be a trap set to lure her into danger.

Or it could truly be a warning that she was in peril of another kind. And the last few words contained the key.

Shar picked up the letter again. Yes, there was the vital clue, the one thing that made the whole message ring true . . . *something that, perhaps, your dreams have already told you . . .*

Whoever had written this must know about her

strange nightmare. Her mother had been a Circle adept in her own right, and one of the skills learned by higher adepts was the sending of true dreams to those with whom they had a personal bond. What greater bond could there be, Shar asked herself, than that between mother and daughter?

She made her decision in that moment. The letter might be genuine or it might not, but unless she followed it through, she would never be certain. She *had* to go to Wester Reach. And somehow, she had to find a way to get there alone.

The sick feeling was fading now, and Shar's mind was suddenly crystal clear. She would be a fool, of course, if she simply went off on this mission without taking what precautions she could. She had a special rapport with the dwellers on the four lower elemental planes; the beings of earth, air, water and fire. They were always willing to help her, and a little scrying might tell her if there was danger in the wind.

The cats watched with interest as she carefully locked her door and fetched from her linen chest a small, carved wooden box. Every Circle initiate had such a box, in which they kept their personal implements for magical work, and though Shar's collection was small as yet, it was enough for her purpose.

The water elementals were the best scryers, so Shar took from her box a small silver bowl and a phial containing an oil scented with the essence of a sea plant. She doused the lamp, for the water beings did not like fire of any kind, then, when her eyes were used to the gloom, she poured some water from her jug into the bowl and sat cross-legged on the floor before it. She focused her mind as her tutors had taught her, and started to murmur a chant, at the same time willing the elementals to hear and come to her.

A cool, silvery sensation flowed over her, and there was a faint sound like rain pattering. Shar smiled, unstoppered the phial and let a few drops of oil fall from it into the bowl. For a moment a ripple clouded the water – then, as the two liquids blended, pictures began to form on the bowl's surface. First there were fleeting shapes like tiny, glinting fish; a sure sign that her friends had answered her call. Then came other images. Shar saw an indistinct figure, who seemed to be walking by the edge of the sea; it faded quickly, and was replaced by a picture of two hands holding something, though it was impossible to tell what. The hands vanished; lightning seemed to flicker silently across the water's surface, and then came an image of a strange, stark building which she did not recognise. Other shapes and pictures followed, but they were cryptic and confusing and Shar could make no sense of them.

Finally there were no more pictures, and with a shiver Shar came out of her trance. Delicate patterns of light were dancing on the room's walls and ceiling, and she could hear the water elementals' voices, thin and sweet and rippling, as they called to her and to each other. She sighed. The creatures had done their best, but if the images they had shown her had any meaning, it was beyond her ability to understand.

She got to her feet, courteously and solemnly thanked the elementals and gave them leave to return to their own world. The water in the bowl agitated briefly then was still, and the patterns faded from the walls. On the bed, Amber made a chirruping noise and Shar felt his mind projecting sympathy. She smiled wryly and said, 'Thank you, Amber. But it was probably foolish of me to try at all. Nothing's clear, not yet, and the elementals simply couldn't help.'

Amber chirruped again, as though agreeing, and the other five cats jumped down to the floor and rubbed themselves around Shar's legs. From the great hall below, Shar could hear strains of dance music, and she sighed again. She really ought to return to the celebration, but she hadn't the heart for it now. She wanted to be alone. No one in the hall would really miss her, except for Kitto and, perhaps, Hestor. She had promised Kitto a dance, but she could apologise to him tomorrow. She wanted to think. She *needed* to think.

The visiting cats picked up the drift of her thoughts and trotted to the door. Shar let them out, then changed into her nightgown and got into bed. Amber settled beside her, purring, and she leaned back against the pillows, trying to make herself relax. She doubted if she would sleep tonight. But tomorrow . . . tomorrow, she would make her plans. And she was determined that nothing and no one would stand in her way.

Shar did fall asleep eventually. In the hall Hestor and Kitto had been debating whether or not to look for her, but by the time they had decided that they should go to her room it was so late that they didn't like to disturb her. So she was left alone . . . and only Amber witnessed what took place an hour before dawn.

The cat knew Shar was dreaming, for he could sense the vague shiftings of her sleeping mind. So he was doubly surprised when, without warning, she suddenly sat bolt upright and then climbed out of bed. Amber mewed a question but Shar did not respond. Instead, she walked slowly but resolutely towards the door, opened it and disappeared into the passage.

Amber's ears flicked with puzzlement. Shar had left the door standing wide open, and after a moment's hesitation he sprang down and hurried after her. He was in time to see her heading towards the main stairs, and abruptly he felt uneasy. What was she doing? He could pick up no messages at all from her mind now; it was completely closed to him. But he knew with his animal senses that something was wrong.

He looked wide-eyed to left and right along the corridor. All the castle's human inhabitants were asleep and there was no sign of anyone. Uttering a small, worried growl deep in his throat, the cat hurried away after Shar.

The castle's main doors were never bolted, so it was easy for Shar to pull them open and go outside. The first moon had set, but the second was still in the sky and silver light washed the courtyard, giving it an eerie, unreal air. Shar was unaware of it, and unaware of the several pairs of almond-shaped eyes that watched her as she walked past the fountain and towards the gates. Amber's unease had alerted the other castle cats, and as Shar neared the gates the little creatures began to gather from ledges and rooftops and doorways. Amber, by now following at Shar's heels, was growing more troubled with every moment. He had never known his human friend behave like this before. Something was *definitely* amiss.

The gates stood open. Shar walked, without pausing, under the black stone arch of the barbican, and emerged on to the top of the rock stack that towered giddyingly above the sea. Tonight the sea's sound was no more than a gentle hiss, but even so there was something threatening and dangerous about it. The wind murmured ominously, lifting Shar's auburn hair back from her face, and the skirt of her nightgown fluttered and tugged around her. Amber thought at first that she was going towards the narrow bridge that separated the stack from the mainland, but quickly realised that he was wrong. Shar wasn't going anywhere near the bridge. Instead, she was heading straight towards the stack's edge, and the lethal drop to the churning tide far below.

Amber's eyes widened in alarm and he yowled, an alert and a warning to the other cats who were now watching curiously from the gateway. As he gave the cry, there was a disturbance in the air above Shar and a cloud of tiny, flittering shapes appeared. Elementals – her friends from the air and fire planes – diving and darting around her head and giving voice to a shrill, agitated chorus. Oblivious to them all, Shar walked steadily on.

Amber didn't pause. He turned tail and, ears flattened

and tail bristling, bolted back towards the castle, with the other cats flowing like a small tide in his wake.

24

THREE

Hestor jolted out of sleep with a yelp as a small, solid weight jumped from the ledge of the open window and landed squarely on his chest. He shot upright in bed, to find himself staring in the pre-dawn gloom into a furry, agitated face.

Amber saw he was awake, and howled. Hestor had never heard any cat make such a sound before and it horrified him. 'Amber!' he said. 'What is it, what's wrong?'

Amber leaped off the bed, ran to the door and howled again. Hestor wasn't good at communicating with cats, but nonetheless a jumbled picture formed in his mind. Open sky, a figure in a nightgown, *danger*—

He scrambled for his clothes and was at the door in seconds. Amber raced out, and as Hestor followed he heard an extraordinary noise. More cats – a great number by the sound of it – miaowing and yowling somewhere below. He ran towards the main staircase, and as he reached it he saw them milling in the hall, tails lashing, heads back and mouths wide as they called their distress.

Hestor pounded down the stairs. He was halfway down when yet more cats came streaking into view – and on their heels was the High Initiate.

'Hestor?' Neryon saw him. 'Do you know anything about this?'

'No, sir!' Hestor replied breathlessly. 'Amber woke me, but I don't know what's amiss!'

More people were appearing, roused by the cats' din. Among them were Eln Chandor, the castle's new senior physician, and Kitto.

'Hestor, sir!' Kitto called. 'I know what's frightened them! It's Shar! There's something wrong!'

The physician said, 'The doors are open.'

'Come on.' Neryon started across the hall, beckoning to them all. 'Hurry!'

With the cats streaming ahead of them, they all ran out into the courtyard. Amber shot like an arrow towards the gates; they followed, and Kitto, who was a fast runner, reached the stack first. As the others caught up they heard him shout. 'Oh, Yandros, *no!*' and they burst out from under the arch to be confronted with a horrifying sight.

Shar stood outlined against a sky turning blood red with the first light of dawn. A storm of elementals whirled above and around her, crying in shrill fear, but she was unaware of them; unaware of anything. Still sound asleep, she was swaying at the edge of the precipice.

Hestor screamed her name, and he and Kitto started to rush forward. But the High Initiate roared, '*No! Don't touch her!*' Neryon's face was white; he raised one hand, fingers extended and pointing towards Shar, uttered the first words of an invocation. The elementals shrieked in desperate encouragement; Shar swayed again, erratically – then Hestor felt a charge of sorcerous energy surge from Neryon. A gust of wind whipped out of the north; Shar's hair and skirt whirled as it snatched at her, then she stumbled backwards and collapsed to the ground.

Hestor and Kitto reached her together, with the High Initiate only a pace behind them. The elementals dived and swooped, hindering. With a sharp word, and tracing a symbol in the air, Neryon commanded them to be calm, and as they fell back he dropped to his knees and gathered Shar into his arms. Her mouth was slack, her eyes open but rolled up and showing only the whites. She didn't seem to be breathing.

'Take her legs,' Neryon ordered harshly. 'Move her to safety.'

The three of them lifted Shar and carried her well clear of the edge. Hestor glanced, once, over the brink, and his stomach lurched as he saw the tide surging and swirling far, far below. *If Shar had fallen* . . . He forced the hideous thought away. They laid her gently on the grass, and as the physician made to join them, Neryon said, 'Wait, Eln. There's more to this.'

He touched Shar's brow, then her mouth, and murmured three words. A peculiar, rattling moan came from Shar's lips but still she didn't breathe, and Neryon swore softly. 'She's in a trance,' he said grimly, 'and she didn't bring it on herself. Hestor, Kitto; keep out of my way.'

The boys fell back, and the elementals were abruptly silent as the High Initiate crouched over Shar. Hestor heard Neryon invoke the name of Yandros of Chaos and saw him make the sign of the seven-rayed star, Chaos's own symbol, above her heart. Then he tensed, concentrating his will and his power. Blue-white light

27

flickered momentarily around Shar – and with a great gasp she sucked air into her lungs and began to breathe again. Her eyelids fluttered, closed, opened once more, and recognition came to her face as she stared bewilderedly at the High Initiate.

'Shar.' Neryon spoke before she could, gently and reassuringly. 'It's all right; there's nothing to fear. You've had a small accident, that's all.' Glancing over his shoulder he beckoned to the physician. Eln hurried forward, and as he examined Shar, talking kindly to her all the while, Neryon moved back to where Hestor and Kitto stood.

'Can either of you shed any light on this?' he asked them sternly.

They both shook their heads and Hestor said, 'The first I knew about it was when Amber woke me and wanted me to follow him. He was projecting images, but I couldn't see them clearly.'

'Kitto?' Neryon turned to the other boy. 'You have a talent for communicating with cats. What did you pick up?'

Kitto looked miserable. 'There *were* pictures, sir, but they didn't make much sense.'

'Whether they did or didn't, what did you see?'

Kitto frowned, thinking hard. 'There was a storm . . . well, lightning, anyway . . . and then I saw someone holding something. I couldn't make out what it was but I got the feeling that it was important.'

'Who was holding it?'

'I don't know, sir. I just saw a dark figure. I think it was wearing a veil. And I felt sure that . . .' He hesitated, and

28

Neryon prompted, 'That what? Tell me – it might be important.'

'Well . . . it was as if Shar herself was dreaming these things, and the cats were trying to tell me about her dream. But I don't know why I thought that.'

'Possibly because it's the truth,' Neryon replied thoughtfully. 'All right. I'll talk to you both again later, but for now we'll take Shar into the castle, and you'd better go back to bed for an hour or two.'

'Sir, we won't sleep—' Hestor began to protest, but Neryon gave him a scorching look.

'Don't argue with me, Hestor. Just do as you're told.'

In other words, Hestor thought unhappily, the High Initiate wanted him and Kitto out of the way while this was investigated. Not for the first time he felt the frustration of being a junior initiate; but he also realised why Neryon was excluding him. This incident was too serious for anyone but the most senior adepts to be involved.

Physician Eln had gathered Shar into his arms and was ready to go. Shoulders drooping, Hestor said resignedly, 'Yes, sir,' and the small procession walked slowly back into the castle. There were more people gathered in the gateway now, but Neryon evaded their questions, saying only that there had been a 'small mishap'. Shar was carried away to the infirmary, Kitto disappeared reluctantly to his quarters and Hestor started up the stairs towards his own room. As he went, he looked back . . . and among the assembly in the hall he saw a face that caught his attention. That musician, Reyni something . . .

suddenly Hestor felt a prickle of suspicion. *What's he doing here?* he asked himself.

Reyni caught his eye at that moment. A flicker of recognition showed in his face, then he turned quickly away. Hestor frowned. Instinct was telling him that something was awry here, and he trusted his instinct. Especially where Shar was concerned.

Something brushed against his leg and he looked down to see Amber sitting at his feet. The cat was calm now, which told Hestor that Shar was in no danger. At least, no *immediate* danger. Pushing his fears and doubts away, he bent and stroked the little creature's head. 'Come on, Amber,' he said. 'They won't want you in the infirmary. You can come with me, and we'll see Shar later.'

Amber responded with a purr. Hestor looked down to the hall again, but Reyni had disappeared. Hestor paused a moment, then turned and continued to climb the stairs.

Shar fell groggily asleep in the infirmary. When she woke, halfway through the morning, she had no recollection at all of what had happened. She was surprised to find herself in Physician Eln's care, and horrified when she learned the details of her adventure. Neryon came to see her, and his questions alarmed her. Had she had any untoward dreams recently? he wanted to know. Had she been dreaming last night? Shar told him, truthfully, that she couldn't remember having had any dreams while she was sleepwalking. But she said nothing about her previous dream – and certainly nothing about the letter.

Shortly before noon, Neryon called Physician Eln and Pellis to his study.

'I don't mind admitting that I'm very concerned about this,' he told them. 'There's nothing physically wrong with Shar, but the trance she was in when we found her was no ordinary stupor. It took a lot of magical power to break it, which can only mean that it must have been induced from outside.'

Pellis, who had now heard the whole story, said, 'You mean that someone cast a spell on her?'

'That's exactly what I mean.' Neryon sighed. 'The question is, who?'

'What about Thel Starnor?' Eln asked uneasily. 'We all know how ruthlessly he tried to use Shar in the plot against you. Could he possibly be trying to reach out to the demonic planes again, and to reforge his link with Shar?'

Neryon shook his head. 'You know how thorough we were when we stripped Thel of his sorcerous abilities. He has no power now; he's safely imprisoned, and his fellow plotters are either locked up or dead. No, Eln, this is something else. It has to be.'

'Shar is very psychically sensitive,' Pellis said. 'If she was under a magical attack I'm sure she would detect it – especially now that she's being properly trained.'

'And she'd have told someone,' Eln added. 'You especially, Pellis – after all, she's looked on you as a second mother since she came here.'

Pellis laughed wryly. 'That's no guarantee of anything!

My own son doesn't confide in me half the time, so there's no reason why Shar should be any different.'

'Pellis is right,' said Neryon. 'So it may be that she *has* had some warning of this but, for reasons which we don't know, isn't willing to talk of it to anyone . . . or at least, to any adult.'

'Ah,' Eln said. 'You mean Hestor and that young rapscallion Kitto.'

'Precisely. Now, I realise there's no point in simply calling the boys here and demanding that they tell what they know. If they've been sworn to secrecy only the gods could make them break their word unless Shar was in real danger, and we can't yet start making assumptions like that. But I'd like you both – and you specifically, Pellis – to be alert for any sign that the three of them are hiding something. Don't watch them too closely; they might be young but they're not foolish, and we don't want to make our scrutiny obvious. Simply keep your eyes and ears open.'

'Should we alert the other senior adepts?' Eln asked.

'No, I think not.' Neryon hesitated, then: 'When Shar uncovered the plot against me, we found that I – and she – had enemies within these walls. I'm not suggesting that the same is true again. But I think it would be wise not to take any chances.'

The others were silent for a few moments. Then Pellis said, 'Yes, Neryon. I understand.' Her expression grew sombre. 'I only hope and pray this is a false alarm.'

'As do we all,' said the High Initiate grimly.

★　★　★

Yandros, highest lord of Chaos, made a slight gesture with one hand, and the small, shining ball of light that floated before him flared once and winked out of existence. His bony, aristocratic face thoughtful and his eyes – which constantly changed colour – narrowed, Yandros crossed the floor to where a tall window looked out over the shifting landscape of the Chaos realm.

'There's no doubt of it,' he said. 'Something's in the wind. And I don't like it.'

A vast comet hurtled across the flickering golden sky outside and vanished with a shriek into a bank of black and purple cloud that boiled on the horizon. It was a reflection of Yandros's mood, and his brother-god Tarod, who had joined him in the tower, watched him with sudden keen interest.

'Can you pinpoint the source of the trouble?' he asked.

Yandros shook his head. 'No. It would be useful, at times, if the absurd human notion that we can read mortal minds and hearts was true – but it isn't, as we both know only too well. I sense something amiss, and I suspect it concerns Shar Tillmer. But I don't know what it is or where it comes from.' His eyes turned from blue to black-flecked crimson. 'I think we should investigate.'

Tarod raised his eyebrows. 'And what about our pact?'

When the Age of Equilibrium had been established, the gods of both Chaos and Order had pledged not to interfere in mortal affairs. The truce had held, after a fashion, for two hundred years. But Yandros, unlike his old enemy Aeoris of Order, believed that rules were made for breaking, or at least bending. He smiled wolfishly. 'I only said "investigate", Tarod. That's not interference. Besides, we have good reason to take an interest in Shar. But for her, the Circle would now be under the control of a tyrant, and that wouldn't please Aeoris of Order any more than it would please us. So he'll have no reason to complain.'

Tarod laughed. 'I doubt if Aeoris will see it like that.'

'Oh, let him grumble to his heart's content, then; he can't do anything unless we actually *break* the pact, and I shan't go that far.' Yandros looked again at the view, decided he was bored with it and made another careless gesture. The window and the tower wall dissolved, the floor under their feet became transparent, and abruptly they were standing on a pinnacle of glass that towered miles above a surging black and silver sea. A flock of birds, like huge gulls but with delicate, cobweb-like wings, wheeled and swooped above them, singing an eerie chorus; over the sound of their voices Yandros added, 'I think a brief visit to the mortal world would be a good idea. I won't go in person; too many of the castle-dwellers would recognise me, and we need to be discreet.' He smiled slyly. 'You, however—'

'Ah,' said Tarod.

'I know, I know. Every time you set foot in the world of humans, there's trouble. And I'd remind you that it's usually you who causes it. However, you have more knowledge and more experience of mortals than our other brothers. You're the obvious choice.'

A gust of wind blew Tarod's black hair back from his face, and his emerald-green eyes regarded Yandros with a mixture of annoyance and amusement. 'All right. If I argue with you, I don't doubt you'll simply order me to go anyway, so I might as well save my breath. What do you want me to do?'

Yandros's smile broadened. 'Just see if you can find out what's afoot. Nothing more. And perhaps have a private word with a certain young man who has been helpful to us once before . . .'

FOUR

Shar was allowed to leave the infirmary later that morning. To stop any speculation, people had been told that her sleepwalking was the result of over-excitement and rich food. But Shar was well aware that Neryon Voss took the matter more seriously – and that presented her with a new problem.

She *had* to go to Wester Reach. The more she thought about the letter, the more determined she was to investigate. And in the wake of this horrifying incident, investigation was even more urgent. She had little doubt, now, that someone or something *was* trying to harm her, and even in the sanctuary of the castle she wasn't safe.

But getting away undetected would not be easy. Neryon would be watching her carefully from now on, and so would Pellis and probably Hestor and Kitto too. She would have to plan her moves very carefully. And her best hope, she decided, was Reyni Trevire.

Hestor and Kitto had been to see her. Neither she nor Hestor said anything about their rift; they had no real wish to quarrel. Shar set the seal on the reconciliation by promising to partner Hestor in the main dance set during the continuing celebrations tonight, and Hestor, relieved, was happy to pretend that the incident with Reyni had never taken place.

However, his relief didn't last for long. Reyni was in the hall that evening, and as soon as he saw the young musician Hestor again felt the instinctive prickle of mistrust in his mind. When Reyni asked Shar to dance, and Shar accepted, Hestor was annoyed . . . and by the time they had danced three sets together without pausing, he was downright angry. Being honest, he admitted to himself that he was jealous. But he also believed there was more to it than that.

'I don't like him and I don't trust him,' he said to Kitto as they stood at the side of the hall and watched Shar and Reyni among the whirling couples. 'Look at the way he's smiling at her. He's *too* friendly, *too* charming. It doesn't ring true.'

Privately Kitto couldn't see anything particularly suspect about Reyni, but, tactfully, he didn't say so.

'Shar keeps whispering to him,' Hestor went on. 'She hardly knows him, so how can she have so much to say?'

Kitto shook his head. 'Your guess is as good as mine; probably better.' He hesitated. 'Shar's been behaving strangely all day, though, have you noticed? As if she's got something on her mind — and not just what happened last night.'

'Mmm.' Hestor considered that. 'You're right, Kitto. In fact it began yesterday, before the banquet. She's become very secretive all of a sudden, and I don't know why.'

'She's hiding something from us,' Kitto declared.

'I think so, too. But what?'

Kitto hunched his shoulders. 'The only way to find

out is to tackle her directly,' he said. 'Though whether it'll do any good . . .'

In Shar's present mood, Hestor thought, it was unlikely that she would take kindly to any probing. But after what had happened last night, he had no intention of letting her attitude put him off.

'I'll try to get her alone,' he said. 'She can't dance with that musician all night; later, when he's out of the way, I'll talk to her. And I'll get some answers.'

Shar, meanwhile, was making cautious but steady progress with her plans.

When Reyni had asked her to dance she'd been delighted. It was the chance she had been hoping for, to get his full and undivided attention without anyone else overhearing what she had to say. While they danced she had asked some seemingly casual questions about his plans, and now, as the third dance set came to an end, she had the information she needed and was ready to make her approach.

Reyni, she had discovered, was leaving the castle at dawn tomorrow. He would return to Wester Reach, stay a few days in the town and then take passage on a ship to his home in Prospect. Shar intended to go with him. She would use any and every means to persuade him to agree; she would charm, she would cajole, she would pay money, she would even blackmail him if she could. Somehow, she would make him take her to Wester Reach.

The set ended. They bowed to each other, then Shar made a show of fanning herself and said that she was thirsty. Could they perhaps have some wine? Reyni agreed, and as they walked to the tables where food and drink were set out she said, 'Reyni, there's something I need to ask you. It's about the letter you delivered to me.'

'The letter?' Reyni was looking at the wine flagons and not really listening. 'Would you like white or red?'

'Oh . . . white, please. Reyni, this is important!'

Flagon in hand, Reyni paused and frowned slightly as her desperate tone registered. 'What is it, Shar? Is something wrong?'

'Not wrong exactly, but . . . I need to ask you a great favour.'

He looked suddenly wary. 'What is it?'

Shar glanced around. No one else was in earshot, so, drawing a deep breath, she told him. Not the details, but only that it was vital she went to Wester Reach. She couldn't make the journey alone, she added, and would be eternally in his debt if he would agree to escort her. Reyni listened to her plea in silence, then when she had finished and looked hopefully at him, he said.

'If the High Initiate has given you permission to go, then surely he'll provide a Circle escort for you?'

Shar flushed. 'Well,' she said, 'you see . . . the thing is . . .'

'You mean he hasn't given you permission?'

She bit her lip, and he saw the answer in her face without any need for words. There was a pause. Then Reyni said, in an utterly different tone,

'Whatever else I may be, Shar, I'm not a complete fool.'

She stared at him. 'What?'

'You heard me. I'm sorry to have to say it so harshly, but my answer is an absolute no, and anyone with a grain of sense would say the same.'

'But—' she began.

'*No*, Shar.' Reyni shook his head firmly. 'If you haven't been given permission to go, then it's out of the question for me to take you. You're a ward of the Circle, and I'd be defying their authority. At the very least I could be arrested for abduction. Besides, I'm going on to Prospect, so who would look after you when I've gone?'

'I can look after myself,' Shar declared.

'You obviously don't know Wester Reach, or you wouldn't say that! It's no place for any girl on her own; it's rough at best, and at worst it can be downright dangerous. I'm sorry, Shar. I simply won't do it.'

Shar argued with him, she pleaded with him, but nothing she could say made any difference. Reyni would not take her to Wester Reach and that was that. At last, defeated, she said stiffly that she had had enough of the revels and was going to bed. Reyni tried to cheer her up a little, asking her to dance again, but she refused. What was the point? she said resentfully, and walked away, leaving him standing by the table.

As she crossed the hall towards the doors Shar seethed with anger. Much of it was directed at Reyni, but a good deal was also directed at herself. That last little retort had been petty and uncalled for; she must have seemed to him like a child being peevish because she couldn't get her own way. But when she looked over her shoulder she saw that it was too late to go back and apologise. Reyni was already talking to another, older girl and didn't even glance in Shar's direction. She had lost her chance and wouldn't get another.

Ruffled and miserable, she had nearly reached the doors when someone moved across her path.

'Shar,' said Hestor. 'I need to talk to you.'

Shar looked at him, and her anger abruptly found a new focus. 'I don't want to talk,' she said belligerently. 'I'm tired, and I'm going to bed.'

Hestor didn't move out of her way. 'This won't take long,' he said. 'I want an answer, Shar. Something's wrong with you – I know it is, and I also know you're deliberately hiding it from me.'

Shar continued to stare at him. 'Don't be stupid.'

'I'm not being stupid! I know you too well to be fooled. Shar, what *is* it? If you're in some kind of trouble, then in the names of all the fourteen gods, why won't you tell me about it? I'm your friend – or have you forgotten that, now that you've got someone else to distract you?'

Kitto, who was standing in the background but close enough to hear, shut his eyes and winced. Hestor had resolved to be tactful, but in his resentment of Reyni his tongue had run away with him, and it was the worst mistake he could have made. Shar's hazel eyes narrowed, and her mouth set in a tight, almost vicious line.

'How I choose to distract myself is none of your business, Hestor Ennas!' she retorted savagely. 'You're not my guardian, and if you think I'm going to answer any of your meddlesome, arrogant questions, you can go to the Seven Hells! Get out of my sight, Hestor, and stay away from me!' And she pushed roughly past him and strode out of the hall.

'Shar!' Hestor would have started furiously after her, but Kitto ran up to him and grabbed his arm. 'Leave it, Hestor! It won't do any good, not while she's in this mood.'

Hestor was breathing rapidly. 'Who does she think she is? Talking to me as if I was dust under her feet—'

Kitto's blue eyes were pensive as he stared after Shar. 'Maybe that's a good question,' he said. 'Who *does* she think she is? Because one thing's for sure; she isn't behaving like the Shar we know.'

His words hit home, and suddenly Hestor's anger vanished. There could be no doubt now that their suspicion was right. Shar *was* keeping a secret. And Hestor felt intuitively that her flirtation with Reyni Trevire was only a very small part of it.

'Give her until tomorrow to calm down,' Kitto suggested. 'Maybe she'll feel differently then, and if she doesn't, we'll have to think again.'

Hestor nodded. 'All right. Though I'd much rather get it out in the open now. If we wait—'

'I think, Hestor, that it would be wiser to take Kitto's advice.'

The new, unfamiliar voice spoke from behind them, and both boys whirled round.

The stranger must have moved up on them while they were talking, though neither of them had heard him approach. He was very tall and dressed entirely in black, with a mane of long, black hair that framed a narrow-boned, aristocratic face. Hestor looked at his eyes – and froze. For those eyes were as green as emeralds, very deep-set and almost cat-like in their intensity. They were not the eyes of a mortal man.

Hestor began nervously, 'Sir, I don't . . .' He meant to say, *I don't believe I know you*, but suddenly his mouth went dry and he couldn't finish. Then he saw that Kitto was staring at the man in horrified awe, and he realised what the other boy, with his deeper sense of superstition, had already sensed.

Face white with shock, Hestor made a reverent bow and whispered, 'My lord!'

Tarod of Chaos made a quick, negating gesture. 'No formality, Hestor! No one knows I'm here, and that's how I – and Yandros – want matters to remain.' He glanced at Kitto, who looked as if he was about to be sick with fright, and his eyes glinted with amusement. 'Really, Kitto, there's no need to be *quite* so terrified! You've faced my brother Yandros and survived, and I assure you I'm a less daunting prospect than he is.'

'S . . . s . . . sir . . .' Kitto stammered.

'My name,' the Chaos god said, 'is Tarod. I want to talk to you about your friend Shar. Come with me, and be casual about it; I don't want to draw attention to us.'

He led them out of the hall, through the main doors and into the courtyard, which was bathed in the tricky, silver-green light of both moons. By the ornate fountain

Tarod stopped and said, 'Now. You both sense something amiss with Shar; am I correct?'

Hestor was getting over the worst of his terrors and his voice was steady as he replied, 'Yes, my lord.'

'We of Chaos are inclined to agree with you. Something is stirring in this world; we don't yet know what it is, but we believe it has some connection with Shar's special abilities, and with the events of a few months ago.' Hestor tensed but didn't speak, and Tarod continued. 'I don't need to tell you that we of Chaos have a particular interest in Shar's welfare. However, we can't take any direct hand in this, for it would be going against the rules of Equilibrium. In fact we're already bending those rules by making contact with you. So you must tell no one of this meeting, and say nothing of our suspicions to anyone; least of all to Shar. But you will help her – and us – greatly greatly if you watch, and listen, and see what you can learn.'

Hestor nodded, then his face clouded. 'But if we discover anything, Lord Tarod, what can we do about it? If Lord Yandros can't intervene—'

Tarod stopped him with a hard smile. 'He can't in any direct sense, as I've already told you. But if matters get seriously out of hand, Chaos won't leave you or Shar to face the consequences alone. That we can promise.' One hand reached into the folds of his black cloak, and he drew out what looked to the boys like a small white candle. 'Take this, and keep it safe. If – but I stress *only* if – you or Shar should find yourselves in real danger, light it, and I will contact you again.' He paused, staring hard into Hestor's eyes. 'Don't use it without very good cause, Hestor. It's a last resort, no more, and Yandros will not be pleased if you call on us without extremely good reason.'

Kitto gulped at Tarod's ominous tone, and Hestor felt his face blanching. 'Yes, Lord Tarod,' he said meekly. 'I understand.'

'Good. Then I'll leave you to enjoy the rest of your celebrations. Be vigilant – and be careful.'

He nodded to them both, turned with a flick of his cloak and walked away. Three paces from them the shadow of the fountain stretched over the flagstones; Tarod stepped into the shadow. There was a strange sound like a pane of glass cracking, and he was gone.

For a minute or more Hestor and Kitto stood motionless, staring at the spot where the Chaos lord had vanished. Then Kitto sat down hard on the edge of the fountain pool and said, 'Great gods!'

'Quite . . .' Hestor pushed one hand through his hair, suppressing a shiver. 'I didn't expect *that.*'

There was a flicker of movement near the fountain and Kitto jumped; but it was only a cat, ghostly white in the darkness, hurrying away on its own business. Kitto couldn't remember seeing a white cat in the castle before, but then the females were always producing more kittens, so it was hard to keep track.

The cat disappeared and Kitto looked at Hestor again. 'We didn't dream it, did we?'

'No.' Hestor held out the candle Tarod had given him. 'Here's the proof.'

'Right. Right, yes . . . but I mean, he was who he said he was – wasn't he?'

'Of course he was.' Hestor pictured Tarod's face in his mind's eye. 'Can you doubt it?'

Kitto couldn't and admitted it. 'But it's funny,' he added, 'I wasn't frightened of him the way I was of Lord Yandros. In fact I quite . . . *liked* him.'

'Yes, well; don't get carried away with that. He's still one of the gods, and we'd better not forget it – or forget what he said.'

Kitto nodded soberly. 'So, what do we do now?'

'Exactly what Lord Tarod told us to. Watch and listen, and don't breathe a word of this to any other living soul; not even to Shar.' He looked towards the brightly lit windows of the great hall. 'We'd better get back to the revels, before anyone finds us here.' Kitto stood up, ready to follow him, and suddenly Hestor turned to face him and held out his free hand. 'Swear to keep the secret, Kitto. Swear it on your life and soul!'

Kitto gripped his fingers, and with his other hand made the splay-fingered sign of reverence to all fourteen of the gods. 'I swear,' he said solemnly.

Their faces were sombre as they walked back towards the main doors.

FIVE

Only a few servants were up and about as Reyni Trevire saddled his horse and led it out into the grey dawn light of the courtyard. The stable-boy wished him gods'-speed and went yawning back to his bed. Reyni mounted, then rode under the barbican arch and out onto the stack. The morning was chilly, with a fresh wind blowing off the sea, and he took good care not to look down as he crossed the narrow rock bridge to the mainland. The mountain tops ahead looked pink in the sun's first light; with the pass dry and the road easy, Reyni thought, he would get to Wester Reach in less than three days. It should be an enjoyable journey.

He didn't see the other horse and rider until he entered the shadows of the pass's first curve. Then suddenly there was movement ahead of him, his own horse shied – and as he got it back under control, Reyni found himself face to face with Shar.

He stared at her. 'Shar, whatever are you doing here?'

Shar's face was serious, and he realised that she was dressed for hard riding, with a saddlebag packed behind her.

'I'm coming with you,' she said. 'To Wester Reach.'

Reyni put one hand to his forehead. 'Shar, I told you last night, I can't take you with me! It would be wrong;

it would lead to all kinds of trouble – it isn't fair of you to ask me!'

'But it's vital!' Shar argued. 'Reyni, *please*. I've *got* to get to Wester Reach, and you're the only person who can help me!'

Reyni's patience was starting to run out. 'And I say again, *no*. Go back to the castle, Shar. If your visit to Wester Reach is that important, then I'm sure your seniors in the Circle will understand. Let them help you, not me. I'll say it one last time, and then I'm riding on, alone. I will *not* take you with me!'

Shar had expected this and during the sleepless night, as she worked out the details of her strategy, she had prepared for it. She had a trump card; one which, she believed, Reyni couldn't counter, and now she smiled at him; a peculiar, almost contemptuous smile.

'If you don't take me willingly, Reyni,' she said, 'then I'm afraid I'll have to force you.'

She raised one hand and called out in a strange, high-pitched voice. There was a *thwack* of displaced air, and to Reyni's shock, a swarm of tiny tongues of fire flashed into being seemingly from nowhere. They whirled and spun above Shar's head, and he felt a rush of tremendous heat that made both him and his horse recoil.

Shar, lit by the orange and crimson glow of the fire creatures, said relentlessly, 'The elementals are my friends, Reyni, and they'll do whatever I ask of them. If you refuse to take me with you, I shall tell them to attack you. And they can *hurt*.'

Reyni looked at the darting creatures, then at Shar again. She expected him to be frightened by her threat, but he wasn't. He was simply angry and disgusted. He had obviously misjudged this girl, he thought. Fame had gone to her head, and for all her special talents she was no more than a spoiled brat.

Quietly and coldly, he said. 'I've no intention of being intimidated, by you or any of your friends. If you think your threats impress me, then you're a foolish child who doesn't deserve to wear the Circle's gold badge. Go back to the castle, Shar. And grow up.'

He jerked on his horse's reins and spurred it forward. For an uneasy moment he wondered if he had misjudged the situation and Shar really would set the elementals on him; but at the last moment she drew back, letting him pass. The dancing tongues of fire flickered, wavered, then vanished. Their light died, and Reyni's last sight of Shar was of a frozen, miserable figure wrapped in shadow.

As the sound of hoofbeats faded, Shar stared blindly at the empty track. She felt sick and stunned, not by Reyni's reaction but by her own behaviour. What had she been *thinking* of? Using magical power to threaten someone was one of the worst misdeeds a Circle initiate could commit! It was as if some awful and undreamed-of side of herself had risen suddenly from nowhere . . . or, worse, as if for one dreadful moment someone or something else had taken her over.

The pass was silent now. Shar looked over her shoulder, but the Star Peninsula was hidden from view by the mountains' bulk. She was horribly torn; part of her wanted to ride straight back to the safety and security of the castle's enfolding walls, while another part wanted to spur her pony into a full-tilt gallop down the track and away. But she couldn't go to Wester Reach alone. The road was too dangerous; there were brigands in the mountains, and they weren't the only hazard. Yet how could she return to the castle? She couldn't solve the mystery of her mother's letter from there. And until she did solve it, there would be no peace for her anywhere.

She was still sitting bewildered and miserable in the saddle when she heard hoofbeats approaching, coming from the direction of the Peninsula. Shar tensed. There were a number of horses, by the sound of it. Surely not a search party? The Circle couldn't have missed her yet! In alarmed confusion she gathered up her reins, but as she was about to drive her heels into the pony's flanks the hoofbeats grew suddenly louder and the newcomers appeared.

She recognised the riders immediately. The Keepers of Light – the sect whose choir had sung at the revels. They still wore the same strange clothes, though now with matching coats over them, and as their leader saw Shar he held up a hand and called out a command to his comrades. The horses slithered to a halt, and the sect leader bowed courteously in his saddle.

'Can we be of some assistance, madam?' Then his eyes widened with surprise. 'Oh! Initiate Shar . . . is something amiss?'

Shar flushed, wishing yet again that she was not so easily recognisable. 'No, thank you,' she began – then paused as she realised that this could be the chance she so desperately needed. Her pulse quickened and, rapidly, she changed tack. 'That is . . . I don't want to trouble you, but—'

'Please.' The leader smiled kindly. 'If we can help in any way, you need only ask.'

'Well . . . I *do* have a slight problem.' Shar was thinking fast. 'I have to go to Wester Reach, you see; I received a message from – from—'

'To Wester Reach?' The leader didn't seem to notice how unconvincing she sounded. 'My dear young lady, you can't possibly go unaccompanied! The road isn't safe for a girl alone, and the town itself is little better!'

'I know,' Shar said. 'But I must get there somehow. The message is – is very urgent, and I – eh – can't afford to delay . . .'

'But surely the Circle should have provided you with an escort?'

Shar's cheeks reddened again. 'I didn't ask for one,' she admitted. 'With everybody so busy . . .' Her heart sank and she thought: *Now they'll insist on taking me back to the castle. I should have known it wasn't even worth trying to fool them.*

The leader said, 'Then you must ride with us.'

'What?' Shar stared at him, confounded, and he smiled.

'We ourselves are bound for Wester Reach, so it's the obvious solution! You'll be perfectly safe with us – oh, and I promise that we won't try to convert you to our beliefs as we travel!'

Several of the sect members chuckled at his joke, but Shar only continued to stare in astonishment, hardly able to believe her good fortune.

'Of course,' the leader added when she didn't reply, 'if the idea of our company is distasteful—'

'No!' she said hastily, as her wits came back. 'Oh, no, no! I'd be delighted – thank you. Thank you very much!'

'Well, then.' The leader looked pleased. 'I suggest we waste no time. Brothers, sisters, if we're all ready?'

The little cavalcade set off again along the track. Shar, riding in its midst, felt dizzy with a mixture of relief and elation. The Keepers of Light might be a little odd, but they were friendly and kind and, above all, helpful; better travelling companions, in fact, than Reyni would have been. Their readiness to come to her rescue was an undreamed-of stroke of luck.

In her excitement it did not occur to her to think that the luck had come her way just a little *too* easily. Nor, as the horses and their riders trotted on, did any of them see the long, lithe shape that crouched on a ledge and gazed after them. The eyes of the huge, white-furred mountain cat held no expression, but there was a thoughtful air about it as it watched. Then, silently, it left the ledge and started to move along a high and narrow path that ran parallel with the road, following in the riders' wake like a shadow.

★　★　★

Shar's disappearance was not discovered until breakfast time, and when her pony was also found to be missing the High Initiate called an urgent meeting in his study.

The searchers had found no clue whatever to where Shar might have gone, and as to *why* she had gone, no one could even begin to guess. Hestor and Kitto were questioned, but it was obvious from their agitation that they were telling the truth when they swore they knew nothing. Neryon was deeply worried, for Shar had been abducted from the castle once before, by Thel Starnor's accomplices, and the pattern of this disappearance looked very similar. But Thel and his co-conspirators couldn't reach Shar now, so if events were repeating themselves, who could possibly be responsible? Neryon thought of Shar's near-fatal accident, and the suspicions he had confided to Pellis. In the light of that, a kidnapping seemed unpleasantly likely. But suddenly Hestor, who was still in the study, frowned and said, 'Sir . . . there was that musician . . .'

Neryon looked at him sharply. 'What musician?'

'The one who played Shar's ballad at the banquet.' Hestor told him about Shar's odd behaviour with Reyni Trevire; their whispered conversations on the stairs and in the dining hall and her secretive and hostile mood afterwards. Neryon listened, then said gravely, 'Hestor, I know how fond you are of Shar. Forgive me for saying so, but don't you think you might be exaggerating this for . . . well, shall we say, personal reasons?'

Hestor flushed. 'You mean I'm jealous, sir? No. Well,

that is . . . maybe in a way I am, but I still think there is something peculiar about it all.'

Neryon studied him thoughtfully for a few moments. 'Very well,' he said at last. 'It may be a false lead, but so far it's the only one we have.' He turned to his steward. 'Find out if Reyni Trevire is still in the castle, and if he is, ask him to come here.'

It took only minutes for the steward to find out that Reyni had left early that morning. No one had seen him go, so it wasn't known whether he had left alone or in company, but when he heard the news Neryon, like Hestor, suspected that there could be a connection. What kind of connection, though? That was the baffling question, and they had no answers.

Messenger birds were despatched to all the major towns in the province, and a party of riders left the castle to search the surrounding countryside. Privately Neryon had very little hope that they would find any trace of Shar; he was more inclined to trust magical methods, and so ordered the Circle's best scryers to do what they could. Hestor's request to help was kindly but firmly refused, and he and Kitto left the High Initiate's study torn between worry and annoyance. Outside in the corridor, Kitto turned to Hestor and said, 'The candle Lord Tarod gave us . . . I think we should light it!'

Hestor, though, shook his head. 'We daren't, Kitto. Lord Tarod said only in a dire emergency, remember? I don't think this is a dire emergency, at least not yet – and I certainly don't want to risk angering the gods.'

'True.' Kitto pushed down a shudder. 'But we've got to do *something*, and if the High Initiate won't let us help—'

'Wait.' Hestor held up a hand. 'I've just had a thought. Something they've all overlooked . . . the cats.'

Kitto's eyes lit. 'Amber! Is he here?'

'I don't know, but if he is, we can find him easily enough. Maybe you'll be able to pick up something from him.'

Kitto had a particular talent for communicating with the cats; something which, in Hestor's opinion, the senior adepts of the Circle didn't take as seriously as they should. His frustration – and, he had to admit, a slight sense of insult – at being excluded from the investigation evaporated at the thought that he and Kitto might learn some vital clue from Amber. If they did, if they *could*, then as well as helping Shar they would also make it impossible for the High Initiate to keep them out of the thick of it. That was what Hestor wanted above all. He needed to do something. He needed to *help*.

'Come on,' he said, grabbing Kitto's arm. 'Let's go and look for that cat!'

They found Amber in the castle kitchens, where he was ingratiating himself with the servants in the hopes of scrounging titbits of food. Scooping him up and ignoring his indignant *wowl* of protest, they carried him to Hestor's room and dumped him unceremoniously on the bed.

'Go on, Kitto,' Hestor said. 'See what you can sense from him.'

Kitto stroked the ginger cat to calm his annoyance, then stared hard into his eyes. Amber blinked, yawned, turned away and started to wash one hind leg, and Kitto looked baffled.

'That's strange. He isn't the least bit worried about Shar.'

Hestor frowned. 'Then he must be the only living creature in the castle who isn't. Are you getting any images?'

'Nothing that's any use. Hold on; I'll try to ask him a question.' Kitto concentrated for a minute or two, then suddenly tensed. 'Wait . . . there's a picture . . . he's showing me what looks like a piece of paper. A letter, or something. Shar, reading it, then hiding it away in her room, and . . .' A pause, then Kitto shook his head exasperatedly. 'No; the rest of it's just about food and having his fur stroked. Typical cat thoughts.'

A letter . . . Hestor chewed his lower lip, then suddenly, startling both Kitto and Amber, jumped to his feet. 'Let's go and look in her room.'

'They've already searched it,' Kitto said.

'Maybe; but that doesn't mean they found everything there was to be found. Come on.'

Amber trotted after them as they made their way along the corridor. Shar's door wasn't locked and, ignoring guilty feelings at the trespass, the boys started to rummage through her belongings while Amber watched with unconcerned interest.

It was Kitto who found the letter. In her haste to leave the castle Shar had forgotten it; it had slipped out from under her pillow and a gust from the open window had blown it under the bed. Hestor read it aloud, as Kitto, though learning, wasn't yet up to reading it for himself. When he finished, the silence in the room was acute. At last, Kitto broke it.

'Great gods!' he said. 'Do you think this is true? Do you think it's *possible?*'

'I don't know.' Hestor was still staring at the letter, half convinced that he had imagined its contents. 'It sounds very plausible, but I'm suspicious. I mean, if anyone wanted to get at Shar, this would be the most obvious way to do it. A lure she couldn't resist.'

'So now we know where she's gone,' Kitto said. 'We'd better tell the High Initiate, and quickly!'

He started for the door, but Hestor said, 'No.'

'What?' Kitto was incredulous. 'But—'

'Wait; listen to me. If we tell Neryon about this, what do you think he'll do?'

'Send a party to Wester Reach, of course, and bring her back!'

'Exactly. And how would that help? Think about it, Kitto. If the senior adepts see this letter, they'll be sure it's a trick; or even if they're not sure, they'll think only of protecting Shar.'

'That's just as well, if the letter is a fake!' Kitto argued.

'Fine. But what if it isn't? What if there is an enemy in the castle, as the person who wrote the letter claims? If this comes out into the open, it will alert them.' He paused. 'Besides, Lord Tarod told us to say nothing to anyone.'

'You're right,' Kitto said sombrely, and frowned. 'So; we know she must have gone to Wester Reach. But where does Reyni Trevire fit in to all this? If he does, that is.'

'Oh, he fits in, I'm certain of it.' Hestor's voice was baleful. 'And I'm going to find out more.'

'How?'

'By performing a ritual, to uncover what really lies behind this letter.'

'Scrying?' Kitto was dubious. 'The High Initiate's already trying that.'

'This isn't scrying,' Hestor told him. 'It's something much more powerful.' He looked searchingly at the other boy. 'Will you help?'

'Well . . .' Sorcery of any kind scared Kitto; but then he thought of Shar, perhaps in peril and, with an effort, nodded. 'Yes. Of course I will.'

'Good. Then we'll do it tonight, in my room. And let's hope it works.'

The safest time for the ritual, Hestor judged, was the hour of the evening meal, when nearly all the castle-dwellers (including Pellis, whose room was next door to her son's) were in the dining-hall. If anyone discovered what they were doing, they would be in dire trouble. But Hestor didn't care. With furniture pushed against the walls, the rug rolled back and Kitto watching from his perch on the bed, he carefully traced a protective circle before lighting a candle and a crucible of incense at its centre. Then, standing before the crucible, he closed his eyes and started to speak the words of the rite. The candle flame began to gutter and sway; shadows closed in around Hestor's figure until he was no more than a silhouette, and Kitto shivered, belatedly wondering if this was a very reckless mistake. But he had made Hestor a promise; and had also sworn a solemn oath that he would never breathe a word to anyone about their intentions. It was too late to back out now; all he could do was listen as Hestor's chanting continued, and try not to think about the oppressive sense of magical energy that was building up in the room.

Hestor was unaware of Kitto's disquiet; in fact he was now unaware of anything except the circle – a bright ring of blue fire in his mind's eye – and the power slowly growing inside it. The ease with which the ritual seemed to be working would have surprised him if he had been able to pause and think about it; Shar's letter, which he held in his right hand, seemed to be quivering and fluttering as though it were trying to pull itself free, and he focused his concentration on it, willing it to yield its secrets. *True or false? True or false?* The question vibrated silently in his head. *Who are you? In the name of Lord Yandros of Chaos, in the name of Lord Aeoris of Order, I command you, show me the truth!*

There was a sudden, sharp singing noise that seemed to come from the back of his skull. Then into his inner vision came a point of light, growing and swelling, as though he were in a dark tunnel and rushing at tremendous speed towards the brightness at its end. Hestor tensed with excitement, concentrated harder—

With no warning, the point of light exploded. Hestor had a split second to register the appalling shape that erupted from it, smashing out of a dimension beyond sanity and hurling itself at him with a roar like thunder. He screamed, reeling backwards; one foot crossed the boundary of the protective circle—

Kitto was thrown back on the bed like a leaf in a gale as a backlash of supernatural power blasted through the room. He saw Hestor scooped up as though a huge, invisible hand had plucked him from the floor; for a moment Hestor's arms and legs flailed madly in mid-air – then the force hurled him across the room. He smashed against the wall with an enormous impact, and Kitto's terrified cry was eclipsed as a howl of monstrous laughter rang out and dinned in his ears like something from the Seven Hells.

Then with a *thwack* as though every atom of air had been sucked out of the room in a single instant, the laughter snapped off into silence. Kitto stared with bulging eyes at Hestor's body lying limp and lifeless as a child's doll on the floor. He wasn't moving. He didn't seem to be breathing. Kitto couldn't move either; panic was trying to batter its way through to his consciousness but he was paralysed with shock and could only keep on staring. A minute passed. Then two. Then—

'*Uhhh . . .*' The awful noise came from Kitto's own throat, and paralysis broke as the panic came surging through. He flung himself from the bed, across the room, clawing for the door. It opened; Kitto stumbled out, fell, scrabbled upright and plunged towards the stairs. He ran

as though a legion of demons were on his heels, and his
voice rang desperately through the castle.

'Help! Someone, anyone – *help me!*'

'Kitto, get a grip on yourself!' the High Initiate said firmly, pulling the black-haired boy away from the door. 'It's all right, do you hear me? Hestor isn't dead; he's just unconscious!'

Kitto gulped and, with a great effort, made his teeth stop chattering. 'N-not . . . d-d-dead?' he stammered.

'No. He's alive.' Though, Neryon thought privately, it was probably more by luck than by anything else. What in the names of the gods had the boy been *doing?*

Neryon and Kitto were in the corridor outside Hestor's room. Inside, Physician Chandor was tending to Hestor; he had allowed Pellis into the room but everyone else had been ordered out until his examination was complete.

'I don't think Hestor's badly hurt,' Neryon went on. 'But I need to know what happened, and quickly. Now, Kitto: do you feel recovered enough to tell me about it?'

Kitto dissembled. 'I – I'm not really sure about anything, sir. I don't quite remember—' He was saved at that moment by the door opening. The physician appeared, and Neryon looked up quickly.

'Eln – how is he?'

Eln's face was unreadable. 'No bones broken,' he said.

'Bruising, but nothing worse. Physically, he should recover in a day or two.'

There was something he wasn't saying. Kitto knew it, and knew why Eln was being cautious. Neryon, though, made an impatient gesture and said, 'Never mind the boy's presence, Eln. Tell me what's wrong.'

Eln sighed. 'He's in a coma, Neryon. And I don't know how to get him out of it.'

Kitto whispered, 'Oh, no . . .' The High Initiate turned a shrewdly thoughtful look on him, and he felt a flush spreading slowly across his cheeks.

'Kitto,' Neryon said, 'I think you'd better tell me everything.' His voice grew stern. 'And I mean *everything*.'

The rest of the evening and the following day were a nightmare for Kitto. Neryon Voss questioned him for over an hour, and by the end of the interrogation he felt miserable and exhausted. His only crumb of comfort was the knowledge that he hadn't broken his promise to Hestor; for though he had told the High Initiate enough to explain the accident, he had not let slip a single word about the letter from Wester Reach. The adepts had been too concerned for Hestor to even notice the piece of paper in his room, let alone examine it, and Kitto had been able to sneak back later, retrieve it and hide it away. So the story he had told, though true as far as it went, was not all the truth. Neryon now believed that Hestor had simply been trying to use sorcery to track Shar down – but though Kitto described as best he could what he had seen when the disaster happened, it was of little use. Clearly Hestor's ritual had gone catastrophically wrong. But how or why it had gone wrong was a mystery.

Hestor did not regain consciousness the following day. Kitto haunted the corridor outside the infirmary but was not permitted to see his friend; and, as Pellis gently pointed out, there was nothing he could do anyway. Eln was hopeful, she reassured; after all, there was no physical damage. It was just a matter of waiting.

Kitto found it very hard to wait, and as he walked dejectedly away from his third failed attempt to see Hestor, he thought of Tarod of Chaos and the candle he had given them. Was *this* a dire enough emergency to warrant lighting it? Eagerness flared in Kitto, but then collapsed as he realised that if he did light the candle, he would have to take complete responsibility. Hestor couldn't help him. He was on his own. Could he face the consequences if his judgement was wrong?

Miserably, Kitto admitted to himself that he didn't have the courage to do it. Maybe he was a coward, but there was no help for it: his fear for Hestor and Shar was eclipsed by the far greater fear of bringing the gods' wrath down on his head. He would just have to wait, as Pellis had said. Wait for Hestor to recover. Wait for him to decide.

He only hoped and prayed that the waiting wouldn't be too long.

Four days after leaving the Star Peninsula, Shar and her

new-found friends arrived in Wester Reach.

It was mid-morning and the sun was shining brightly, though a brisk south-westerly wind made the air chilly. Shar was enchanted by her first sight of West High Land Province's capital with its fine stone towers and bustling streets. Many buildings were still decorated with pennants and garlands after the Quarter-Day celebrations, and the whole town had a festive air that she found exhilarating.

They crossed the broad river that ran through the heart of Wester Reach, then turned on to a wide thoroughfare that followed the river's path towards the sea. Boats of all kinds and sizes sailed downriver on the tide or bobbed at their quayside moorings, and in the distance Shar could just see the wall with its four great arches that marked the boundary of the inner town.

It seemed that the Keepers of Light were well known in Wester Reach, for no one stared at their strange hair and clothes; indeed, many people smiled or greeted them as they passed by. One of the party, a woman called Amobrel who had become Shar's special companion on the ride, was chatting cheerfully about the sights to be seen, but Shar was suddenly preoccupied. She now had some decisions to make – and dismay filled her as she realised that she was completely unprepared for them. She had left the castle in reckless haste, thinking only of the letter and the mystery to be solved. But she had nowhere to stay, and didn't know a single person in the town. Nor did she have the least idea where the Bronze Bell Tavern was, or what she should do when she found it . . . and Reyni had told her that Wester Reach was a dangerous place for a girl on her own.

She glanced sidelong at Amobrel, who was now pointing out a large and impressive spritsail barge gliding by. Amobrel and the others had been so kind to her; if she asked them for help she was certain that they would give it gladly. But dare she ask? The letter had urged the utmost secrecy; somewhere there were unknown enemies, and for all their apparent benevolence it would not be wise to trust even the Keepers of Light with her secret. Besides, if they knew what she really meant to do here, they would probably be horrified and, for her own safety as they would see it, take her back to the castle.

What, then, was she to do? Shar considered trying to give her companions the slip and lose herself among the town crowds. But that ploy was unlikely to work. There must be a better way.

Her worried thoughts were interrupted as she heard Amobrel speak her name, and she turned her head to see that the woman was smiling at her, eyebrows raised as though she had asked a question and expected a reply.

'I'm sorry,' Shar replied in confusion. 'I wasn't concentrating. What did you say?'

Amobrel continued to smile. 'I just asked where you'll be staying while you're here. Do you have relatives in the town?'

'Er . . . no,' Shar said. 'Not relatives.' *Or have I? I don't know yet . . .* 'Just – um – some friends.'

The group's leader, Jonakar, was looking back over his shoulder, and Shar thought that he and Amobrel exchanged a look before he nodded very slightly. Then Amobrel said, 'If you haven't yet made arrangements, we'd be delighted to offer you accommodation with our community. We welcome guests, and we'd make you very comfortable – at no charge, of course.'

In one sense it was the answer to Shar's dilemma, but as Amobrel spoke she felt suddenly wary, for she suspected that there was more to the offer than met the eye. Jonakar was still watching them. He looked interested, almost eager, and a cold feeling moved in the depths of Shar's stomach.

'Thank you,' she said. 'It's very kind, but my friends are expecting me, and—'

She was interrupted by Jonakar, who, with a strange, gentle smile, said, 'I don't think they are, Shar.'

Shar jerked on her pony's reins and brought it to an abrupt halt. She stared at Jonakar. 'What do you mean?' she demanded.

The others had also stopped, and they were all looking at her now. All smiling.

'It's all right, Shar; we're not your enemies and there's nothing to fear,' said Jonakar. 'But there is something we haven't told you.'

Shar's heart was starting to pound. But before she could speak again, Jonakar continued, 'I'm sorry we deceived you, Shar, but we couldn't take any chances. We know about the letter, and we used Reyni Trevire to deliver it because it seemed safer not to risk drawing any attention to ourselves.'

'*You* used him?' Shar whispered incredulously.

'Yes. The letter was written at our mission house. Your mother is there, Shar. She has been with us for some time now – and she is waiting for you.'

The house that the Keepers of Light called their 'mission' was just outside the main town, among the jumble of docks and wharves that made up the busy main harbour. It was a large building, set in its own garden and courtyard behind a high stone wall.

As she rode with the others through the gates and into the courtyard, Shar's stomach churned with nervous sickness. She was still struggling to take in all that Jonakar and Amobrel had told her. Some months ago, they'd said, a group of their members returning from Empty Province had found a woman lying by the road. She was badly injured, so they had brought her back to Wester Reach. They tended her until she recovered – and then she told them who she was. They had been dubious at first, Jonakar said, for Shar's exploits at the castle were well known, and they suspected that the woman might be a trickster with some dark motive. But time and careful delving had convinced them that she was telling the truth. So when she begged them to help her make contact with Shar, they had of course agreed.

The Keepers were also convinced that Shar's mother was right in her belief that she and Shar were still in danger. The nature of the danger wasn't for him to reveal, Jonakar said, but with Shar's arrival in Wester Reach, he prayed to Lord Aeoris that they would both be safe in the mission house. And if there was anything at all that the Keepers of Light could do to help, Shar need only ask.

The gates closed behind the party, and they halted. Shar hardly dared look at the house's front door, and wondered if, when the moment came to enter, her nerve would fail. She took a grip on herself; this was what she had come for, after all, and to baulk was ridiculous. *Face it*, an inner voice said angrily, and to steady her mind she looked across the courtyard to where a white cat sat sunning itself on a wooden bench. She tried to project a telepathic greeting but there was no tingle of response; either she was too keyed-up to concentrate or the animal simply wasn't interested.

Then the front door opened. Shar tensed as two figures emerged from the house. One was an elderly, patrician-looking man with his clipped white hair swept back from his face. The other was a woman, who was not dressed in the zig-zag patterned clothes of the Keepers. She looked at Shar. She stared. Her eyes widened. Then—

'*Shar!*' A radiant look came to the woman's face. 'Oh, Shar, Shar, it's really you!'

She rushed forward, arms outstretched and eyes shining with joy. Shar took in her face, her hair, everything she could assimilate in a single instant – and something inside her locked and froze. She couldn't think, couldn't speak, couldn't react in any way at all. Though she had no memory of her mother, she had expected to feel *something*. But she did not. There was only a huge, choking sensation inside her, an awful sense of disillusion and misery that verged on despair. For she was looking at a total stranger.

Jonakar's kindly eyes saddened, and Amobrel, at Shar's side, said softly, 'Oh, Shar . . . don't you remember?'

Hardly aware that she did so, Shar shook her head. 'No . . .' she replied in a tiny, crushed voice. The woman – she couldn't even think the word *Mother* – had stopped and was gazing unhappily at her. Wetness glittered on her cheeks and Shar felt tears welling in her own eyes, too. 'I'm sorry . . .'

The white-haired man moved towards her. 'My child,' he said in a gentle, sympathetic tone, 'This has been a shock to you, I know. Come, now; dismount, and let's all go inside. And Giria, my dear,' turning to the woman, 'don't be too downhearted. It's understandable that Shar does not remember you. We must be patient.'

Giria nodded but did not speak. She turned and went back into the mission house, and numbly Shar allowed herself to be helped down from her pony. The white-haired man put an arm around her shoulders and said, 'My name is Lias Alborn. I am the leader of our little group, and on behalf of us all, Shar, I welcome you to our home. There is a very great deal to tell you, but there's also plenty of time. Don't feel overwhelmed, my dear.' He smiled into her eyes, then with his free hand made a sign that Shar recognised as a reverence to the gods of Order. 'With our Lord Aeoris's guidance, you will understand the truth soon enough.'

★　★　★

Hestor finally regained consciousness two days after the disastrous ritual. For another day Kitto wasn't allowed to see him, but on the third morning he was at last permitted to visit the infirmary.

Hestor was weak but alert, and the moment Physician Eln left the two boys alone he grabbed Kitto's arm and hissed, 'You didn't tell them, did you? You didn't tell them what we found?'

Thankful that he had not given way to temptation, Kitto shook his head. 'Of course I didn't! But Hestor, what *happened?*'

Hestor let out a breath. 'I don't know. Everything was going fine, just as I expected. Then suddenly . . .' As best he could remember it, he told Kitto the details, and when he had finished Kitto looked grave.

'I don't like this,' he said. 'I thought about lighting the candle Lord Tarod gave us—'

'Great gods, you didn't do it, did you?'

'No! What do you take me for?' Kitto didn't mention the fact that it was only lack of nerve that had stopped him. 'But honestly, Hestor, there's something very weird going on, I'm sure of it. What you said – what you described – it sounded like . . .' He suppressed a shiver, unable to say it directly. '*You* know.'

'The Sixth Plane.' Hestor dropped his voice to a whisper. 'Yes. I agree. It's got some horrible comparisons with what happened a few months ago, hasn't it? And that makes me wonder . . .'

'What?'

'I've got no evidence. But it makes me wonder if Thel

Starnor is really as powerless as the Circle think.'

Kitto frowned. 'They should have cut his head off and had done with it!'

'Yes, well; the Circle haven't executed anyone for nearly two hundred years, and they never went in for beheading anyway. So whatever the rights or wrongs of it, Thel's still alive. And though he's in solitary confinement on a prison island, and his sorcerous skills are supposed to have been stripped from him, I'm starting to wonder if he's behind this.'

'What about Sister Malia?' Kitto asked. 'It could be her.'

Malia, former Senior at the West High Land sisterhood cot, had been one of Thel's major accomplices in the plot. She too was imprisoned, but she claimed to have repented and was being kept at the Matriarch's own cot, where, with time, it was hoped that the truth or otherwise of her remorse would be proved. Certainly Malia was in a better position than Thel to make mischief, but all the same Hestor shook his head. 'I don't think so. She's only a seer; she hasn't got abilities like Thel's. No; if anyone's at the back of this, everything points in just one direction.'

Kitto considered for a few moments. Then: 'Maybe we should talk to the High Initiate after all.'

'We can't, Kitto! Remember what Lord Tarod said?' We mustn't breathe a word to anyone, not even Neryon Voss.' Hestor made an effort to sit up in bed, but his strength wasn't up to it and he fell back against the pillows. 'This is stupid! I'm so *feeble* – if I could only get my strength back, I'd go to Wester Reach straight away and see what I could find out!' Then he sighed. 'Oh, what's the use thinking that? The senior adepts will be watching me like hawks from now on. I'd never get away from the castle.'

Kitto's eyes glinted. 'Maybe not,' he said. 'But I could.'

'You?' Hestor started to look interested.

'Why not? Getting a horse is no problem; I often exercise them for the grooms. I could pretend I was doing that, and by the time anyone finds out the truth it'll be too late to catch me.' Kitto leaned forward eagerly. 'I can find Shar, I know I can!'

He probably could, Hestor thought. Kitto hadn't forgotten all the tricks he had learned during his years with the brigands. But there was another consideration, and he said uncertainly, 'You haven't got any magical skills. If Thel *is* up to something, you could be running into danger.'

'Fine,' Kitto countered. 'So you can't go because you're too weak, and I can't go because I haven't learned any sorcery. Where does that leave us?' He snorted. 'I can look after myself. I'm not scared.'

He was right; it was their only chance. 'All right,' Hestor said, the last of his doubts vanishing. 'How soon can you be ready?'

Kitto grinned. 'Give me ten minutes.'

Aeoris, highest lord of Order, loved symmetry, and so the shimmering hall to which he had summoned his six brothers was a masterpiece of flawlessly matching curves and angles and colours. Seven golden chairs were set at precisely equal distances from each other, and mellow light shone in at the tall windows, creating a nimbus around Aeoris's flowing, pure-white hair. Beyond the hall the faint sound of birdsong could be heard; but though the birds of Order's realm were far more beautiful and sang far more sweetly than any in the mortal realm, it was clear that their song wasn't pleasing Aeoris at this moment. The god's stern, handsome face was creased by a frown, and his eyes – which had no iris or pupil but were orbs of glowing gold – burned with an angry light.

'I have no doubt of it,' he said. 'Despite the pact he made and pretends to believe in, Yandros is meddling in human affairs again. And I am not prepared to tolerate it!'

His six brothers nodded. Unlike the lords of Chaos, they all looked identical to Aeoris in every way – and also unlike the Chaos gods, they never presumed to argue with their leader.

'It was bad enough that he took matters into his own hands when the High Initiate's life was threatened,' one put in. 'The Circle would have appealed to us for help as well as to Chaos, but Yandros stepped in and turned the situation to his own advantage before they could take any action!'

'And, as always, went about it by devious means,' Aeoris said. 'Manipulating that young initiate Hestor Ennas . . . who now, of course, feels an obligation to Chaos that he does not feel to Order. As do many others who were involved. Including Shar Tillmer.'

There was a faintly resentful note in his voice as he spoke Shar's name. As both a Dark-Caller and a Daughter of Storms, Shar had strong natural links with Chaos, and the fact that she was now looked on as a heroine did not please him at all. The lords of Order had been as anxious as anyone to see Thel's plot foiled, but the fact that it had been done in the name of Chaos rather than Order was annoying. Now, to make matters worse, it seemed that Shar – and the Chaos lords – were taking centre stage once again.

Aeoris steepled his fingers together and stared at them. 'We know,' he continued, 'that Yandros's brother Tarod has already paid one visit to the castle. We can't see clearly enough, either into Chaos's realm or into the mortal world, to be sure of his motive. However, we *do* know that something untoward is stirring, and we suspect it has a connection with the events of a few months ago. It seems likely that our friends of Chaos have sensed the same thing, and Yandros is trying to find out what's afoot. This time, though, he hasn't waited for even a very junior initiate to ask for his help. That, as I see it, breaks all the rules of Equilibrium.'

Another of his six brothers leaned forward. 'In which case we could justifiably intervene. If one of us were to go to the Star Peninsula—'

But Aeoris held up a hand before his brother could finish. 'No,' he said. 'If we visit the castle, we will also be breaking the rules, and I have no intention of stooping to Yandros's level. Besides, we would show our hand and

Yandros would realise that we're taking an interest. I don't want him to know that yet. We have other friends in the mortal world – friends who put their allegiance to us before anything else. For the time being at least, they will be our eyes and ears. And what we learn from them will help us to decide how and when to make our move and better Yandros at his own game!'

SEVEN

'I'm sorry that we had to use stealth to bring you here, Shar,' Lias Alborn said. 'But when you hear your mother's story, I think you'll understand why we dared not approach you too openly.'

They were all together in a small, neatly furnished sitting room; Shar and Lias and Amobrel . . . and Giria, who so far had not spoken but only gazed intensely at Shar. A jug of tisane had been brought to them but Shar couldn't drink any; her throat was tight and her stomach felt churned-up and queasy. *Your mother*, Lias had said. She kept looking back at Giria and thinking of the drawing in the castle archives that was the only image of her mother she had ever seen. There were so many differences – but the drawing had been made years ago, and people changed as they grew older. *Could* that picture and the woman sitting in this room be one and the same person? Shar simply didn't know.

She said, 'The letter claimed that we're both still in danger. I don't understand that. My uncle and the others—'

Giria made a small, choked sound and put one hand to her face. Lias glanced at her sympathetically.

'I know it still pains you to speak of Thel Starnor, my dear,' he said. 'But I think that you should tell Shar

77

everything, just as you told me. Beginning with the murder of your husband.'

Giria nodded and swallowed. 'Yes, Lias. You're right . . . she must know.' She looked at Shar, her eyes intense, and continued with an effort. 'I told you in my letter that Thel murdered your father. But that was only the beginning of it . . .'

Thel had made Shar's father's death look like an accident, Giria said, but she suspected the truth – and the plotters knew it. A few nights after the murder they abducted her from the castle, laying a false trail that suggested she had jumped from the stack in grief. Thel's motive had been simple. He wanted control of Shar's special powers, and the surest way to achieve that was to have control of Shar herself. With both her parents gone, Thel was her closest living relative and thus her rightful guardian. He had taken her far away from the castle to Summer Isle, and there he waited patiently until she was old enough for her powers to be useful to him.

While Shar grew up, Giria had been kept prisoner in a house in a remote part of Empty Province.

'I still don't understand why Thel didn't simply kill me, as he had killed your father,' she said. 'But when I challenged him he only laughed and said that he had good reasons, which I would find out when the time was right.'

'*Did* you find out?' Shar asked.

Giria shook her head. 'No. I suspect that he intended to use me in some way after the High Initiate's

78

assassination, but I don't know how. And then, of course, his plan went wrong . . .'

She had had a jailer at the house, she continued. He had always been kind to her in his way, and then one day a few months ago he came to her room and told her that he was setting her free. 'It's all over for Thel,' he had said. 'He won't be coming back. There's a horse saddled and waiting outside; take it, and go.' Stunned, Giria tried to ask him what had happened, but he refused to listen to her questions and ran from the room. Minutes later she heard the fast drumming of hooves dwindling away, and realised that he had fled.

Another horse was waiting as the jailer had promised, and, bewildered and frightened, Giria made her escape. She had no idea where she was; all she could do was set out and hope to find a town or village. But the countryside was barren and lonely; she rode all afternoon without seeing another living soul. Then, just as the sun was setting, she was attacked.

'I thought in the first few moments that they were brigands,' she said sombrely. 'But I was wrong. They weren't bandits. They weren't even human – they were demonic creatures, with warped bodies and clawed hands, and – and they had no faces; where their faces should have been was just a hideous blankness.' She shuddered at the ugly memory. 'The instant I saw them I knew, somehow I *knew*, that they had been deliberately sent to attack me.'

Shar's eyes were wide. 'How did you escape?' she asked.

'I didn't,' Giria replied grimly. 'When they pulled me

down from my horse I tried to fight them – though I've lost a lot of my adept's skills I still remember my training, and I tried to combat sorcery with sorcery. But it was useless. They were too powerful. When I realised that, I tried to run, but they came after me and caught me, and the last thing I remember was a flare of light – an awful, ugly light – and a high-pitched shrieking sound. Then I . . . I must have lost consciousness. If it hadn't been for Lias's people, I think I would have died.'

Lias took up the story. A group of his followers on their way home to Wester Reach found Giria lying at the roadside. She was so badly injured that at first they thought she was dead; but a faint heartbeat was detected and in great haste they brought her to the mission. Thanks to Lias's healing skills she recovered, but it took a long time, so she had only recently learned of the momentous events at the castle and the part Shar had played.

Giria spoke again. 'My first impulse was to go to the castle and be reunited with the daughter I lost so long ago,' she said. 'But I realised that that could be a deadly mistake. Whatever attacked me on the road was sent by someone with real sorcerous power, who knew who I was and what I intended to do. There had to be a connection with Thel. That could only mean one thing – that the chain of evil he created isn't yet broken. You're still in danger. And so, now, am I.'

Silence fell, while Shar stared at Giria. The others exchanged tense glances but she was unaware of them. She didn't know what to think. She didn't know what to say.

'Please, Shar,' Giria urged, 'you *must* believe what I've told you! In my letter, I said that your dreams might already have warned you—'

Shar interrupted sharply. 'How do you know about my dreams?' The question had been disturbing her since the letter's arrival, and the possible answers made her skin crawl. Giria looked helplessly at Lias, who said,

'We didn't know for certain, Shar. But we – the Keepers, that is – used our scrying skills in an attempt to help Giria unravel this mystery, and what we learned made us suspect that you were already under some form of magical attack.'

Such as almost sleepwalking off the edge of the stack to her death . . . Shar quelled a violent shiver and asked more quietly, 'What else did you learn?'

Lias shook his head ruefully. 'Nothing definite, I'm afraid. As a Circle initiate you must have scried for yourself, so you know how frustratingly cryptic the answers can be. But though we could unearth only a few enigmatic hints, they were enough to convince us that Giria's fears are real.'

Shar's eyes narrowed and a frown creased her face. On the surface, and in the wake of her own recent near-disaster, this sounded unpleasantly plausible. But there were still some things that didn't add up.

She said, 'If you believe I *am* still in danger, why didn't you simply send word to the High Initiate?'

'Because we couldn't risk making contact with anyone at the castle,' replied Lias. 'Our scrying warned us that there may still be traitors among the adepts; powerful traitors who would destroy anyone who tried to stand in their way. We didn't dare take the risk of alerting them. We didn't even dare warn Neryon Voss, in case any message we sent was intercepted.'

'So that was why you used Reyni to deliver the letter.'

'Yes. Even to make contact with you through our choir would have been hazardous, for we already have a link with your mother. Reyni, though, was a harmless stranger.' Lias smiled with faint humour. 'And you are both attractive young people. Anyone seeing you together would simply draw the obvious, if wrong, conclusion. No; Reyni Trevire was an innocent courier, no more. He has no further involvement in this.'

Shar nodded, wondering privately whether or not to believe him. Her body felt cold and there was an ugly, clammy sensation in her mind; a mingling of doubt and wariness with a creeping undercurrent of fear. Perhaps sensing it, Lias continued with sudden gravity,

'We don't yet know the nature of this new threat, Shar, and in truth we can't prove that it even exists. But we are convinced it is there. And we believe that your uncle is still a major player in the game.'

'But Thel's powerless now,' Shar countered uneasily. 'All the plotters are either dead or imprisoned.'

'Are they?' Lias's eyes took on a steely look. 'Can you be sure?' He paused. 'I don't doubt that the Circle were efficient in rounding up the culprits, but even they are not perfect. For example, Giria's jailer was never captured. If one escaped the net, how many others might there be – possibly with real power, and not mere servants?'

Giria spoke up quietly. 'This isn't over yet, Shar. You *must* be protected. Even at the castle your safety can't be guaranteed; you must go into hiding, and this is the only secure place. There's nothing to link either of us with the Keepers, and they have the strength and the will to shield us.'

'We can offer you a safe haven,' Lias added. 'Possibly the only safe haven there is at present. Please, Shar, believe me when I say that you need help!'

With an awful, lurching sensation Shar realised that she did believe him. For she had one piece of evidence that was far more potent than any words. The unknown force that had invaded her mind as she slept, and had drawn her helplessly, relentlessly towards that horrifying drop to the sea. But for the castle cats, the attempt would have succeeded . . . and she might not be so lucky a second time.

She said cautiously, 'Perhaps if I were stay for a little while . . . say, a few days . . .'

Lias looked pleased and relieved. 'You'll be very welcome. And I'm glad that you feel able to trust us enough to accept our offer.' He smiled. 'I promise you, Shar, we won't let you down.'

Shar couldn't get to sleep that night. She had been given a room of her own in the mission house, and everyone seemed to assume that the question of her staying was fully settled. But Shar herself had no such certainties. She felt confused, unhappy – and frightened.

Could she believe what she had been told? Were these

people what they seemed? The sudden and very convenient reappearance of her long-lost mother could so easily be a trap. So, was Giria an imposter? They had talked together for a long time that afternoon, and Shar had to admit that everything she said suggested that she *was* Giria Tillmer Starnor. She knew all about life at the castle, about the adepts and their rituals, and spoke of old friends whom Shar herself knew. She remembered Pellis, Hestor's mother, and Hestor himself as a baby; she spoke of Neryon Voss, who had been twenty years old when she was abducted, and of his father, the old High Initiate. And when she talked about Solas, Shar's own father, her words and her voice were so loving and sad that it was all but impossible to believe she was lying.

Yet still Shar couldn't completely shake off her doubts. Maybe, she thought miserably, she didn't dare shake them off; for if she built her hopes too high and they were then dashed, the disappointment would be unbearable. She couldn't think clearly, not yet, and she wished desperately that she had someone to talk to whom she could really trust. Hestor and Kitto, for example. Or Neryon Voss, or Pellis. Even Amber, for his feline instincts were always reliable. But they were not here, and as yet Shar didn't dare take the risk of returning to the castle. Just in case Giria and the Keepers were telling the truth.

She needed time, she told herself. Time to think . . . and time to make some investigations of her own. She would be safe enough here for a while; even if the Keepers were enemies they obviously didn't intend to move against her yet, or they would not have gone to such lengths to pretend friendship. If she could perform a little sorcery without anyone knowing of it, she might ask her elemental friends for help. They, above all, would be able to show her where the real danger lay.

With that thought Shar felt a little better. She sat up in bed and, to settle her mind, performed a small ritual; nothing complicated, just a simple spell of protection, followed by a silent and personal prayer to the gods, and to Yandros in particular. If the Keepers detected it, it would rouse no suspicions. And it was a small safeguard.

She fell asleep at last, with the night sounds of the docks and the river a faint and somehow reassuring murmur beyond the mission wall.

Each night before retiring to bed the Keepers of Light gathered in a square, white-painted room on the ground floor of the mission house, to make obeisance to the gods of Order. The room had been set out as a shrine, and on one wall, dominating the scene, hung a huge painting that depicted Aeoris himself. The god was dressed in white, with a golden cloak flung over his shoulders; behind him a gory sun filled the rose-red sky, and he stood with one hand outstretched while the other made a sacred sign. Lamps were set at either side of the painting, and a third, burning with a clear, cool light, hung above it, highlighting Aeoris's stern face.

Led by Lias, the group began with a formal prayer, then everyone knelt down on the bare stone floor and silence fell as they concentrated on silent devotions.

After a few minutes Lias rose to his feet, signalling that the time for contemplation was over. A small brazier stood in front of the hrine, with a bronze dish heating on the coals. bias sprinkled some grains of incense into the dish, and as pale, scented smoke began to curl gently from it he stretched out his hands, palms upwards, and said:

'Lord Aeoris, greatest of the true gods, we ask your guidance for Shar Tillmer, daughter of our friend Giria, in her time of need. The shadow of evil has fallen upon her, and her life is in peril. But doubt and fear have blinded her, and shadow stands between her and the light of understanding. We beg you, great Aeoris, to grant us the strength to shield her from the darkness and reveal to her the true way – the way of Order.'

The others began to chant softly: '*The strength of Order. The truth of Order. The way of Order.*'

'We pledge ourselves to Shar's protection,' Lias continued. 'And we pray for the wisdom to unmask the evil that has come among us, and the courage to face that evil, and the power to defeat that evil and banish it from the world forever.'

'*Wisdom and courage and power,*' the Keepers chanted. '*Wisdom and courage and power.*' As the sound swelled through the room Lias turned to face them and his voice rose above theirs. 'Brothers and sisters! In the name of Lord Aeoris, I charge you all to—'

Suddenly, shockingly, all the lamps went out.

The chant collapsed in a backlash of gasps and cries as the room plunged into a darkness so intense that it was like a solid wall crashing down. People were scrambling to their feet, groping, colliding; someone wailed in fear, and Lias hastily gathered his wits. 'Be calm!' he called. 'There's—' But before he could get any further, Jonakar's voice cut through the babble, high-pitched with alarm.

'Lias! The painting – *look at the painting!*'

Lias spun round. The tall, gilded frame of the picture was eerily visible in the dark – but the figure and the scene inside it had vanished. Instead, the rectangle within the frame was starting to glow a dark, hot and unearthly gold. Slowly the glow intensified, pushing back the blackness, lighting the stunned faces of the Keepers who were now all staring in transfixed silence. It was like watching a strange and ominous sunrise; it was turning to a glare now, hurting their eyes. But they couldn't turn away. They couldn't move. Lias, his mind whirling, tried to fight the paralysis; he was the leader, the strongest, and with a tremendous effort he made his hands unclench, started to raise them—

A bolt of white lightning exploded from the centre of the painting and tore through the room. It struck Lias full on; for a moment his figure was wreathed in a blindingly brilliant halo – then he toppled like a felled tree and crashed to the floor.

'*Lias!*' Jonakar rushed to the leader's side, Amobrel and several others on his heels. The eldritch glare from the picture vanished, winking out and shrouding them in darkness again; with a shocked oath someone can for flint and tinder, and shaking hands re-lit the lamps. As their more natural glow filled the room, the group all gathered around Lias, calling out to him and to each other.

'He's breathing!' Jonakar's voice made itself heard above the rest. 'He's alive!'

'Thank Aeoris!' another said fervently. 'Fetch water, someone — Amobrel, help me raise his head!'

Amobrel moved to obey . . . then stopped, gazing wide-eyed at Lias's face. 'What's that?' she cried. 'There — on his forehead!'

They all looked. Then stared. Faces paled, and Jonakar whispered incredulously, 'The sign . . . the gods' own sign . . .'

Across Lias's brow, a white mark like a scar made a long, zig-zag pattern. The shape of it was unmistakable. It was a lightning-flash — the symbol of the lords of Order.

Then, even as the Keepers continued to stare, the mark began to fade. It grew fainter and fainter, and within seconds it had vanished altogether. As the last trace of it disappeared, Lias's eyelids fluttered open.

'Lias!' Awe and relief mingled in Jonakar's voice. 'Are you all right? Can you speak?'

Lias gazed up at the ceiling. For a moment his lips quivered with a spasm, then suddenly his voice croaked unsteadily from his throat.

'*The gods have . . .*' Another spasm; he coughed, and his followers waited with bated breath for him to recover. '*They have spoken to me . . . The lightning . . . it was th-the light of a revelation, and I know . . . I know now . . . what we must do!*'

And in a room upstairs, Giria's head turned from side to side on the pillow and her breathing grew quicker as she stirred restlessly in her sleep.

EIGHT

The black gelding that Kitto had 'borrowed' from the castle stables was really far too big for him, and skittish from lack of exercise into the bargain. But Kitto was sure he could handle the animal. Besides, it had the two qualities he wanted: it was built for stamina rather than speed, and it didn't belong to anyone in particular and so would not be missed for some time.

By evening he was deep among the mountains and a satisfactorily long way from the castle. He had given the horse a rest earlier and it was still fairly fresh; rather than stop just because the sun was setting, he thought, he'd keep going until the animal grew tired, then make camp for the night. He had a bag of oats, food and a blanket for himself, and there were plenty of springs to provide water. All in all, he was doing very well.

The sun's last rays were shining rose and crimson on the tops of the peaks, but the gorge through which he rode was heavy with shadows. They played tricks with the eye, looking more tangible than they really were; a sharp edge of darkness slanted across the next bend in the track, and as he approached it Kitto could easily have believed that he was heading towards a solid black wall.

Suddenly the horse jinked. Its head jerked up and it flattened its ears, snorting as it slithered to a halt. Kitto said a word that wasn't permitted in the castle and kicked its flanks, telling it to 'Get *on!*' But the animal only shied again, stamping. Then it whinnied shrilly – there was something unnerving about the way the sound echoed between the gorge walls – and Kitto's arms were jerked nearly out of their sockets as it snatched at the reins, trying to pull its head free.

'What's the matter with you, you stupid beast?' Kitto yelled. 'Come on! *Forward!*' He kicked again, harder, and the horse danced sideways, stiff-legged, jolting him violently.

'Behave, blast you, *behave!*' Half unseated, Kitto fumbled for a lost stirrup, at the same time struggling to get the horse back under control. It was that wall of shadow ahead; the idiotic brute thought it was something real, lurking beyond the bend and waiting to—

The shadow moved, and Kitto almost fell out of the saddle in shock.

'*What in the names of*...' He heard his own voice, heard it tail off and echo slowly, eerily away through the pass. It faded into silence, and with a peculiar, unreal feeling in the pit of his stomach Kitto found himself sitting rigid on the horse's back, staring along the track and unable to move a muscle. The horse was motionless, too, frozen, as though something had pinned its hoofs to the ground. It was trembling.

And the shadow had doubled in size.

No, Kitto told himself ferociously. *I'm imagining things. It hasn't changed. It can't have done.*

The loud slither of iron on shale made him jump

almost out of his skin. The horse had taken a step backwards. And another. And another. Kitto could *feel* its terror now, like a charge of psychic energy pulsing through the reins. It set up an answering fear in him, gripping him, swelling—

With no warning the horse uttered a shriek of blind panic and reared, forelegs raking the air. Caught completely unawares Kitto was flung backwards; he made a wild grab for the saddle pommel, but his hand closed on nothing and he pitched from the gelding's back. He hit the ground with an impact that punched the breath out of him; rolling, he saw the blur of the horse's great, dark bulk above him, then a flailing hoof glanced stunningly across his skull, and he sprawled with his face in the dust as the animal slewed around and bolted.

For some seconds Kitto couldn't move as pain surged like waves in his head. But instinct came to his rescue and with an effort he raised himself enough to lift his face from the dust and look with blurred vision along the track.

Slowly but unmistakably, like a creeping black tide, the wall of shadow was flowing towards him. Kitto's eyes bulged, and bile rose in his throat as a gust of hot, foul air, like the breath of something from the Seven Hells, wafted chokingly over him. The shadow was growing, bloating, stretching out towards him with a hideous life of its own; within moments it would reach him, and when it did—

From the depths of the shadow something laughed, horribly, cruelly. Pure terror hit Kitto like a hammer-blow and his voice bubbled from his throat: '*No-o-o! No, get back – oh, help me, HELP!*'

Panicking, floundering, he tried to scrabble to his feet. His one instinct was to run – anywhere, it didn't matter, he just had to get *away* – and he kicked out, jackknifing himself upright and spinning round in the same instant—

Something white and fast-moving smeared across his vision, and a shattering roar dinned in his ears and resounded through the gorge. Kitto had time for a single scream – then the whiteness launched itself at him, and he crashed to the ground again under its onslaught as the entire world blanked out.

Shar heard the news of Lias's revelation when she woke the next morning. The mission house was in a ferment, and none of the Keepers had even thought of their beds; only Shar, incredibly, had slept through all the excitement.

Lias himself had fully recovered and was none the worse for his experience. But there was a new light in his eyes and a new resolve in his voice; and when Shar learned of his intentions, she felt a stirring of deep unease.

The gods of Order, Lias said, had given him a clear and unambiguous warning – for in the moments when he lay unconscious after the lightning strike, he had had a vision. He saw a golden brooch, the badge of a Circle adept; then the brooch grew and became a ring of pure, shining fire with Shar's smiling face at its centre. But then the vision changed; darkness crowded in like a vast fist closing, Lias felt an enormous sense of evil, and the Circle cracked and broke apart, shattering into fragments, as Shar's face was replaced by the image of Thel Starnor, with other shadowy figures behind him.

Lias had no doubt of the vision's meaning. The Circle believed that Thel could no longer perform sorcery; but they were wrong. Somehow, he had kept control of his powers; from his prison he was starting to plot and work again, and he had friends to help him. Lias had not been shown who those friends were, but one thing was certain; it was *vital* that Shar should be protected. To that end, he declared, the Keepers were ready to pledge their strength, their skills and, if necessary, their lives to help her. All he asked in return was that she would place herself in their hands, and trust them completely.

Shar did not know how to react. She didn't doubt Lias's sincerity; it was clear that the vision had been real. But had the warning really come from the lords of Order, as he believed? Or did it have a different source?

She tried to point out her doubts to Lias, but he was adamant. The vision had been sent to him, and only to him, because the gods wanted him to be Shar's protector. There could be no question of her returning to the castle; the risks were far too great. She *must* stay at the mission, where the influence of Order's powers would keep her safe. He would pray to Lord Aeoris for guidance, and with the gods' strength to help him he would set out to unmask Thel and his accomplices.

Shar realised then that to agree to what Lias wanted would be to become, effectively, a prisoner. In the mission house she would be watched, guarded, defended — she would have no privacy and precious little time to herself.

Investigations of her own would be impossible, for the Keepers would know her every move. Shar didn't want that. She wasn't even sure, yet, that she could trust Lias and his friends.

Yet what else could she do? She knew no one else in Wester Reach, and to take a room, alone, at a tavern would be foolhardy. The Keepers of Light had offered her shelter, they were unfailingly kind and friendly, and so far they were her only hope of unravelling this new and possibly deadly mystery. In truth she had no choice but to stay, at least for the time being. So, hiding her uncertainty, she solemnly thanked Lias and accepted his offer.

Later that day, Shar decided to go out. She simply wanted to explore her surroundings. She didn't *need* to know her way around Wester Reach, but if anything should go wrong – in other words, if the Keepers turned out to be less benign than they appeared – that need might suddenly change. As she approached the gate in the wall, however, she was stopped by Jonakar, who appeared seemingly from nowhere. His face was smiling, but his words were firm. They couldn't hear of allowing her to venture out alone. The streets were unsafe for any unaccompanied girl, and under the present circumstances they would be more dangerous still for her. If she wanted to see something of the town, he added, he and Amobrel would go with her. He seemed pleased by this solution – but Shar was not, for it was a clear signal that the Keepers were watching her very closely indeed. They didn't intend to relax their scrutiny for a moment. They had psychic powers, too; enough to detect any attempt she made to use her own skills. That made it impossible for her to contact her elemental friends as she had planned . . . and it also raised a twinge of suspicion.

She was careful not to let Jonakar see her dismay. Instead she said pleasantly that there was no need for him and Amobrel to trouble themselves. All she had wanted was a little fresh air, and she could get that well enough by walking in the mission garden. Satisfied, Jonakar went inside the building, and as she gazed after him Shar saw another face at one of the windows. Oh yes; she was being watched all right . . . Well, there was no point in trying to sneak out, that was obvious. She would just have to bide her time until she could think of another plan.

To keep up appearances, she started to stroll around the garden. Everything was neat and well tended, with straight paths between the beds and not a single leaf out of place. It was so tidy that the effect was faintly oppressive, and after a few minutes Shar found herself becoming irritated. She wanted to disrupt the orderliness of it all; tip up a pot or kick some earth onto the path; make it less *perfect*. She knew the real reason for her frustration, but that didn't make her feel any better. Somehow, she had to solve this new problem and find a way to escape from the Keepers' surveillance.

Suddenly she jumped as a shape dashed out from the shrubs in front of her. It ran a few paces ahead then stopped and looked back, and Shar saw that it was the white cat that had been sunning itself on the wall when she arrived yesterday. Green-gold eyes stared hard at her for a second or two, then the cat blinked very deliberately and walked away. No telepathic message came from its mind, but Shar had an overwhelming feeling that it wanted her to follow.

Her pulse quickened and she set off after it. The cat strolled slowly and apparently aimlessly along the path. Twice it stopped and waited for her to catch up, raising its head to be stroked and responding with a purr. It was impossible to be sure, but Shar suspected that it was trying to show her that she should appear casual; so she slowed her own pace, pretending to look at the flowers as she walked.

Suddenly the cat turned off the path and dived into the shrubbery again. It moved so fast that for a moment Shar lost sight of it; then a white tail waved somewhere near the high wall and she heard a soft but urgent chirrup.

She pushed her way in among the bushes and found the cat at the foot of the wall, staring pointedly upwards. She followed the direction of its gaze. The wall was about twice her height and obviously very old, for the stones were rough and worn. But there was nothing especially interesting about it.

The cat chirruped again, impatiently, as though she were being very obtuse. Then it reared up on its hind legs and put its forepaws against the wall, as high as it could reach. Shar looked more closely . . . and realised what it was trying to tell her. The wall was rough and rubbly and the mortar crumbling, and from bottom to top, at regular intervals, someone had gouged out a series of footholds. It had clearly been done a long time ago, and the reason for it was impossible to guess; but the purpose was obvious and Shar felt her heart skip with excitement. She was more than agile enough to climb to the top, and provided there was a way down on the other side, this was the answer to her prayers.

She looked over her shoulder and to her delight saw that the mission house was hidden from view. If she could not see the Keepers, they could not see her, and quickly she set one foot in the first toehold, gripped a protrusion on the stonework, and started to haul herself up.

The climb was easy. She reached the top of the wall in less than two minutes and cautiously peered over into the street beyond. There before her was the sprawl of the docks, carts rumbling, people hurrying on their business, the twin masts of a ship, its sails furled, gliding down the river towards the sea. No one looked up, and leaning further over she saw to her enormous excitement that a matching line of footholds zigzagged down the wall on the other side.

So; she could get in and out of the mission, and no one would be any the wiser! Shar slithered back down the wall, dropping to the soft earth with a thud. The cat stared up at her, its eyes inscrutable, and she crouched to stroke its small, white head.

'Thank you!' she said heartfeltedly. 'I don't know where you came from or why you did this for me, but I owe you a debt!'

The cat arched its back with pleasure and started to

purr again, and to emphasise her gratitude Shar tried to project a telepathic message. However, there was no response, and after a few moments she frowned, puzzled. She wasn't especially good at communicating with cats, but her efforts always provoked *some* reaction, however slight. With this creature, though, there was nothing at all.

Ah, well. Doubtless the cat knew she was grateful. When the next meal was served she would save it a special titbit from her plate; but in the meantime she had plans to make. It was likely that someone would be looking for her by now; best to get away from this spot before any suspicions were aroused.

A minute later, Amobrel, who had been sent to the garden to check on Shar, saw her playing with a white cat. Cats weren't encouraged in the mission – they were, after all, creatures of Chaos rather than of Order – but the sect preached kindness to all living things; and besides, they kept away the mice that would otherwise eat all the newly-planted seeds. Amobrel couldn't recall seeing this particular cat before, but new ones were always coming in from the docks. She watched its antics for a few moments, then smiled and, satisfied that Shar would come to no harm, went back into the house.

Kitto regained consciousness to find himself lying on dry, hard-packed earth, with a shaft of cold light shining on him. For a horrible moment he panicked, thinking, *I'm dead – the thing that attacked me carried me off, and this is its lair in the Seven Hells!* But then reason came back.

99

He couldn't be dead, for his head ached fiercely and he could feel bruises all the way down his spine. So where was he?

The light, he realised, was the glow of the moons, and when he looked around he saw that he was in a cave. Still in the mountains, then. What had *happened* to him? The last thing he recalled was trying to run from the horror on the track; he had turned, and something white had hurled itself at him . . .

Kitto's eyes widened as he remembered what he had glimpsed in the instant before he lost consciousness. He sat bolt upright in a flurry – and from the deep shadows at the back of the cave came a soft, rumbling growl.

His heart thumped so hard that he thought it would break through his ribs. *It was here! The creature, the thing –* panic gripped him; he tried to make himself look round but he was frozen. Then he heard movement. *It* was padding towards him; he could feel warm breath on his neck, and in despair he shut his eyes tightly, thinking: *It's going to kill me, it's going to tear me to pieces – oh gods, oh Yandros, help, help—*

Something whuffed by his ear and Kitto was nearly sick with terror. But then a new sensation invaded his mind. A message; not words but a feeling, faintly amused, faintly pitying . . . and friendly.

Hardly daring to believe it, Kitto found the courage to turn his head.

It was the biggest mountain cat he had ever seen. Nose to tail-tip it must have been at least twice the length of a tall man, and its fur was silver-tipped white, shading to grey only on its muzzle and haunches. For a few seconds it gazed at him with calm interest. Then it stretched forward, sniffed his face, and licked his forehead.

Kitto was stunned. He had always been terrified of these giant cats, despite the fact that they hardly ever attacked humans and in fact kept well out of humans' way. But now, face to face with one for the first time in his life, his fear vanished. The cat was a friend; he knew it as surely as he knew anything. In fact it had saved his life.

Tentatively he stretched out a hand towards it. 'Th . . . thank you,' he stammered. It was impossible to tell whether the cat understood, but he suspected it did. It whuffed again, then padded towards the cave entrance and stood staring out. Kitto made to follow, but stopped as the animal turned and gave a soft, warning growl. Was there something out there? The cat was very alert, as if it expected trouble, and Kitto started to wonder about the attack on him. Who had launched it – and how had the cat been able to defeat a supernatural power? It was only an ordinary animal . . .

Or was it? A sharp tingle went through Kitto as he realised that his rescuer couldn't possibly be any normal creature. Just as someone had sent the crawling dark shadow to devour him, so someone else must have sent the cat to protect him. But who?

The answer was obvious and made him tingle again. Cats had strong links with Chaos, and strong links with Shar. This was all beginning to make *sense*.

'Please . . .' He inched forward on hands and knees,

not daring to go too close to the cat. 'Is Shar safe? Do you know where she is?'

The animal turned its head and looked at him, and a clear image flicked into Kitto's head. He saw Shar walking in a garden, with a small white cat at her heels. A pale aura shone around her as though protecting her; but in the background was another figure, a faceless human silhouette that lurked and followed, and from which Kitto sensed a wave of evil.

The vision faded and Kitto shivered, but he thought he understood. Shar *was* safe, at least for now. The darkness was close behind her, though, and if its chance came, it would strike.

Kitto felt suddenly angry and helpless. He wished Hestor was here, and for a moment thought of going back to the castle. But he couldn't risk alerting the Circle – and anyway, it would take too much time. He had to get to Wester Reach. He had to find Shar.

The mountain cat was still looking at him, and he spoke to it again. 'Please,' he said, 'warn Hestor! Let him know I'm all right, but tell him to be careful. They'll try again, I know they will, and next time he might be the one in danger.' The cat didn't react and he wondered if it understood. '*Please!*' he entreated again. 'Please, tell him!'

In the distance among the peaks there was a rumble. At first Kitto though it was thunder, but then, listening, he heard something else; a thin, high-pitched wailing, as if a hurricane was rushing in from far, far away. Then a flicker of eerie, crimson light swept across the cave entrance, momentarily eclipsing the glow of the moons, and his pulse quickened. A Warp – one of the great supernatural storms from the realms of the gods! Was it an answer to his plea?

A wall of wild green light flashed through the gorge outside; thunder sounded again and the wailing was growing louder. Kitto huddled back against the cave wall; he had always been frightened of Warps and couldn't break the habit even now. But the cat raised its head eagerly, and a snarl of excitement vibrated in its throat. Then, as the wailing rose to a demented shriek and the third thunderclap exploded almost overhead, it opened its mouth and uttered a shattering roar – a roar of challenge and resolve, that rang out in turbulent harmony with the din of the breaking storm.

NINE

The dream was one of the most vivid that Hestor could ever remember having, and he was certain that it was no coincidence.

To his annoyance he had been forced to spend another night in the infirmary; though he protested that he was perfectly well now, Physician Chandor would take no argument. Another day, he had said, and then he would see. Grumpy and frustrated, Hestor had no choice but to obey.

This dream, though . . . he woke from it just as dawn was breaking, and as he sat up in the chilly half-light he found himself wet with perspiration. In the dream, Kitto had been in danger. Where and what the danger was Hestor had no idea, but he *knew* that it was about to strike, and he was running through the castle's maze of corridors, looking for his friend and desperate to warn him. But every time he found Kitto and tried to call out to him, someone interrupted and distracted him. It happened time after time, and the people interrupting were always different; his mother, two of his friends, the High Initiate, even, crazily, a jovial visiting dignitary whom he had briefly met at the Quarter-Day festivities. Then suddenly he found himself thinking: *these people all look different – but are they?* In the illogical way of dreams

Hestor began to suspect something amiss, and then became convinced that they weren't different at all. They were all the same person, in disguise. But who was it? *Who?*

Suddenly the dream changed, and Hestor found himself in the Marble Hall. Its mists swirled around him; in the distance the seven statues of the gods towered, and he dared not look down at the mosaic floor because it was trying to suck him in. Then footsteps echoed, and Kitto appeared. The two boys faced each other in the eerie, shifting light. Then Kitto said, 'It's all right. It didn't work. Watch out for the white cat, Hestor. They're sure to try again soon, and we don't know which one of us it'll be next time.'

He turned and started to walk away. Hestor shouted, 'Kitto!' but Kitto didn't even turn round.

'Kitto! What do you mean? What are you talking about? Kitto, come back! *Come*—'

And Hestor had woken.

He couldn't unravel the dream's meaning, but he was absolutely certain that it was trying to tell him something. Had someone sent it? Not Kitto, certainly; he had no sorcerous skills at all, let alone the high level needed for dream-sending. Shar, too, was ruled out, unless she had had help from the elemental planes. Yet somehow this didn't feel like an elementals' message.

Hestor wondered about the woman who claimed to be Shar's mother. Giria Tillmer Starnor had been a high-ranking adept, and if she *was* alive, she might still have the power to cast a dream spell. But what did it mean?

Kitto in danger; then Kitto safe. What was going *on?*

Hestor made up his mind then. Whatever Physician Chandor said, he couldn't sit idly by; if Kitto was in trouble, he had to do something. No one had noticed the black-haired boy's absence yet, but Hestor pushed away the idea of telling the Circle and asking them for help, for the dream suggested that so far Kitto was coping. The moment he was allowed out of bed, he would try to make contact with the elementals. Whether he could actually do it was another matter, for he didn't have Shar's talent. But he would try, and if he succeeded he would ask them – beg them if necessary – for the answers to some very urgent questions.

There was a clear sky the following night and both moons were near the full. It was not ideal, for the moonlight in the garden would make Shar all too visible from the mission house windows. But cloudy nights were rare at this time of year, and she wasn't prepared to wait any longer than she had to.

Getting out of the house was simple; all she had to do was wait until everyone was asleep, then tiptoe downstairs and let herself out through the kitchen way. The Keepers did not believe in locking doors, and the house was so well cared for that no squeaking hinge would give her away. Reaching the garden she headed for the place that the cat had shown her, and forged in among the bushes. The wall was in deep shadow but the toeholds were easy to locate by feel, and Shar climbed to the top without mishap.

A busy port town like Wester Reach never truly slept; at this hour, though, it was quiet enough to ensure that no one saw her scramble down the other side of the wall and set off along the paved street towards the docks. She had chosen clothes that made her as inconspicuous as possible; her old coat over loose wool trousers and leather boots, and her hair tied in a knot at the back of her neck. At a glance she could be taken for a boy, which was safer; all the same she glanced frequently over her shoulder as she walked, and her pulse was racing.

The dockside area was a bewildering jumble of wharves and jetties and storehouses. There was more activity here; tides took no account of the time of day and three coastal barges and a passenger barque had come upriver on the flood to unload their cargoes. Shar veered away from the bustling, shouting figures all lit by the flare of torches, and hurried on to a quieter section. Here, buildings were unlit and boats bobbed unattended at the quays; rats scrabbled and rustled in dark corners but there was nothing else to disturb the night's stillness.

Between a shuttered tavern and a tall warehouse, Shar stopped and looked around her. Just a few paces away the river slid past, shining darkly with reflected moonlight, and her resolve wavered. The river had seemed the ideal place for a summoning of the water elementals, but now that she was close to it she felt daunted. It looked so deep and relentless; more frightening than the sea, beside which she had lived all her life. And if enemies were near, an 'accident' would be all too easy to arrange. One slip, one splash, and the river would keep the secret of her disappearance for ever.

Shar began to shiver, and was tempted to turn and run back to the sanctuary of the mission house. With an effort she took a grip on herself. What sort of coward was she, to lose her nerve because of a mere atmosphere? Her fellow adepts would laugh at her, and rightly so. *Be calm*, she commanded herself silently and fiercely. *You're not a child, to be afraid of the dark. The night is a friend, not an adversary!*

Touching her tongue to dry lips, she moved towards the edge of the quay. The tide was going out now, exposing weed-covered steps down to the water. Still there was no one in sight, and Shar took a deep breath before starting carefully downwards. The steps were treacherously slippery; several times her feet nearly slid from under her and she had to grab a mooring ring to save herself. At last, though, she was close enough to the water for her purpose, and hidden from the view of anyone who might pass by.

She sat down on the step, ignoring its unpleasant sliminess, and words formed in her mind. *Little friends of the water . . . it is Shar who calls to you. Hear me, little friends; hear me and answer. I need your help tonight.*

The river slapped against the wall, sounding sinister and dangerous, but there was no other response. Shar quelled a shudder and tried again. *Little friends. Remember me, come to me. I need you. I summon you, creatures of water.*

Still there was only the murmur and glide of the river. The elementals had not heard her, or did not choose to answer. Shar summoned every scrap of willpower she could muster and projected a powerful, desperate plea: *HEAR ME, PLEASE HEAR ME!* But there was no tingling in her mind, no sense of a presence, *nothing*. She felt tears welling and bit them back. What was wrong? In the past her friends had always come when she called to them. They had never let her down. Now, though . . .

From above her came a low hiss. Shar started and almost lost her balance on the step; then looking up with a thudding heart she saw a small face, pale in the moonlight, peering over the edge of the quay.

It was the white cat. Its eyes glowed with a peculiar reflection; seeing her turn it mewed, urgently, and Shar felt a twinge of excitement.

'What is it? she whispered. 'Do you want me to follow you? Is that what you're trying to say?'

The cat mewed again. Hastily Shar scrambled up the steps, and at once the cat set off along the quayside, moving fast so that she had to run to keep up. Within minutes they had left the jetties and the buildings behind, and the last edges of Wester Reach were giving way to untamed country. It was utterly deserted, but when Shar looked longingly back at the dwindling lights of the town, the cat yowled an imperative order, urging her to hurry. She wavered for a moment, then hastened on. The cat had helped her once – she could only trust it to help her again.

Abruptly the little animal veered off the rough path and trotted towards the river. There was a sharper edge to the bank here, a drop into deep water, and Shar approached cautiously. A short way from the bank the cat stopped. It looked intently at her, then at the river. She followed its gaze but saw nothing and, puzzled, turned to ask it what it was trying to convey.

The cat wasn't there. In the time it took Shar to glance towards the water and back again, it had vanished without trace. Shar stared quickly around, but there was no small, white shape running away in the moonlight. Incredibly, impossibly, the cat was gone.

Then behind her the steady rippling sound of the river was disturbed by a splash.

Shar spun, her heart lurching fearfully, and was in time to see a sleek shape break the water's surface. It was far too big to be a fish; and anyway, fish had scales, while this was . . . it was *furred*.

Suddenly two heads appeared in midstream, rising from the current, and a sweet, wailing song shimmered out across the river. Shar saw the huge, dark eyes, the whiskered muzzles, the brindle pattern of the coats, and understanding came, together with an enormous surge of excitement. Her call *had* been answered, but not by the beings of the water plane. Something far stranger had come to her aid; something mortal and corporeal, yet wiser – and more elusive – than any elemental. The fabled creatures called fanaani, which lived their mysterious lives in the deep-sea world and neither asked nor gave any bond of allegiance, had come to her.

Shar sank to her knees and stared in awe as the fanaani swam slowly towards her. They were the size of a man, lithe and powerful and graceful, and their flippers and broad tails cut through the water with scarcely a ripple.

They didn't sing again. Instead, they stopped a short way from the bank and turned on their backs, floating easily and gazing at her with mild interest. Then, as clearly as if someone had spoken aloud, she heard words in her mind.

No need for fear. No danger yet.

Shar shook her head in astonishment. She had heard that the fanaani had incredible telepathic powers, but this – it was greater than anything she had imagined, let alone experienced! Leaning precariously out over the bank's edge, she called to them in an eager whisper.

'Where does the danger lie? Please, can you tell me?'

The nearer and larger fanaan blinked languidly, and its reply echoed in her head. *Danger is all around. But the sea protects. The sea is good. There are many answers in the sea. Many answers over the sea.*

The sea? Instinctively Shar looked downriver, but even by the moons' light she could see only a little way; certainly not to the distant coast. The river's estuary, she knew from her studies, formed a natural anchorage that channelled out into the open waters of the Western Sound. But what lay beyond that?

Then it fell into place. Across the Sound was an island known as the Brig. A prison island, hardly used for the past hundred years but now inhabited again by one man.

Thel Starnor.

Stifling a sudden surge of queasiness Shar again turned her gaze to the fanaani where they floated near the bank.

'Please,' she asked them, 'Who can I trust to help me?'

The larger animal rolled placidly over in the water. *Trust us*, it replied. *Trust cats. And other friends.*

'What friends? The Keepers of Light?'

The fanaan almost seemed to shrug. *Who knows? Men are good and evil, wise and foolish. How best to judge?*

'What about my – Giria – the woman who claims to be my mother . . .?'

Ah. The mother. Strangeness and sorrow and confusion. We cannot see. We cannot tell.

'I don't understand what you mean!' Shar said desperately.

But the fanaan did not reply directly. Instead it started to drift out into the current, which was now moving faster as the sea-tide ebbed. Fainter now, its voice sang in her head. *To understand is hard.*

The second animal was swimming to join the first. Shar cried, 'Please wait! I need your help! I need—'

As one, both fanaani dived. There was barely a ripple to mark their going; one instant they were visible, the next they had vanished, and all that remained was a last whisper that touched her mind like a fading breath.

All around . . . yet over the sea. Listen to the sea. Listen . . .

Then all trace of the fanaani was gone, as though they had been nothing more than a dream.

For a long time Shar crouched on the river bank, staring at the water and hoping against hope that the creatures would come back. At last, though, she admitted defeat. The fanaani had come in answer to her plea, but no power in the world could hold them against their will. They would not return.

She rose to her feet. Upriver the lights of Wester Reach looked distant and dim, and curls of groundmist were starting to rise along the marshier stretches of the bank. The first moon had set and the second was close to the horizon; it was hard now to see the pathway, and with a shiver that wasn't entirely due to the chill Shar started back towards the town as quickly as the rough ground allowed. Several times she stumbled, but her fear of a turned ankle was suddenly less than her fear of the night. Everything was so quiet – *too* quiet, she thought uneasily, for there were no sounds of nocturnal birds, no whispers of wind, not even the smallest ripple from the river itself. There was only an absolute and unnatural silence.

Then, in the reeds that now lay between her and the water, something rustled.

Shar stopped in her tracks, staring towards the river. The sound stopped, too, but she had an awful feeling that an invisible presence was watching her. The fanaani? Hope surged, then died. This had nothing to do with the benign sea-creatures, her instinct was horribly sure of it. This was far more ominous.

Trying to breathe evenly, she made herself walk on again. The night seemed darker all of a sudden; so dark that she could hardly see the ground in front of her. And the mist was thickening . . .

When the rustling began again she forced herself not to stop and not to so much as glance at the reeds and the river beyond. Whatever was there kept pace with her, and now there was a splashing as well as a rustling, as though it was wading along the shallows at the water's edge. At first she had thought it was something small. Now, though, she was not so sure.

There was a denser patch of mist ahead, lying right across the path, and it also looked darker than the rest. Shar slowed uncertainly as she neared it, half convinced that she had glimpsed a shape moving in its depths. It blotted out the town lights . . . and abruptly she had an ugly conviction that if she walked into that drifting darkness, she might not emerge on the other side.

She halted again, trying not to notice the unpleasant fact that the furtive noises from the river ceased at the same moment. What to do? In her Circle training she had learned some protective spells but they weren't especially powerful, and if this was something stronger than a low elemental, to use them could make the situation worse.

Torn, she hesitated.

Then, slowly but unmistakably, the patch of darkness began to move towards her.

Shar took a lurching step backwards and a whimper of fear broke from her throat. She clapped a hand to her mouth, frantic to silence her voice, not draw attention to herself – but it was too late for that, because the mist was coming, flowing, spreading—

From behind her came a hiss of fury, and Shar spun round.

The white cat stood on the path, ears flat, back arched and the fur on its spine and tail bristling. Its eyes flared like twin fires and it hissed again, showing its teeth in an open-mouthed snarl. It was staring past Shar; then before she could react, it launched itself forward and shot past her, straight at the encroaching shadow.

Shar cried out in a mixture of shock and fear for the cat's safety. Her human reactions were far slower than an animal's; she turned, instinctively reaching out to grab at the cat—

She was in time to see the flick of a white tail as the cat darted into the scrubland stretching away from the river. And the patch of darkness was no longer there.

Shar stared in amazement. The mist had *gone* . . . and with its vanishing, so too the sense of thick, brooding menace had evaporated as though it had never existed. A nocturnal bird called with a long, churring note and was answered by the hooting and almost comic cackle of a water-fowl. The river current rippled, the second moon shone serenely down and the lights of the town and the docks showed clear and steady.

With her heart and pulse thundering Shar looked for the white cat. But it had gone. She was alone, and there was nothing here to threaten her.

At least, until next time.

A cold, deep-seated shiver ran through her marrow and she began to run towards the sanctuary of Wester Reach.

By the time she reached the mission house, Shar was feeling a good deal better. There had been no more incidents, and no one to trouble her as she hurried through the now quiet docks. She found the footholds in the wall, climbed them without difficulty, and glided across the garden to let herself into the dark, silent house.

She had reached the entrance hall and was tiptoeing

towards the stairs when a light glimmered suddenly from beyond a half-open door. A figure carrying a lantern loomed – and Shar found herself face to face with Giria.

'*Shar!*' Giria looked as shocked as she was. 'Shar, where have you *been?*'

Thinking quickly, Shar tried to dissemble. '– I was thirsty,' she said. 'I came downstairs for a drink of water . . .'

'In outdoor clothes? Oh Shar, don't lie to me! I saw you running across the garden. What have you been doing?'

She couldn't talk her way out of it, Shar realised, and at once she became defensive. 'It was something private,' she said. 'I don't want to discuss it.'

'But if you went outside . . . the danger . . . Lias would be horrified!'

'It's none of Lias's business,' Shar countered. 'He doesn't have any authority over me.' She was starting to feel angry and added, 'And though I don't want to be rude, neither do you.'

Giria's face creased unhappily. 'How can you say such a cruel thing? I'm your *mother.*'

Shar stared steadily at her. 'Are you?'

Giria shrank back as though she had been stung, and for a moment Shar thought she was going to cry. Then she got herself under control and looked away, her eyes filled with pain. 'I'm sorry,' she said indistinctly. 'I must remember how hard this is for you. It's too soon to expect you to trust me.'

'I'd like to go to bed now, please.' Shar didn't let herself unbend. 'May I pass?' She stepped forward, and Giria started to move out of the way. Then suddenly she clasped Shar's arm in a tight, urgent grip.

'Shar, please – I won't ask you to tell me where you went tonight or what you've been doing. But I beg you to be careful! You're so young, so inexperienced, and I'm afraid of what could happen to you! If you'll only trust Lias and confide in him, he'll help you! It's what he wants; it's what we *all* want. *Please*, Shar – can't you do that, for me?'

Shar looked away and gently but firmly pulled her arm free. 'No,' she said. 'I can't.' Then she looked up again with a challenge in her eyes. 'And if you tell anyone that I went out tonight, I'll leave for good.'

Giria bit her lip, then her shoulders slumped. 'Very well. I won't say a word. But I'm so frightened for you!'

'I can look after myself.'

Giria laughed softly, hollowly. 'I pray with all my heart that that's true . . . Go to bed, then, my dear daughter. Dream sweetly, and may the gods watch over you.'

She touched Shar's face briefly. Her fingers were cold, and the touch made Shar shiver with a twist of painful emotion. Then she turned and went back into the room from which she had come, closing the door quietly behind her.

TEN

'So you understand, I'm sure,' Lias finished, 'why I must place this restriction on you.' He smiled at Shar kindly but with a hint of reproach. 'I *do* see your point of view; but my conscience wouldn't rest easy if we didn't take every possible care for you. To allow you out on your own – and especially at night – is simply too dangerous. I hope you'll try to understand, and not feel that we're being unfair or unkind.'

The look that Shar flashed across the room to Giria showed her reaction without any need for words. Giria looked away and Lias added, 'Try not to be angry with her, Shar. It's only natural that she should put your welfare first, even if it meant breaking a promise.'

Shar did not answer. There was no point; nothing she could say would make any difference. Giria had told Lias about last night's episode, and as a result of it the Keepers meant to ensure that it wouldn't be repeated. From now on, Shar would be watched more closely than ever. There would be no more chance for secret investigations, for in the daytime there would be someone constantly with her, and at night her door would be locked.

She felt a momentary urge to flare up, tell them all exactly what she thought and storm out of the mission before anyone could stop her. But she pushed the impulse

118

down. If she was to find a way out of this predicament she needed to be subtle, pretend to give in and then look for a chance to catch her protectors off their guard and escape. Her protectors. Were they? she wondered. Or did they have another motive for wanting to control her?

At least they hadn't found out where she had gone or what had happened to her. Lias had tried to question her but she refused to answer, and at last he had abandoned his efforts. Nor, as far as she knew, did they have any idea how she had got out of the mission, which still left her with an escape route if the chance came to use it.

So she made a pretence of submitting and, relieved, Lias declared that no more would be said about the matter.

'And of course this doesn't mean that you can't go out at all,' he told her. 'If you wish to see the town, you need only ask and someone will go with you.'

'Thank you,' Shar replied meekly as her mind latched on to the possibilities of that. 'I'll remember.'

For the rest of the morning and half the afternoon Shar tried to think of a means of getting away from the Keepers. At last she decided on an experiment which, if nothing else, would test the water, and asked Amobrel and Jonakar to come out with her, to show her something of Wester Reach. They were happy to agree, and the three of them left the house together, turned away from the docks and walked under the arches in the great stone wall, to the main part of the town. Despite her preoccupations Shar was absorbed by the sights and sounds of Wester Reach, which she had been in no mood to notice properly on her arrival. She had never visited any of the province capitals before; throughout her life she had known only the elegant peace of Summer Isle, then the seclusion of a Sisterhood cot and, after that, the remote world of the castle. This bustle and noise and sheer *busy*-ness was completely new to her. Houses, taverns and markets all crowded together along a maze of streets that looked even more complex than the castle's passages, and the streets themselves were a hurly-burly of people and horses and wagons. There was so much to look at that Shar all but forgot her dilemma – until, as they passed one of the larger taverns, she glimpsed a face that looked vaguely familiar.

He was just going into the tavern, and for a few moments Shar couldn't place him. Then, with a mental jolt, memory came back.

It was Reyni Trevire.

'Shar?' said Amobrel. 'Are you all right?'

Shar had stopped in her tracks and was staring at the tavern door. In a flashing moment she took in the painted sign; a ship's bell against a background of rigging, with a dull patina shining on its surface.

The Bronze Bell tavern . . . Of course, she thought. Reyni would only have arrived in Wester Reach a few hours ahead of her, and he had said that he would be here for a few days before going on to Prospect Province. This must be where he was staying. That was how he had met Giria . . .

'Shar?' Amobrel said again. Shar's mind snapped back

120

to earth. Reyni had disappeared through the tavern door, and though both her companions were staring at her curiously, they clearly had not seen him.

'I—' She searched feverishly for something to put them off the scent and, thankfully, found it. 'I was looking at the inn sign. The Bronze Bell.' She smiled sadly. 'It was where my – where Giria's letter told me I would find her.'

'Ah, of course.' Amobrel smiled compassionately, and Jonakar added, 'Thanks be to our lord Aeoris, it wasn't necessary for you to go to such lengths.'

'Yes,' Shar replied blandly. They walked on, but her brain was still working with sharp energy, and a wild idea had come to her. Above all else she wanted to get a message to Hestor and Kitto, but to use the messenger-bird service was too risky, for if she did have enemies at the castle, they might intercept her letter when it arrived. Would Reyni be willing to play courier a second time? She could pay him well, and musicians always seemed short of money. If she could just find a way to meet him and talk to him in private . . .

Something brushed against her leg. She looked down, and saw the white cat pacing beside her. It was gazing up at her face; its look was very intent, but as soon as it was sure she had noticed it, it darted away. Anxious not to alert her companions Shar slid her own gaze sidelong and saw it run straight to the door of the Bronze Bell. Its tail flicked once, urgently, then it ran back to her.

Its meaning was as clear as any words. It was telling

her that Reyni *could* be trusted, and that her wild idea was not wild at all.

Amobrel and Jonakar were unaware of the cat. Jonakar had started to tell a story about a time, five springs ago, when unnaturally high tides on the west coast had sent an enormous bore-wave upriver and half Wester Reach had been flooded; but Shar wasn't listening. The cat was trotting beside her again now, still staring up, and she tried to project telepathically to it: *How can I meet Reyni? Amobrel and Jonakar won't let me out of their sight!*

As before, she felt no answering tingle from the animal's mind. Instead it veered away from her and suddenly ran across Amobrel's path, almost tripping her up.

'Whatever – Amobrel began, righting herself. Then she saw the cat. 'Look – it's the animal that keeps coming to the mission garden! I'd recognise it anywhere, its colour is so unusual.' She held out a hand, making soft sounds in her throat. 'Here, little one! Do you remember me?'

The cat started towards her. In the road behind them a heavily laden cart was about to pass, its wheels rumbling like thunder on the cobbles. The cat drew nearer to Amobrel, tail high – then without any warning it streaked past her, straight into the road in the path of the cart.

'Jonakar!' Amobrel's voice rose in a horrified shriek. 'Catch it, catch it, oh, no—'

She and Jonakar both dived for the cat but missed, and Amobrel cried out again as it seemed the little creature would be crushed. But the cat shot like a crossbow bolt between the trampling hooves and the grinding wheels, and gained the safety of the far pavement. It looked back at the stricken Amobrel, a look of amusement, almost of triumph. Then with an impudent flick of its tail it melted into the bustle of the town.

And when Amobrel and Jonakar turned to where Shar had been standing, she was no longer there.

From the shadowed entrance of a narrow alley Shar watched Amobrel and Jonakar zigzagging through the crowds as they searched for her. She could hear them calling her name, but they were moving away in the opposite direction and within minutes they had disappeared in the throng. Cautiously, Shar emerged from her hiding place and looked around her. The Bronze Bell tavern was a short way back along the road, and her first thought was to go there in search of Reyni. But it wouldn't be wise to face him breathless and dishevelled, and with no story prepared; she needed to think up a tale that wouldn't raise his suspicions. Besides, she recalled with a pang of conscience, they had not exactly parted on the best of terms, so if she wanted his help she would have to make peace first, and that might not be easy.

The first and most important thing was to prepare her message for Hestor and Kitto. Luckily she had her purse with her, so she could buy writing materials. All she needed was a way to stay safe from discovery while she wrote the letter. Then, and only then, would she steel herself to meet Reyni.

She made her purchases, and with a gleam of inspiration also bought herself an oiled hide coat with a hood, of the kind worn by boat crews. Many women here in the north went out fishing, so a girl in such a coat wouldn't draw attention; and with the Keepers no doubt combing the town for her by now it would lessen the chances of being recognised. Feeling more confident, she returned to the riverside and looked for somewhere where she could sit down and blend in unnoticed. She soon found the ideal place; a cluster of booths with tables and benches set around them, where traders were selling food and drink. With two passenger ships newly arrived at the quay, trade was brisk among sailors looking for something more appetizing than sea rations. Shar bought herself a crab and a hunk of barley bread, then sat at one of the tables to write to Hestor and Kitto.

She was still working at her letter when two burly sailors sat down at the table beside her. They were close enough to read what she had written, so Shar put the letter away and turned to her food. As she ate, she couldn't help but hear their conversation.

The sailors were discussing their next voyage, and Shar, only half-listening, didn't register the significance of their talk for a few moments. But then two stray words lodged in her brain and her stomach clenched suddenly.

The words were: *The Brig*.

The island where Thel languished was, Shar knew, uninhabited but for its solitary prisoner. With his magical powers stripped and no means of leaving the island, he did not need guards or jailers; once a month a ship took provisions to him, but apart from that he was left to shift for himself. These sailors, it seemed were about to make that voyage. They clearly didn't relish it; seamen were notoriously superstitious and, knowing what the island contained, none went there willingly. But, as one grumpily remarked, at least they wouldn't have to sail within sight of the accursed place again until another month had passed. Out on tonight's tide, he added, and the sooner it was over and done with, the happier he would feel.

Shar pretended not to be interested in the men's talk, but inwardly her heart was pumping and her mind raced. An idea had formed in the back of her brain; an idea so impetuous, so audacious and so foolhardy that if she stopped to consider it she would dismiss it as mad. But she didn't let herself stop, for the idea had already taken hold of her and she could not shake it off.

There are many answers over the sea, the fanaani had said. And only one person in the world could tell her whether her mother was dead and Giria therefore an imposter. *Over the sea* . . . If she was to have her answers, Shar must confront him – and the sailors had given her the opportunity.

The men had finished their food; they stood up and one smiled agreeably at her before they walked away. To Shar's feverish imagination the smile was like a sign. To contemplate this was *insane*, she told herself. But even as a part of her said it, another part knew that the decision was already made. She knew the supply ship was called the *Margravine*, for the sailors had mentioned it. She knew when they would be sailing. She only needed to find a way to get on board without being caught.

Slowly Shar unfolded her half-finished letter. She wished that her message could reach Hestor and Kitto before she embarked on this venture, but the only way to alert them in time was by messenger-bird, and that was too risky. All she could do was tell them of her plan; then if anything went wrong – though she didn't let herself dwell on that possibility – they would at least know what was afoot.

If it isn't too late by then, said a small voice inside her. Shar forced it away. She picked up her stylus and began to write.

Reyni Trevire was surprised when a tavern potboy knocked at his door and told him someone was downstairs asking for him by name. He was even more surprised when, as he came down the stairs, he saw Shar.

'Reyni.' Hoping that she looked more confident than she felt, Shar plunged in before he could say a word. 'I've come to apologise for what happened on the day you left the castle. And I – I've come to ask – properly this time – for your help.'

It wasn't an ideal approach, but it was the best she had been able to think of in a short space of time . . . and it worked. Reyni wasn't the kind to bear a grudge, and once he had got over his first suspicion that she might try to magically coerce him again, he was willing to listen. What she asked of him seemed harmless; it was an easy commission and (as she had suspected) he could well use the generous payment she offered.

'You just want me to ride to the castle and deliver the letter?' he said. 'Nothing more?'

Shar shook her head. 'Nothing. Except that you *must* give it *only* to Hestor or Kitto, and be sure that no one else knows about it.'

'That's simple enough. Very well, then. A few more days won't make any difference to my plans; there are plenty of ships sailing to Prospect and I can change the passage I've booked. So: Hestor or Kitto. I know what they both look like; I'll find them.' He paused, then: 'Shar, is everything all right with you? I don't want to pry, but . . .'

She smiled. 'Everything's fine.'

'Well, then . . . I'll leave first thing tomorrow. I should be at the Star Peninsula within three days.' Suddenly, impulsively, he put his hands on her shoulders and kissed her cheek. 'Good luck, Shar, and the gods go with you. I hope we'll meet again before too long.'

'So do I,' said Shar, and meant it.

She thought he was watching her from one of the tavern windows as she hurried away towards the quays, but she did not let herself look back. She had made up a vague story about some trouble with a distant relative who was involved with the Keepers of Light, and of whom the High Initiate did not approve, pleading family loyalty as the reason for her secrecy where the Circle was concerned. It explained the earlier letter that the Keepers had entrusted to Reyni, and it had seemed to convince him. Even if he did suspect something amiss,

Shar felt confident that he wouldn't act on his suspicions. The white cat had shown her that he could be trusted.

It did not take Shar long to learn that the *Margravine* was berthed in the storehouse district below the town walls. Making a careful detour to avoid passing the mission, she found the ship, a three-masted barquentine, loading her cargo at one of the deep-water quays. With the tide only just turned from the ebb the *Margravine* sat low in the water, and men were rolling barrels noisily down a gangplank, watched by a fair, bearded man sporting a shipmaster's silver arm device. Shar eyed the master. He looked stern and short-tempered, and it was hard to imagine that he would treat stowaways kindly. She would just have to make certain that she wasn't found.

The sun was westering and it would soon be dusk. What time was high tide? Shar calculated, remembering her adventure of the previous night, and judged that the *Margravine* was likely to sail at about first moonset. That meant she should be on board and hidden while both moons were still in the sky. With luck there would be a lull between loading and sailing, and that would give her her chance.

She found a vantage point from where she could see the ship, and settled herself on a pile of coiled ropes to wait.

Reyni was awake before dawn the next morning, and by the time the sun had cleared the horizon he was saddling his horse ready for the journey to the Star Peninsula.

Shar's letter was stowed in his saddlebag. He had been sorely tempted to break the seal and read it, for this mystery intrigued him and he would have liked to help Shar in some other way if he could. But a promise was a promise; and besides, it was none of his business. Pity, though. He liked Shar. Ah well; if their paths crossed again, perhaps they would have more time to get to know each other.

He mounted his horse, rode out of the tavern yard and away towards the edge of the town. The streets were fairly quiet at this hour, so when he saw the small, dark-haired figure walking towards him he naturally looked more closely—

And reined in with an exclamation of surprise.

He knew the boy's face immediately, for he had spent half the night committing it and another face to memory, so that there could be no mistakes when he arrived at the castle. Yet here that same boy was, plain as daylight, hurrying alone one of the main thoroughfares of Wester Reach.

The boy was nearly level with him now, and Reyni said sharply, 'Kitto?'

Kitto stopped in his tracks and looked up at the figure on horseback. He frowned, momentarily baffled – and very wary, Reyni noticed – then recognition dawned.

'Oh . . .' he said. 'You . . .'

He sounded hostile, but Reyni ignored that. 'What are you doing in Wester Reach?' he asked.

Kitto's blue eyes narrowed suspiciously. 'What's that to you?'

'Quite a lot, as it happens. That is, if you're looking for Shar.'

Ah, yes; he had hit the target. Kitto tensed like a cat, his hands clenching at his sides, and in that instant Reyni noticed his state for the first time. He was dirty and dishevelled, his hands and face were grazed and there was a huge, purplish-black bruise on his forehead and spreading over one eye. He looked as if he had either been fighting or had taken a bad fall. And he also looked exhausted.

Reyni slid down from the saddle. 'What's happened to you, Kitto? Is something wrong?'

The alarm in his voice allayed some of Kitto's suspicion but he was still distrustful. 'Never mind me,' he retorted. 'What did you mean about Shar?'

'Then you *are* looking for her?' Swinging back to his horse Reyni fumbled in his saddlebag. 'I was about to set off and look for *you*. Shar gave me this, for you and Hestor.'

He handed over the letter and explained the story in a few sentences. As soon as he heard the gist of the tale Kitto broke the seal and tore the letter open. He stared at it, mouth moving silently and eyes squinting with concentration . . . then said something under his breath.

'What is it?' Anxiety was starting to squirm in Reyni. 'What does she say?'

Kitto looked at him defensively. 'It's private.' But his face gave him away and Reyni abruptly realised the problem.

'Kitto, can you read?'

Kitto's face reddened. 'I'm learning . . .'

'But you haven't learned enough to read that letter. Then give it to me, quickly!' He reached for it; Kitto snatched it away and Reyni added urgently, 'For the gods' sakes, Kitto, if Shar trusted me with it, so can you!'

Kitto hesitated for a few seconds – then handed the letter over. Reyni looked at it. His eyes widened and he whispered, '*Oh, by all the Seven Hells . . . she can't*—'

'What?' Kitto's voice went shrilly up the scale. 'What can't she do?'

Reyni's eyes were stark. 'She's going to the Brig,' he said. 'She means to confront her uncle. And she's doing it alone.'

ELEVEN

'Why – didn't – she – *wait?*' Kitto's words came jerkily, breathlessly as he ran as best he could beside Reyni, with the horse trotting at their heels. Kitto was limping badly now; a legacy of two days' and nights' walking and scrambling on the mountain tracks with only the briefest of rests when he was simply too exhausted to go on. 'All she – had to do was – send us the letter – and we'd . . .' But his words tailed off as he realised that he didn't know what he and Hestor could have done. Stopped her, he thought grimly; that was what. Stopped her from running headlong into what might well turn out to be the worst danger she had ever faced. But how *could* they have stopped her? For Kitto was certain that an outside force was working on Shar; working to snare her and trap her. And she was caught in its lure and would not have listened to reason.

Reyni wasn't paying attention to Kitto. Instead he was scanning the dockside as they ran, looking at the moored vessels. A supply ship – it would be a barquentine or brigantine; possibly a big schooner, though that was far less likely. Which one, though? Shar had given no clue in her letter. And the port was so busy, it could take them half the day to cover it all. Time was against them – secrecy or no, he would simply have to ask someone.

A group of men in sailors' oilskins came into view, and Reyni shoved the horse's reins into Kitto's hands. 'Wait here!' he said.

He sprinted away and Kitto waited, thankful for the chance to rest. He felt queasy and light-headed, and the busy scene seemed to swim before his eyes, as though everything around him was a dream. He was incredibly tired, and if his stomach hadn't been churning with fear for Shar he would also have been ravenously hungry. The only food he had had since leaving the castle was a share of the mountain cat's raw kill. That had been before his trek began; for the past two days he'd had only water, as the cat led him over the mountains, avoiding the road and taking a shorter but arduous path through the peaks. Kitto had wanted at first to return to the castle, but the cat refused to let him and had shepherded him instead towards Wester Reach. Now, he knew why.

Reyni came running back. 'I've found out the name of the supply ship,' he said. 'The *Margravine* – she's berthed further downriver; or at least she was last night.' He took the horse's reins again. 'My mare can carry us both, and it'll be quicker if we ride. Come on!'

He legged Kitto into the saddle and sprang up after him. The streets were becoming busier and people scattered out of their path as they cantered recklessly towards the arched town wall, ignoring the curses and shaken fists in their wake. Within minutes they were through the shore arch and among the maze of wharves beyond.

Reyni slowed the mare to a halt. There were at least a

dozen large vessels moored at the quays, and Kitto, who didn't know a barquentine from a dinghy, stared in helpless bemusement. Reyni, though, was looking for something else, and after a few moments he found it; a glimpse of a crimson sash that denoted a harbour official.

'Sir!' He spurred the mare into a trot, waving to attract the official's attention. 'Sir, we need your help!'

The man stood with fists on hips as they approached. 'What do you want? If it's information, then you should go to—'

Reyni interrupted. 'I know, sir, and I apologise, but this is an emergency! We're looking for the *Margravine*, the supply ship for the coastal lighthouses. I understand she's berthed in this area.'

'She *was*,' the official corrected. 'She sailed on the night tide, just after first moonset.'

Reyni's face whitened. 'Sailed?'

'That's what I said. She's going on down coast, so she isn't due back for eighteen days. If you've business with her, it'll have to wait until then.'

He walked away, leaving them silent and stunned. Kitto's gaze strayed downriver and he felt as if something inside him had crumbled. Too late. The barquentine was gone, with Shar aboard, and nothing could recall her. She probably wasn't far away yet; maybe hadn't even reached the open sea. But for all the difference it could make to them now, she might as well have sailed to the Seven Hells.

The messenger-bird that arrived at the Star Peninsula

that same morning bore the Matriarch's device, and carried a private letter for the High Initiate. Neryon read the letter, thought hard for some while, then sent for Hestor's mother.

When Pellis arrived, he said, 'I've had some disturbing news from the Matriarch. And I think it might involve Shar and Hestor.'

He showed her the Matriarch's letter, and as she read it Pellis began to frown. The news concerned Sister Malia, Thel's co-conspirator in the plot against Neryon. Malia had been making great progress, the Matriarch said, in her efforts to reform, and it had been hoped that in time she might prove herself enough to be pardoned. But matters had taken a new turn. To put it bluntly (as the Matriarch always did), Malia was going mad.

It had begun with monstrous nightmares. At first Malia woke shrieking from her dreams in wild terror, but before long that changed and she did not wake, nor was it possible for anyone to rouse her. The Sisters would hear her screaming in the night, run to her room and find her still asleep but with eyes wide open, thrashing and babbling as though fighting to escape from an unknown horror. Sometimes she stumbled from her bed and flailed around the room, and on two occasions she had to be stopped from hurling herself through the window to the cobbled courtyard below.

In her waking hours, Malia remembered nothing of what had happened. The Sisters had used their seeing skills to try to find the cause, but without success; in fact every time they tried, their scrying-glasses came up against a peculiar and unnatural void. The Matriarch had never encountered such a thing before, and that, combined with the nature of Malia's babblings during the nightmares, had prompted her to write to the High Initiate.

For Malia's dreams involved Shar. How, the Matriarch could not say; in her fits Malia was incoherent and her words made no rational sense. But she cried out Shar's name again and again. And just lately, she had also begun to rant and rave about Hestor.

'So,' Neryon said quietly when Pellis finished reading, 'you see why I'm concerned, and why I wanted to talk to you before I alert the Circle council. The Matriarch knows about Shar's disappearance, of course; I sent word to every Sisterhood cot. She clearly fears that there could be a connection with Sister Malia's affliction – and I'm inclined to agree.'

Gravely Pellis nodded. The search for Shar hadn't yielded the smallest clue so far, and everyone in the Circle was becoming increasingly worried. But the Matriarch's letter wasn't the only new development. There was something more, something discovered only this morning.

Kitto had also gone missing, she told Neryon. He wasn't in the castle; in fact no one could remember having seen him for the past three days. Pellis had questioned Hestor, but he claimed to know nothing about it; he said that he and Kitto had had some kind of a quarrel and had been avoiding each other, so he hadn't realised that anything was amiss.

'Did he tell you what the quarrel was about?' Neryon asked.

'No. But I'd hazard a guess that it had some connection with Shar.'

Neryon pondered. If Pellis was right, then it seemed likely that Kitto had gone in search of Shar; and that meant that he must have some idea where she was. The High Initiate would also take any wager that Hestor was in on the scheme. The boys hadn't quarrelled; that was just Hestor's way of trying to put the Circle off the scent. But if they *did* know something, why in the names of all fourteen gods had they taken matters into their own hands, instead of coming to him?

He said, 'I think I'd better talk to Hestor. Don't worry; I'm not angry with him.' *Not yet, anyway*, he thought. 'I simply want to know a little more about this rift, to see if it can shed any light on both these pieces of news.'

'You think there might be a connection?' Pellis asked uneasily.

'I don't know. But my intuition is telling me there is. And I know better than to ignore it.'

When Kitto woke, it was past midday and Reyni hadn't yet returned. For a minute or two, still groggy, Kitto lay staring at the ceiling of the musician's room in the Bronze Bell tavern. Where was Reyni? Why was he taking so long? He shook his head and sat up, pushing away a surge of panic. Boats weren't that easy to come by unless you had plenty of money, and their combined fortunes hadn't amounted to much. It would take time to find something that could be hired at a price they could afford. And in the meantime, Kitto had a decision to make.

It was vital that Hestor should know what was happening – but Kitto couldn't tell him, for he wasn't going back to the castle, at least not yet. Hestor *had* to have Shar's letter. But the only way to deliver it was by messenger bird, and that carried the risk of interception. Kitto had gone to sleep worrying at the problem like a dog worrying prey, but now, with his head clearer, he realised that he had no other choice. The risk must be taken.

He took the letter from the table beside the bed, then picked up a stylus of Reyni's that lay nearby. Slowly and laboriously, he wrote his own addition under Shar's signature:

HESTAR – SHARS GON BUT WER GOWIN AFTER HER RENI AND ME. KEEP WACH AND DONT FEGET WAT TO DO IF TRUOBL. PREAY FOR US. KITTO.

He stared at what he had written, wondering if he had missed anything. For some reason his thoughts strayed to his own rescue in the mountains, and then, abruptly, he recalled a small incident at the castle. A creature in the courtyard; one he hadn't seen before but which he noticed because it was so unusual . . .

A sharp instinct clicked into place and Kitto wrote: *WITE CAT IS A FREIND.*

He put the stylus down, and as he did so there was a clatter of feet on the stairs and Reyni came in.

'Ah, you're awake!' Reyni came in and shut the door. 'I've found what we need.'

'How much?' Kitto asked.

'He wanted thirty gravines at first, which was outrageous. I beat him down to twenty-one.'

'Twenty-one – lucky number,' Kitto said with superstitious hope.

Reyni raised wry eyebrows. 'Not for him. He thinks it's only a day's hire. Still, by the time he finds out he's wrong there'll be nothing he can do about it.'

Kitto nodded. Twenty-one gravines seemed like a very great deal of money. He still had his own coin, for it had been in his belt-pouch when his horse threw him, but it was nothing like that sum.

'Thank you,' he said heartfeltedly. 'I don't know what I'd have done without your help.'

Reyni grinned. 'Don't worry about it. It's an adventure. Something to write a balled about.'

If we get through it, Kitto thought. But he kept the thought to himself.

They left the tavern soon afterwards and Kitto went to the nearest messenger-bird post to dispatch Shar's re-sealed letter. It would reach the Star Peninsula that evening, so Hestor would receive it while he and Reyni were at sea.

Kitto wasn't looking forward to sailing. It was all very well for Reyni; his father was a lighthouse-keeper and he had virtually been born with a tiller in his hands. But this would be Kitto's very first voyage, and he didn't relish the prospect. Indeed, as he followed Reyni along one of the lesser quays to where a number of boats rocked at their moorings, he was already starting to feel queasy.

There was some parley with a squat, swarthy man who had a scar half-closing one eye; then came the clink of coins and Reyni beckoned Kitto towards the nearest of the boats. The tide was high and it was only a short step down, but the boat swayed alarmingly as Kitto climbed in. Reyni steadied him, grinning. 'Don't worry. Just sit down; you'll soon get used to it.'

To Kitto the boat seemed terrifyingly small for a sea voyage. It was less than three times his own length, and had one mast and no cabin, only a tiny, cramped sail-locker. He sat down carefully amidships, gripping the gunwale with both hands. Reyni ran up the mainsail, then turned and looked at him. 'Ready?' he asked.

His face was calm, his eyes steady, and suddenly Kitto felt ashamed. Here he was, frightened just of going to sea, while Reyni was willing to face another and far greater danger that, in truth, was none of his concern. Reyni didn't *have* to do this – but he was doing it, for friendship's sake. If their positions had been reversed, Kitto thought miserably, he doubted if he could have been so heroic.

He looked at his feet, knowing his face was reddening and not wanting Reyni to see, and nodded. 'Yes. I'm ready.'

Shar heard the sound of shouted orders, felt the change in motion as the *Margravine* started to alter course, and knew that the voyage was almost over.

She breathed a sigh of relief, though she was not home and dry yet. Getting on board the barquentine had been easy; she had merely walked across the gangplank in the general bustle of loading, her hood up and her head bent so that anyone seeing her would take her for one of the crew. But hiding, and staying hidden, was far harder. After several heart-failing moments of near-discovery, she had crawled under the tarpaulin-shrouded lifeboat that rested on its blocks on the deck. Barring a disaster, no one was likely to disturb her here, and as the ship ploughed on across the Western Sound she had watched the booted feet tramping back and forth, listened to the sounds of sea and wind, the creaking, booming, rattling of masts and sails, and tried to quell the fear that was building up in her like a threatening storm.

She was starting to rue her rash impulse. If she came face to face with Thel, what would she say to him; what would she do? If she believed for one moment that he would willingly answer her questions, then she must have been born without a single gravine of sense. Why had she *done* this? What kind of madness had got hold of her, and driven her reason away?

But it too late for second thoughts. Rightly or wrongly, she had come this far and there could be no turning back. The barquentine, she realised, was going about, for she could feel the faint judder of the hull turning against the current. She risked a cautious peek out from under the tarpaulin. It was pitch dark – the voyage had taken a little less than a full day – but the night was brightened by a pale glare that smeared across the sky. Faintly amid the ship noises Shar thought she could hear waves breaking, and realised that they must be passing close to the lighthouse on its solitary rock off the Brig's southern tip. The harbour, such as it was, lay ahead. The *Margravine* would anchor before long.

Feet came pounding along the deck and she ducked quickly out of sight again. Activity would increase from now on, so she must stay well hidden and rely on sound alone her to tell her what was happening. She wouldn't have too long to get ashore. The captain would not linger here; as soon as his duty was done he would want to be away from this brooding place, so she must take the first chance she could.

Concentrating on that helped to push Shar's terrors into the background as the *Margravine* sailed slowly in to harbour. Within minutes Shar heard the gangplank thump down and the rumble of barrels being rolled across it, then several pairs of feet tramped past in unison. That must be the militia detachment who would deliver Thel's supplies. Shar lifted a corner of the tarpaulin, but it was like trying to peer through a tiny window; she could see only a small section of the deck, and she didn't dare pull the cover back any further. She would have to make her move soon.

She drew a deep breath, eyes straining in the gloom . . .

And something small and white flicked past at the edge of her vision.

The cat! How it had got here? Shar couldn't even begin to guess – although she had no doubt, now, that it was no ordinary animal. It had slipped into the darkness

142

between two bollards, but moments later it emerged again, paused and looked directly at her, then moved quickly, silently towards the bows of the ship.

Shar didn't hesitate. She slid out from under the tarpaulin and was after the cat in an instant. The little creature ran along the deck, keeping just ahead of her. But it wasn't heading for the gangplank; it was—

The *Margravine's* bo'sun, carrying a lantern, loomed suddenly before her. Panic flared; she swerved, despairingly, certain she was about to be caught as the bo'sun raised the lantern high. But then his voice boomed out,

'That's it, boy! Catch the beast!'

The cat had streaked past him, but suddenly and with astonishing agility it twisted round and into Shar's path. Unable to stop in time, she tripped over it and went sprawling, and as she measured her length on the deck she found that her hands were clasped around the cat's body.

The bo'sun chuckled. 'Well done, boy. Pick yourself up and put the animal ashore, before it starts a fight with the ship's cats. Move, now!'

Put the animal ashore . . . Hardly able to believe her luck, Shar scrambled to her feet, said smartly, 'Sir!' and ran for the gangplank with the cat in her arms.

No one took any notice of her as she hurried across the old granite quay. The militiamen were piling barrels onto a handcart, helped by two sailors, while the *Margravine's* captain and mate were talking to an older man, doubtless the lighthouse keeper, nearby. The glare of the distant lighthouse beacon stained the sky and cast eerie, distorted shadows; by its light Shar could see the foursquare outline of a large building on the high ground that rose beyond the cliffs to the northward side of the bay. It looked like a grim, bleak fortress, featureless and forbidding, and a prickling shudder ran the length of her spine at the thought of what she must face there.

A sound behind her snapped her out of her uneasy thoughts and she turned to see that the militiamen were setting off with their handcart, heading towards a track that made a pale swathe through the heather and scrub of the island. The white cat wriggled suddenly in her arms; she bent quickly to put it down and it trotted after the cart. Reaching the beginning of the path it looked back, mewed once, though Shar couldn't hear it over the sea's hiss and murmur . . . and, like a candle winking out, vanished.

Shar blinked in shock. Where had the creature gone? It couldn't just have . . .

The question faded as she realised that the white cat could probably do anything that it chose to do. No normal animal indeed . . . but it was a friend. And on this desolate island, with its unknown and untested dangers, it was the only friend she had.

She looked back, once, at the quay and the tall masts of the *Margravine*, tilting against the night sky as the ship rocked gently on the water. Back there lay light, human company, *safety*. Ahead . . .

She didn't allow herself to dwell on it, but turned her face resolutely and set off along the path.

TWELVE

Though he had intended to summon Hestor to his study earlier, the High Initiate had been too busy. First the council had to be told of the Matriarch's letter, and the Circle's response discussed. That took up more than half the day, and then a second messenger-bird had come in from Wishet Province with a query from the Province Margrave that needed an immediate reply. Having missed the midday meal, Neryon was among the first in the great hall when food began to be served in the evening, and only when he finally returned to his study did he have time for other matters.

He was just about to send for Hestor when the third messenger-bird of the day arrived. It spiralled in to land, and moments later Neryon's heart sank as he saw, through his window, the falconer come running towards the main doors. Something for his attention, no doubt; falconers never ran for anyone of lesser importance.

He was right – but when he saw what had arrived, his irritation vanished instantly. The bird had come from Wester Reach, and among several letters in its pouch was one addressed to Hestor.

Normally, Neryon would not have dreamed of prying into a private message, not even that of a very junior initiate. This, though, was not a normal circumstance, and he thanked the falconer for his sense in bringing the packet to him. When the man had gone, he looked at the letter. The writing was familiar, and with a quickening pulse Neryon broke the seal and started to read.

When he had finished, he got up from his chair, went to the window again and stared out over the darkening courtyard. His mind was in a turmoil of fury and fear together, but at this moment fury had the upper hand, and with it a sense of new urgency that made his thoughts as sharp as a blade.

Suddenly he swung round and yanked at the bell-pull that would summon his steward. When the man appeared he said curtly, 'I'll be leaving for Wester Reach tonight. Tell Pellis Bradow Ennas that I want her to come with me; and we'll need an armed escort – two will be enough. Pack the minimum I'll need for fast travelling, then send birds ahead to request that fresh horses be ready for us on the route.' He paused. 'This is urgent, so anything that can be done to speed our journey is vital.'

He was thankful that the steward was experienced; he didn't dither or ask questions but only bowed crisply, said, 'Yes, sir,' and made to leave.

'One more thing,' Neryon added. 'Please send word that I want to see Hestor Ennas in my study, *now*.'

Another bow and the man was gone. Neryon waited, drumming fingers on his desk and looking again at Shar's letter. He had no doubts now that his intuition had been right, and that her disappearance and the developments at the Matriarch's cot were connected. Intuition was also telling him that he should ride straight to Southern

Chaun, where Sister Malia was, but for once he refused to heed it. Shar's plight was urgent, and deadly. It was too late to stop her from trying to reach Thel – but if Neryon could do anything to help her (or save her; though he did not let himself dwell on that ugly thought), Wester Reach was where he must go.

Thel and Malia. He shouldn't have been so lenient, Neryon thought. He should have had them both executed, as his predecessors would have done before the age of Equilibrium, and then none of this could have happened.

The angry train of thought was broken by a hesitant knock at the door, and Hestor came in.

'Hestor.' The High Initiate's voice gave nothing away, but his eyes were cold and unnervingly steady. 'Sit down, please. I intend to ask you a question. And I expect nothing less than the truth in reply.'

Hestor's face lost some of its colour. He lowered himself gingerly on to a chair, and Neryon continued.

'What do you know about the disappearance of Shar and Kitto?'

The rest of Hestor's colour vanished. He opened his mouth, but no sound came out.

The High Initiate smoothed one hand over Shar's letter where it lay on the desk before him. 'I'm waiting for your answer, Hestor.'

'I . . .' Hestor faltered. 'I don't . . .'

Neryon's face hardened. 'Be careful, boy. "Don't" may be a dangerous word for you to use at this moment. I said the truth, and I meant the truth. Now. Speak.'

From the corner of his eye Hestor could see the letter, and as he glimpsed the style of the writing his courage, and with it any plan he might have had to brazen this out, crumbled. A slow, deep flush started to spread across the whiteness of his face; his gaze dropped away from Neryon's and in a small voice he replied, 'Shar went to Wester Reach. Kitto followed her.'

The silence that followed seemed to Hestor to last for half a lifetime, though in fact it was only a few seconds. Then Neryon said ominously, 'I see. And you, knowing this and knowing why, saw fit to say nothing to anyone, but instead let them both run senselessly into what could well prove to be a peril even greater than the one we all faced only a season ago!'

Hestor's face was agonised. 'But, sir, I didn't—'

'I'm not interested in excuses!' Neryon's clenched fist came down like a hammer on the desk top. Then with difficulty he got a grip on his fury and continued, his voice less violent but still ferocious, 'I think you have a great deal to tell me, boy. Begin – and I warn you now, if I find out that you have withheld one snippet, one *iota* of information, I will make you regret the day you were born!'

So, with Hestor hunched miserably on the chair before him, Neryon heard the story. When all was told, Hestor went to fetch Giria's letter and mutely handed it over, and when he read it, the High Initiate's attitude softened a fraction. Small wonder, he thought, that Shar had been unable to resist the temptation to do what the letter asked. And it proved Hestor's claim that he and Kitto had not known about her plans. However, it did *not* excuse Hestor's own secrecy, and the High Initiate had no intention of sparing him the full brunt of his anger.

'Your stupidity and disobedience are almost beyond belief!' he said wrathfully. 'Such behaviour from an initiate of the Circle in *intolerable* – and this isn't the first time that you have ignored your superiors and taken matters into your own hands! Well, you've had fair warning, and my patience has run out. You are suspended from the Circle.'

Hestor's jaw dropped in horror. 'Sir—' he tried to protest.

'*Be silent!*' Neryon snapped. 'Don't dare to interrupt me! You are suspended, until such time as I decide whether or not you have any future as an initiate. My decision,' he added with a fine sting, 'will depend greatly on your own actions from now on. I suggest you think very hard about that, Hestor. *Very* hard! Now, get out of this room and out of my sight.'

Hestor stood up and, shoulders drooping, moved slowly towards the door. On the threshold he paused and looked back. 'Sir, please . . .'

The pitiful note in his voice moved Neryon just a little and he replied curtly, 'What is it?'

'Shar . . . is she all right? Is she safe?'

So he had recognised the writing on the letter. The High Initiate stared at the paper for a moment, then abruptly picked it up and held it out.

'Read it.'

Nervously, Hestor obeyed. His eyes widened as he took

in what Shar had said, and saw Kitto's clumsy addition. At last he looked up at Neryon.

'Now,' Neryon said sternly, 'you see what your foolishness has led to.'

Hestor swallowed. 'I'm sorry, sir.'

'Sorry is as sorry does,' Neryon told him, unrelenting. 'Which in your case means doing nothing. Your mother and I will be leaving for Wester Reach tonight – and if, while we are away, you attempt to meddle one more time, in any way at all, you know what the consequences will be.'

Hestor hung his head. 'Yes, High Initiate,' he said dejectedly, and left the study.

All the way up the main stairs and along the corridors Hestor wrestled inwardly with himself. Despite Neryon's warnings there was one thing he hadn't revealed, and that was the tale of his encounter with Tarod of Chaos. A promise to a god couldn't be broken under any circumstances, after all. And the candle Tarod had given him was still in his room, unlit, waiting.

Was *this* a dire enough emergency? he asked himself. The thought of Shar coming face to face with Thel made him feel sick with fear for her. But was she truly in danger yet? She might be found and returned to the mainland before she could set foot on the prison island. Or Kitto and Reyni might catch up with her and take her back. The High Initiate was going to Wester Reach, and Hestor's mother with him. They were far from powerless; they would be able to do something. *Don't use the candle without very good cause*, Lord Tarod had said. *It's a last resort, no more, and Yandros will not be pleased if you call on us without extremely good reason.* Hestor shivered. Unless he was absolutely sure of his ground – and he wasn't, not yet – then surely this didn't count as a dire emergency. Or did it? He simply didn't *know*.

He was halfway along the passage that led to his room. There was a window ahead of him, and on the sill something was sitting. It moved suddenly as Hestor approached, and he saw that it was a cat.

A white cat.

The white cat is a friend. The words of Kitto's note came sharply back to Hestor, and he stared at the animal with quickening eagerness. It gazed back for a moment, then very deliberately jumped down from the sill and started to walk away.

'Wait!' Hestor hissed after it. 'Come back! Hey, cat, little one—'

The cat looked over its shoulder, seemed to shake its head, then broke into a run. Calling 'Wait!' more loudly, Hestor ran after it. He saw it swerve into a side passage; quickly he followed—

And stopped. The passage was empty. The animal had vanished.

Hestor's heart began to thump. The corridor ahead of him was a long one, so even at top speed the cat couldn't possibly have reached the far end by the time he arrived. Nor was there a single cranny big enough for it to hide in. Yet it was gone without trace. That was impossible. Unless . . .

The white cat is a friend. Hestor thought he was beginning to understand what Kitto had tried to tell him. His mind recalled the image of the cat looking over its shoulder, shaking its head. He had been thinking about Tarod's candle, asking himself, trying to decide . . . well, he had his answer. The cat had told him.

He stared for a few seconds more along the corridor, but the white cat did not reappear, and at last he turned and headed slowly for his room.

'If I didn't know better,' Reyni shouted, over the ramping noise of wind and sea, 'I'd say that the gods had taken a strong dislike to us!'

Kitto didn't answer. He didn't have the energy to spare, for one arm was hooked and locked desperately around the boat's mast, feet braced hard against the thwarts, while with his free hand he was frantically – and pointlessly, it seemed to him – trying to bale water back over the side where it belonged. All around was a pitching, rolling, saturating mayhem of shrieking air and surging water, that seemed bent on the destruction of them and their small craft.

The first part of the voyage had gone well. The day was balmy, and when night fell they had sailed under a calm, starry sky with the breeze and the current in their favour. But an hour or so before dawn, there was a sudden and shocking change.

At first Kitto had thought that the roaring from the north-west was the herald of a Warp storm; now he wished it had been, for even a Warp with its howling thunder and lightning and vast, wheeling bands of grim colour could have been no worse than this. As the sea began to rise Reyni had sworn ferociously at the crazy impossibility of it – a clear sky, no rough weather forecast, and gales didn't *come* from that direction at this time of year! Kitto knew then, in the marrow of his bones, that *something* was trying to stop them from reaching their destination.

A grey-green wall rose like a nightmare before Kitto's eyes, and he ducked his head and braced himself anew for the crashing, pummelling deluge as the bows ploughed through the waves. He was so wet already that another soaking made no difference, but the water's impact snatched away what breath he had and left him gasping and gagging. His eyes were streaming and there was a roaring in his ears, almost drowning Reyni's yell from the stern, where he wrestled with the tiller, 'Kitto! Keep baling!' Kitto wielded the baler with all the strength he could muster, but he was losing the battle; the boat was filling faster than he could empty it. This was hopeless – they hadn't chance, they were going to be swamped, they were going to capsize, they were going to *drown*—

'Oh, Lord Yandros!' He choked out the god's name as panic whirled through his head. 'Lord Yandros and Lord Tarod and all the gods of Chaos, if you can hear me, if you can see us, help us, oh, please, help us now!'

His answer was a renewed screaming from the wind, through which, an instant later, came a whiplash crack and a shout of alarm from Reyni as the boom broke free from its lashing. The heavy wooden spar swung like a sword cutting the air, and Kitto flung himself flat in shin-deep water as Reyni grabbed for it. He caught it, but its impetus snatched his other hand from the tiller, and the swing of the boom dragged him off balance and half over the side, so that he hung, horrifyingly, over the heaving sea.

'Reyni!' Kitto bawled his name but didn't know what to do. With one hand he tried to reach to Reyni, but the distance was too great and he was too frightened to let go of the mast. Reyni clung grimly to the boom, but his scrabbling feet could find no purchase; he was falling, he was—

A pale blur surged out of the churning water, and with a yell of astonishment Reyni was pitched back into the boat by a solid body that struck hard against him. He fell in a tangle, miraculously still holding the boom, and as he scrambled to right himself, a sweet, shiveringly eerie sound rose above the noise of the elements, like a chorus of unearthly voices. Kitto's skin prickled; he had never heard such a sound in all his life – but Reyni had, and his eyes widened with astonishment and awe.

'It's the fanaani!' he shouted.

'What?' Kitto couldn't hear.

'Fanaani!' Reyni gestured wildly towards the sea and almost lost his balance again. 'Great gods, there they are, look, look!'

This time Kitto did get the gist of it, and his head whipped round. Four of them – no, five – fast and sleek and graceful, cutting through the water alongside their boat. Their heads were raised above the waves, their mouths open, and the spine-tingling harmony of their song surged through the gale's madness. It soared louder, sweeter, clearer . . . and Kitto realised that the wind's scream was failing, the force of it dropping, dropping, as though the fanaani's song was a challenge that it couldn't meet.

Then, in less time than it took to draw breath, the gale vanished. One moment they were in the midst of the elements' uproar; the next, the uproar was gone. The wind was no more than a breeze. The sky was utterly clear. The sea was utterly calm, its blue tinged pink by the light of the early sun. It was incredible, impossible . . . but it had *happened*.

'I don't believe this,' Reyni said. 'I'm dreaming. I *must* be.'

Kitto was still too shocked to speak, but he looked over the side. The fananni were there, at a distance but still keeping pace with them. And one of them was white . . .

'It was them . . .' he found his voice at last, though it sounded as if it belonged to someone else. 'They sang the storm away . . .'

'There's no other possible explanation,' Reyni agreed, awestruck. 'But – they can't have calmed the sea, Kitto. The sea doesn't calm as quickly as that; it *can't*. After a gale it's rough for hours, days – it – it—'

Even Kitto knew that much, and he nodded sombrely. 'You said the weather wasn't natural,' he reminded Reyni. 'Looks like you were right, doesn't it?'

'Yes . . .' Reyni licked salt-whitened lips. For a few

moments his face became introverted and he seemed to be looking at something very private. Then he shook himself and turned his attention to the boat.

'No sense in wasting time. Get the worst of that water baled out while I run up the mainsail; then we'll check our bearing and—' the words broke off as he glanced westward. 'Great Yandros and Aeoris, Kitto, look! Look where we are!'

Kitto followed his gaze. The sun had just cleared the horizon, and its low-slanting rays cast a haze over the sea. Through the haze, looming like the humped back of some huge, sleeping sea-creature, the outline of a coast showed almost dead ahead.

Kitto stared. 'What is it?'

'If I'm not mistaken,' said Reyni, 'and I don't think I am, it's the Brig.'

'But you said it would take—'

'At least a day and a night. I know. *And* the gale was blowing us right off course.'

'So how—'

'Don't ask me.' Reyni looked to where the fanaani had been, but saw only the smooth emptiness of the sea. He licked his lips again. 'I was going to say, ask them. But they haven't waited around to be asked – or thanked.'

'People say, don't they,' Kitto ventured, 'that the fanaani are creatures of Chaos.'

'Yes. They do.'

And one of the creatures had been white. So Yandros *had* heard him, and had chosen to answer. Kitto felt a peculiar thrill go through him, and suppressed a shiver.

He was wet and cold, that was all. He wasn't really frightened. He didn't even feel sick any more.

'Come on,' Reyni said, suddenly brisk. 'Get busy with the baler.' He eyed the distant coastline again. 'Wind's from the east now; if it keeps up, we'll make harbour in less than an hour.'

Kitto narrowed his eyes. 'How long a start will Shar have on us, do you think?'

'It's hard to say; depends on whether the *Margravine's* captain was in a hurry or content to take his time.' Reyni was unlashing the foresail. 'That's assuming, of course, that she wasn't discovered on board.'

Kitto hoped fervently that she had been. But he also knew that the hope was a slender one. If his suspicions were right, luck – or something disguised as luck – would be running with Shar, as it seemed to have done from the start of this venture. All the perils, so far, were befalling her friends. What would be next? *Who* would be next?

The mainsail was going up now, and Kitto tried to forget his thoughts. There was no point in speculating about what might lie ahead. In a short while they would find out for themselves, and, as the castle's head groom was so fond of saying, only idiots jumped fences before they could see them.

Reyni said, '*Baler*, Kitto! If my feet get any wetter, I'll start drowning from the toes up!'

The musician's calm confidence was back; he looked for all the world as though he were simply out for a morning's leisurely sail. Kitto wondered for a moment whether he should envy him or feel sorry for him. Then he remembered the castle groom again, picked up the baler and set to work.

THIRTEEN

From the shelter of a rock outcrop Shar watched the militiamen approach the fortress gate. The sound of a key grating in the lock carried loudly in the quiet night; the gate creaked open, and the handcart was manoeuvred through.

Two men remained on guard, putting paid to Shar's hope that she might slip through undetected. No matter: there were other ways. She would simply have to wait a little longer.

She concentrated, instead, on the granite building itself. From the outside it looked as daunting as the cliffs of the Star Peninsula, and even grimmer, for there was an air of desolate hopelessness about this place that seemed to taint everything around it. The glare of the lighthouse beacon was desolate, too, blotting out the stars and dimming the moons, and Shar tried to imagine what it must be like to be imprisoned here, alone, without another living soul for company. She could almost pity Thel.

The first moon was setting by the time the militia party finished their task. Huddled in the rocks' shelter Shar had fallen into a doze, but the noise of the gate opening roused her immediately, and she peered from her hiding place in time to see the men emerge with the handcart, loaded now with empty barrels. Words were exchanged, then laughter rang out in a harsh echo, as though someone had made a joke to relieve tension. The gate was locked again, then the small procession set off back down the twisting path towards the harbour. They passed the outcrop where Shar crouched, and she watched their dwindling figures and bobbing lanterns with impatience surging in her. Until the *Margravine* had departed she dared not make a move for fear of attracting attention, and she silently willed the men to hurry, hurry, *hurry*. Finally they reached the quay, and minutes later, like a great bird riding on the water, the *Margravine* began to make way towards the open sea.

Shar wasted no more time. The second moon was dropping below the horizon now, and there was less than an hour to go until dawn. As she hurried along the track towards the fortress her heart started to thud erratically and she felt keyed-up with excitement. The grim granite wall loomed; as she approached it she slowed and studied its towering face carefully in the reflected glow from the distant lighthouse. High up, at intervals, narrow embrasures had been cut into the stone; lookout points, probably, which meant there were likely to be steps down to ground level on the other side.

Turning from the wall she gazed over the bleak vista of island and sea. The wind was stronger up here, and a faint grey glimmer showed on the eastern horizon; the false dawn before true sunrise. Shar faced the glimmer, spread her arms wide and closed her eyes. Her mind focused on images of air: vast, open skies, scudding clouds, autumn leaves blowing and whirling – she could feel the wind in her face and she welcomed it, called to it, urged it to grow stronger, as she summoned her friends of the elemental plane.

'Creatures of air and sky! Little ones, hear me – it is Shar who calls to you, Shar, your friend and a Daughter of Storms! Come to me, little ones! Come to me, and help me in my task!'

Three times she called, accompanying her summoning with a surge of love and eager affinity. Even the Circle's highest-ranking adepts could not match Shar's ability to communicate with the elementals of air, fire, water and earth; it was a skill born in her, a part of her nature, and as she whispered the words for the third time she felt a power and a presence answering. The wind rose suddenly, dancing and gusting – then a host of tiny forms exploded out of the air like a starburst. Frail faces, translucent hands, fluttering wings – Shar was wreathed in their small, shrill tornado as the wind snatched at her clothing and whipped her hair to a frenzy.

'Little friends!' Shar cried joyously. 'Help me, now! Help me!' With all her willpower she visualised what she wanted the elementals to do. They understood; their cries swelled, there was a renewed rush of wind, and a hundred unearthly hands and talons caught hold of Shar and swept her up, up, soaring to the top of the fortress wall. Carrying her as though she weighed nothing, they swooped over the parapet. For a moment the world turned giddily below her, then she saw the steps that led up to the embrasure, gave a silent command, and the elementals lowered her gently down, to land on the top stair.

Gasping, exhilarated, Shar leaned against the wall as she caught her breath. The elementals danced above and around her, eager for more games, but she held up her hands in a calming gesture and their whirlwind settled to quietness, allowing her to look down, for the first time, into the prison compound.

The scene below her was sunk in shadow, but enough light reflected from the sky to show the bare stone courtyard and squat central keep, with a single plain door. Windows were studded in its walls like pockmarks, but no lamps burned in them; the keep was still and silent and looked as though no living creature had set foot in it for decades. More staircases led up to the other embrasures around the enclosing wall, and Shar scanned the whole compound carefully. If Thel was awake, he must be aware of her arrival but had chosen not to show himself. Very well; then she must flush him out of hiding.

The air elementals still drifted around her, their presence like a light breeze on her face. Eastwards, the light was growing stronger and the sky was taking on a blood-red tinge, heralding sunrise. Shar closed her eyes and whispered her thanks to the elementals. The beings winked out with a soft *hush* of air, and Shar rose to her feet and moved to the stairs. As she began to descend she felt a brief, psychic flicker of something unpleasant, and for a moment the sun's first blood-red rays seemed to dim. She stopped, trying to attune her senses. But the uneasiness had gone and the light was back to normal. Shar continued downwards, and as she stepped from the last stair and into the flagstoned courtyard, she raised her voice and called loudly and clearly:

'Thel Starnor! There is someone here to visit you. Come out!'

Her challenge echoed away and away into the morning. Silence followed and she waited, her senses sharply alert. Had he heard her? She was about to call again when the door at the foot of the tower moved. There was a click, a scrape of wood on stone, then the door opened and a figure emerged into the courtyard. A wave of heat and cold went through Shar as, for the first time since the night of the double eclipse, she looked into the face of Thel Starnor.

Memory and familiarity hit her like a slap. Here was the face she knew so well, the uncle who had brought her up as though she were his own child. But there were changes. He was much thinner, his dark hair and turned grey and he moved with a strange stiffness that looked slightly – and disturbingly – unnatural. What he thought, what he felt, at being confronted with the sight of Shar was impossible to guess, for his expression gave away nothing. For several seconds he stared at her, his eyes narrow and half-hooded, and peculiarly intense. Then he said, 'How did *you* get here?'

His voice was almost as Shar remembered it – almost, but not quite, for there was an underlying tremor that hinted at enormous strain. Her mouth suddenly dry, Shar replied, 'Hello, Uncle Thel.' She couldn't offer any pleasantries; 'How are you?' would have been ludicrous. She realised how much she hated him.

He said harshly, 'I asked you a question. How did you—'

'I heard you.' Anger and disgust had risen suddenly in Shar and her voice was as combative as his. 'I came on the supply ship.'

He considered that for a few moments, then laughed a peculiar, unpleasant laugh. 'How very resourceful of you! And would it be too inquisitive of me to ask *why?*'

There was no point in dissembling, she thought. 'Because I want answers to some questions.'

'Questions? Well, well.' Thel turned slowly on his heel, surveying the courtyard. 'That might present a problem. You see, trapped as I am in this *delightful* place, I am just a little out of touch with the world, so I rather doubt that I can tell you anything you don't already know – or think you do.' Abruptly he faced her again. 'And more to the point, my dear niece, why should I want to? What makes you think that I would cooperate with you in any way at all?'

Shar said, 'Oh, you might, Uncle. If I could do something for you in return.'

'I see. And what sort of bargain do you have in mind? My freedom, in exchange for information? I rather doubt it!'

Though his words were cynical, an underlying hungry, almost desperate, edge in his tone gave Shar a vital clue. His freedom. This soulless, solitary imprisonment must be a living nightmare, and though Thel was strong-willed, the strain was showing. In time, it would break him; he knew it. And he was afraid.

'I can't promise that much,' she said, putting a slight but deliberate emphasis on the word *promise*. 'But there are ways in which I might help you. For instance . . . what would you give for the chance to get away from here? Maybe to another prison – but somewhere less isolated?'

Thel stood very still, and a new, searching light crept into his eyes. Then he said, 'You've changed, Shar. You've grown up.' His lip curled. 'The Circle must have taught you more than I imagined – including trickery and cunning.'

'If I've learned that, Uncle Thel, then I learned it from you,' Shar countered.

He bowed mockingly. 'Thank you for the compliment! Well, at least it gives us some common ground, if nothing else. So, Shar, what do you want to ask me? What is so important to you?'

Shar replied, 'I want you to tell me about my mother.'

There was a sharp silence before Thel asked warily, 'What about her?'

She drew a deep breath. 'Did you kill her?'

'*Ha!*' Thel swung away. 'The Circle convicted me of her murder, as you well know!'

'Yes. But you didn't admit to it; you never have. And her body has never been found.' Shar paused. '*Did* you kill her, Uncle?'

A second and much longer silence fell, during which Thel seemed to be weighing her up – or weighing up some very private thought; it was impossible to judge which. At last he spoke.

'I think, Shar, that we have a great deal to discuss . . . and, perhaps, an agreement to make.' He indicated the door of the keep with a courteous gesture that, for the first time, had no mockery in it. 'I'd suggest that we talk inside, where we can at least sit down and make some pretence of civilisation. If you will . . .?'

Shar hesitated, wondering if this could be some sort of trap. But her psychic senses could detect no danger. Not yet, anyway . . . And her heart was beating like a drum under her ribs; beating with excitement and with hope.

She nodded wordlessly, and let him usher her into the keep.

Thel poured water from a flagon into a cup and pushed it across to Shar, who shook her head.

'No,' she said. 'Thank you.'

'Some wine, then?' He reached for a second flagon, forcing a humourless, almost painful smile. 'Even prisoners are permitted small comforts.'

'No,' she said again. 'I don't want anything.'

He shrugged and poured wine for himself. As he sipped it Shar looked uneasily around. They were sitting on opposite sides of an enormous table in the keep's main hall, which in the past, when large numbers of prisoners had been held here, had been the refectory. Now it was Thel's sole domain, and there was something very bizarre about sitting in this small oasis of comfort he had created, yet surrounded by the hall's damp, bare and gloomy vastness. It felt somehow unreal.

Shar looked again at Thel. At close quarters he looked ill, his skin pockmarked and unhealthy, his eyes dull. A peculiar scent hung around him, too; an odd, acrid smell, like something charred. He had drunk the wine-cup's contents and was pouring more; when he finished he looked at her.

'Well, niece. You asked me if I killed your mother. You must have a reason for wanting to know the answer, after all this time.'

'Yes,' Shar said, 'I have.'

A pause, then Thel raised his eyebrows wryly. 'But you're not prepared to tell me, yet, what that reason is. However, you *can* tell me one thing. Does your willingness – or ability – to help me depend on the nature of my answer?'

Shar smiled thinly. 'No,' she lied.

Thel uttered a sharp, derisive laugh. 'I haven't *quite* lost enough of my wits to take your word for that! But no matter; for I think the truth will favour me anyway. Very well: did I kill your mother? No, Shar. I did not.'

Shar stared at him across the table as his words sank in, and her mind raced. Was he telling the truth? She so desperately wanted to believe him, but if she did, would she be making a terrible mistake? She simply didn't know!

Then Thel smiled, and it took her unawares, because the smile was tired and so bitterly sad that it almost moved her to pity.

'You're not as surprised as I expected you to be. I thought as much. Something's happened, hasn't it?

Something that drove you to come here and confront me . . . and I think I can guess what it is.' He sighed. 'Was she found at the house in Empty Province? Or did the jailer set her free when he realised that he was no longer going to get paid for his work?'

A wave of heat followed by a wave of cold surged through Shar. He couldn't have known about that part of Giria's story. Not unless it had actually happened. He *was* telling the truth. Her mother was alive – and she had found her.

With a huge rush of emotion that she couldn't hope to control, Shar burst into tears. She slumped forward over the table, covering her face with her hands and sobbing wildly as all the fears and hopes and griefs that she had been storing up for so long poured out. Thel watched her, his face expressionless, one hand gripping the stem of his wine cup. He didn't speak; he only waited until at last the storm within Shar's mind was exhausted and slowly, shakily, she raised her head. Her cheeks were blotched, eyes reddened and puffy, and through lashes still wet with tears she gazed at him.

'Tell me everything,' she whispered. '*Please.*'

He did, and as she listened Shar's certainty grew, for every detail of the story he told matched Giria's own account of her imprisonment. At last, when Thel stopped speaking, she lowered her gaze from his and said, very softly, 'Thank you, Uncle. Thank you.'

Thel gestured towards the cup of wine which she had refused earlier. 'Drink a little now. It will calm you.'

She nodded, sniffed, and picked up the cup. As she

raised it to her mouth she saw her own reflection in the wine's surface . . . and abruptly she paused. Something was nagging at the back of her mind; something that she had overlooked. What *was* it? She couldn't think clearly; she was still dazed, and very emotional. But there was *something* . . .

Then it came to her, and she could have screamed aloud at herself for a blind, stupid fool. When her mother had escaped and fled from Empty Province, *someone* had known about it – and that same someone had launched a sorcerous attack on her which, but for the Keepers of Light, would have killed her. The Keepers' scrying had warned of danger, and the fanaani had confirmed it. And Thel knew what that danger was. Of course he did – for *he* was at the root of it!

The cup in her hands was suddenly unsteady, and the mirror image of her face shivered and broke apart. Very, very carefully Shar set the cup down and said, struggling to keep her voice even, 'No, I . . . won't have any wine.'

'Oh, come.' Thel sounded impatient – or frustrated. 'It will do you good. Drink it.'

Why was he so anxious for her to drink? Was there something in the cup? 'No,' Shar said, more sharply, and started to stand up. 'I think I will . . . have some fresh air.'

Thel was on his feet so quickly that she jumped. Her head jerked up – and in the moment before he could mask it she saw something hideously alien looking out of his eyes. She took a step backwards and he said, 'What's wrong, Shar? You look frightened.'

'No . . .' she said, trying to deny it to herself as well. But in the last few seconds the atmosphere in the hall had begun to change. The light coming in at the windows seemed dimmer, drawing the shadows out from their corners, and Shar could feel a crawling sense of oppression starting to build up. The sense, almost, of another presence, watching and listening . . .

'Come, Shar,' said Thel, and now there was just a faintly frenzied note in his voice. 'You've nothing to fear from me. Nothing at all.'

There's something else here with us . . . As the certainty struck her, a gust of air whisked through the room. It blew the door open wider, like a warning – and suddenly premonition surged in Shar. She spun round and plunged for the doorway – and with a mad snarl Thel flung himself after her. For all Shar's youth and speed, he was faster; he reached the door an instant before she did, and with a pistoning kick of one foot, slammed it shut in her face.

Unable to stop her headlong flight Shar crashed into the door, rebounded, and staggered backwards to collide with the table. Thel, breathing hard, stood in front of the door, between her and freedom.

'*Help me!*' Shar cried. '*Friends of air, friends of fire, help me!*'

Thel smiled. He looked insane. 'They can't get in, Shar. Once this door is shut, they can do *nothing* against the power that reigns here.'

Her heart lurched. 'Power . . .?'

'Yes. Oh, yes. *Real* power, Shar, not the paltry conjuring

tricks of the Circle! Haven't you realised yet? Haven't you *felt* it?'

Another presence . . . The ominous, suffocating feeling was building up like the simmering pressure before a massive thunderstorm. Suddenly Shar realised that it was horribly familiar, calling back her nightmares. Darkness. Malevolence. Hatred. *Evil* . . .

Thel saw her look change from fear to horror, and gave a soft, cruel laugh. 'Yes, you understand now, don't you? The beings of the Sixth Plane don't forget, you see, and nor do they forgive. They remember how you thwarted and cheated them. And they want *revenge*.' He laughed again. 'They can't touch you themselves, not unless you should invite them into your mind. You should have drunk the wine, or even the water; my hospitality is *their* hospitality, you see. If you had accepted it, you would have given yourself to them. As I have done. It would have made things *much* easier.' A pause. 'But it doesn't matter. They still have me to help them, and I can do what they cannot. I can give you to them, Shar. I can give them your soul, to play with for eternity!'

One hand moved, fast, and Shar found herself confronted by the glinting blade of a knife. It must have been hidden in his sleeve . . . she tried to take a step back, but the table barred her way. All right: she could still move forwards or sideways. Her only hope was to make a feigned dash for freedom, trick him into coming after her and get past him to the door . . .

Heart crashing against her ribs, she judged her moment, then suddenly darted to her right. Thel's face twisted in fury; with a yell he sprang at her – and Shar spun on one heel and hurled herself towards the door.

Her bid almost succeeded, for her hands had clawed round the latch when Thel caught her. They reeled back from the door together, Shar flailing, screaming, trying to kick him. But Thel was far stronger. With one hand he pinned her against the wall. The other hand rose. And the knife-blade glittered as his arm came shearing down—

FOURTEEN

Kitto and Reyni were approaching the fortress when what looked like a tornado exploded into the air above the granite wall.

'*What the*—' For one shocking moment Reyni thought it *was* a tornado, and as it speared towards him he flung up his hands, staggering backwards. Tongues of fire roared in a blast of wind, stones rolled and danced down the track at them, and a shower of rain, dust and grit hurled itself in their faces. Reyni yelled, 'Kitto, look out!' but Kitto, hair streaming and eyes stung by the flying debris, was staring wide-eyed at the frenzied spectacle.

'It's the elementals!' he shouted above the mayhem. 'Shar's friends – she's in trouble!'

Without waiting to see if Reyni was following, he pelted towards the fortress gate. Invisible hands snatched hold of him as he ran, whirling him along faster, and he skidded to a breathless halt at the portal.

The gate was locked, and no amount of wrenching and banging and kicking could move it. Reyni, panting up in Kitto's wake, pulled him back, calling, 'Kitto, you're wasting time! Give me a grapple, *quickly!*'

They had brought a coil of sturdy rope, a marlinespike and two grappling-hooks from the boat; Kitto flung one of the hooks over and Reyni tied it to the rope with two deft half-hitches. Then he ran back from the gate and pointed to the top of the towering wall. 'If I can catch the grapple in one of those embrasures, we'll get in that way!'

With the elementals shrilling urgently, Reyni started to swing the hook round and round above his head. He threw; the hook soared up with the rope snaking behind it – and dropped back like a stone as the aim fell short.

'Let me try!' Kitto was almost dancing with fear and frustration. 'Maybe I can – *AAH!*'

The elementals weren't about to wait for anyone to make a second attempt, and the ground dropped away from under Kitto's feet as he was whisked vertically into the air. The stones of the wall flashed past his eyes; he saw Reyni's legs kicking as he too was snatched up, and there was a moment's terrifying glimpse of the harbour far, far below, before they both flew over the top of the wall. The air-beings didn't trouble with the staircase but plummeted them straight down into the compound, arresting their descent with a violent jolt just before they hit the ground. Kitto sprawled; Reyni, on his feet but only just, tottered over the flagstones—

And a scream of terror echoed from beyond the keep door.

Reyni regained his balance and raced for the keep. His shoulder cannoned into the door as Kitto scrambled upright; the door juddered – then it burst open and Reyni all but fell inside. Kitto heard him yell, '*Shar!*' and then another voice, a man's, roared out in a bellow of insane rage.

Kitto catapulted across the courtyard – but the elementals were faster. With shrieks of triumph they hurtled in a single, arrowing mass towards the doorway. The man's bellow changed to a scream of fear, and as Kitto reached the door he saw Thel in the midst of a wild maelstrom, arms flailing as he tried to beat the creatures off.

Then Reyni appeared. He was pulling someone with him, and Kitto could have shouted aloud with relief as he recognised Shar. She was dazed, stumbling; Kitto grabbed her other arm and together he and Reyni hustled her across the compound. As they neared the wall Reyni gasped, 'How are we going to get out? Unless the elementals help us again—'

Kitto flung a glance over his shoulder at the mayhem in the keep, then slithered to a halt. 'Shar!' He shook her. 'We need your friends! Can you call them off, can you make them listen?'

Shar shook her head giddily. 'Oh, gods . . . I don't know . . .'

'Try! Or we'll be trapped here!'

She shut her eyes tightly, pressing both hands to her temples in an effort to concentrate. 'Little ones! Little ones, hear me!' With all her strength she tried to project her message through the elementals' fury.

Suddenly there was a rush of air and the whole mass of creatures erupted from the keep. But they had not come at Shar's bidding, for as they burst out she felt a wave of fear surging from them. And behind them, another figure was stumbling to the keep's threshold.

175

'No!' Shar raised her hands, warding the elementals off as they made to grasp hold of her and Kitto and Reyni. 'No, wait! *Wait!*'

The elementals subsided and an eerie, chilly silence descended on the courtyard. Thel had reached the keep doorway now. He stopped, and stared at the three. Then, in a voice cracking with horror, he called, 'No! No, you can't get away, you can't leave, I won't allow – *uhh!*' The words cut off in a gasp of pain and a spasm racked him. '*No – oh no, it's not my fault, I'm not to blame, I'm not, I'm not!*'

He collapsed to his knees. His face had warped into an expression of abject horror; his mouth hung open, working violently, but for several moments no sound came. Then it began – a moaning, gargling noise, rising up the scale, growing louder and shriller, a sound of terror, of agony—

'Uncle!' Shar made as if to run towards him, but Kitto grabbed her arm. 'Shar, no! Don't go near him!'

The elementals added their own clamorous warning, and Shar froze, staring at Thel. He was clutching his own upper arms now, swaying back and forth, and suddenly he uttered an appalling howl. '*No!* I tried, I did all I could, you know I did! You can't—' Another howl, as though he were being torn apart from within. '*Oh gods, help me, help me!*'

He was answered by a hideous, malevolent rumble that seemed to squeeze itself from the walls and echo across the compound. The stones beneath Shar's feet shifted – she *felt* them move – and Thel's cries rose to an ear-splitting pitch as an invisible force snatched hold of him and wrenched his body into an incredible contortion. His spine bent, his neck twisted; for an instant Shar glimpsed what looked like dark, gigantic fingers clamped crushingly around him – then he was picked up, spun around three times and flung with bone-cracking force to the ground.

'*Uncle!*' This time Kitto couldn't hold her back and she ran to where Thel lay. As she reached him he raised his head slowly, painfully. His skin was grey; blood ran down his chin, and his eyes in the hollows of their sockets burned with agony and insane terror.

'*Damn you . . .*' Distorted, hardly recognisable, his voice croaked from his throat. '*I tried and I failed and now it will punish me . . . Damn you to the Seven Hells, and damn her and all she has . . . all she has . . .*' He choked. '*Oh, but there's still one. Yes, yes . . . There's still Malia. Malia will . . . she will make you all sorry . . .*'

He started to laugh, and as the awful sound of it bubbled from him there was a renewed rumbling, this time from deep below the ground.

'Shar!' Kitto and Reyni were at her side. 'Shar, come away! Get away from him – quickly, before it's too late!'

Shar felt as if something inside her was shrivelling up. *There's still Malia . . .* She couldn't move. Her feet were rooted. And a darkness had begun to flow out of the ground, flowing around Thel, enfolding him, engulfing him . . . His laughter cut off abruptly. His eyes bulged in their sockets. '*No . . . please, not that, not that . . . oh, no-o-o . . .*'

'Shar, *run!*' Kitto yelled. He and Reyni didn't pause; they grabbed Shar's arms between them and hauled her bodily across the courtyard. Behind them, the darkness was coalescing, rising – then like a whirling tide a cloud of air elementals plunged down on them. Again came the seizing grasp, the dizzying climb – Kitto didn't cry out this time – and then they were clear of the fortress, speeding away with the ground spinning far below. Twisting in the elementals' grasp Shar looked back and saw a tower of shuddering blackness swaying above the keep. From the heart of the blackness a despairing voice seemed to echo briefly, like the moan of a lost soul. Then came a wail of pain that faded, faded . . . and as the black tower collapsed, there was nothing left but the noise of the wind.

The elementals set them down on the harbour quay. Shar was shaking, crying, and though Kitto was too shy to put his arms around her and hug her, he held her hands tightly until the worst of the reaction was over.

Reyni, grim-faced, had returned to the boat and was raising the foresail. When the others joined him he looked briefly at both their faces. There was so much to say, so much to be explained; but now was not the moment for it, so he only said, with a lightness that didn't deceive anyone, 'I don't know about you, but I don't want to stay here any longer than we have to. If the weather holds' – he exchanged a wry glance with Kitto – 'we can be back in Wester Reach tomorrow morning.'

Kitto nodded, relieved, but Shar said: 'No. I'm going to Southern Chaun.'

'What?' They both looked at her incredulously.

'Southern Chaun,' she repeated. 'I have to see Sister Malia.' Her lower lip started to tremble, but Kitto, who knew her well, suspected that it stemmed from anger and not from any threat of tears. 'Before he . . .' She swallowed, not wanting to say the word *died*. For Thel *was* dead, she was sure; and sure, too, that she knew what had killed him, and why. 'He told me that my mother *is* alive.'

'Shar, you can't believe anything he—' Kitto started, but again she shook her head.

'I can, Kitto. He knew things that he couldn't have known unless they were true. The woman I met in Wester Reach *is* my mother. Thel tried to kill her but he failed, just as he failed to kill me just now. But the power that was using him is using someone else, too.'

Kitto said softly, 'Sister Malia?'

'Yes. That's why I must go to Southern Chaun.' Shar had a stony look; stony, and faraway. 'I *must*.' Abruptly then she turned her gaze on Reyni. 'You've already done so much to help me, I can't ask any more of you. But—'

'Wait.' Reyni held up a hand. 'If I sail you back to Wester Reach, then as soon as we land you'll simply set off for Southern Chaun. Isn't that so?'

Shar nodded. 'I *must*,' she said again.

'All right. Actually, the north–western tip of Southern Chaun isn't that much further from here than Wester Reach, if you include the journey upriver. The wind won't be so favourable, but if it's so important to you . . .'

179

He shrugged and grinned, though the grin took an effort. 'If nothing else, it'll make a good ballad one day.'

Shar looked nervously at Kitto. 'Kitto . . .?' she said tentatively.

Not for the first time Kitto wished that Hestor was here to help him. He was frightened; the shock of all that had just happened hadn't really hit him yet, and when it did he knew that it would strike hard. But Hestor wasn't here, and neither was the High Initiate, or Yandros of Chaos, or anyone else. He had to make his own decision – and he couldn't let Shar down.

'Yes,' he said. 'If Reyni's willing, I'll agree.' And thought: *Gods preserve me for a fool. But I don't know what else I can do.*

'Truly, Jonakar, I can't see the point,' Giria said unhappily. 'Lias has already tried so hard to find Shar, and his efforts have failed. He'll only exhaust himself. And he's not a young man.'

'He's fit enough,' Jonakar reassured her with a gentle smile. 'And he doesn't want to give up. Let him do this, my dear. Who knows; this time he might succeed.'

She nodded, though her face was still troubled. 'I suppose if he really can't be dissuaded . . .' A pause. 'May I come to the sanctuary?'

'Of course, if you wish to.' Jonakar looked pleased. 'Lias is praying now, but the rite will begin as soon as he has finished his devotions. I'll send someone to fetch you.'

Compassion filled Jonakar as he watched Giria walk

away. He fervently hoped that this newest attempt to track Shar down would succeed, for it was almost the only chance left to them now. In the hours after her disappearance the Keepers had scoured Wester Reach, but had found no trace of Shar herself, nor any clue to where she might be hiding. Lias had then called upon all his seer's skills to find her, but after a day and a night without sleep he had discovered nothing at all – until a new thought had occurred to him.

He had used his scrying-mirror to search Wester Reach and the land around it, but he had not yet considered the sea. Could Shar be on board a boat, and thus much further away than they had assumed? Excitedly, Lias had declared that he would make one more attempt to find her. It would take all his skill and energy, but it might just work.

Jonakar hadn't been surprised by Giria's reaction. She was almost convinced now that Shar would never be found, and so, to her, Lias's attempt didn't seem worthwhile. He hoped they could restore her faith, before she lost heart altogether.

A little while later the Keepers all gathered in the sanctuary. The shutters were closed and the brazier lit; a sweet, woody scent of incense filled the air, and the three lamps that framed the painting of Aeoris burned steadily. When Giria came in, Amobrel beckoned her to a seat on a bench at her side; she squeezed her hand encouragingly but Giria only managed a pallid smile in return. For perhaps a minute there was silence. Then, when everyone had stilled, Lias rose from his seat and knelt down before the painting. He bowed his head, spreading his arms wide, and his voice began to whisper through the room in the words of a devotional chant. After a few moments the other keepers took up the litany. It had a hypnotic rhythm, and soon Lias began to sway gently from side to side. He was slipping into a trance, and as it took hold of him, two of his followers moved silently to place before him a large scrying-mirror of smoked glass. Lias's face reflected distortedly in its curved surface; his lips still moved but his eyes were glazed over – he was deep in the trance now, oblivious to everything and everyone in the room.

Then suddenly the chanting stopped. The last words fell away into silence and all eyes focused on Lias. He didn't seem to be breathing – but then, slowly, slowly, he raised his head. His mouth opened . . .

'*Sha-a-a-ar.*' He uttered her name in a long, steady exhalation. '*Sha-a-a-ar. We are seeking. We are calling. In the name of our Lord Aeoris, we exhort and command the veil of mystery to draw aside and reveal the truth to our sight.*'

He brought his hands slowly together and a third acolyte stepped forward, holding a brimming chalice. Lias took it – not a drop was spilled – and raised it to his lips. '*I drink from the cup of vision! I call upon the powers of light, to shine through the veil of darkness and show us the one we seek!*'

'*Sha-a-a-ar . . .*' the Keepers chanted in unison. '*Sha-a-a-ar!*'

The surface of the scrying-mirror began to change. Lias's reflection vanished; in its place dark colours swirled like fog – and there were shapes in the fog. They were vague as yet, but there were glimpses of a cat's face, then what looked like two hands clasping something, then a fluttering thing that could be a bird's wing or even a sail. Lias was staring into the mirror, still holding the chalice, muttering now; and on the bench beside Amobrel, Giria leaned forward, straining to hear his words over the rhythm of the chant.

Then Lias cried out in triumph, 'Ah! I see – I see her!'

He dropped the chalice and clutched at the sides of the mirror, peering into its depths. Jonakar and another Keeper ran to his side and crouched down, steadying him as he began to shake uncontrollably; they too looked into the mirror, then Jonakar gasped triumphantly, '*Yes – she is there!*'

Giria was on her feet in an instant, eyes wide, scrambling to join him. Jonakar caught hold of her shoulders, almost hugging her. 'Look!' he breathed. 'Look in the glass!'

She looked. The dark colours were whirling like a maelstrom now, but at their centre, clearly visible, was the image of a small boat with three figures on board. Two of them were strangers to Giria. The third was not.

'Shar!' she cried, then turned frantically to Jonakar. 'Where are they *going?*'

A harsh cry from Lias startled them, and they turned quickly to see that the old man's eyes had snapped open, though they weren't focusing. Between sharp, rapid breaths Lias said, 'I see . . . an island. But that is not their destination, for they have already . . .' He frowned, shaking his head. 'It is not clear!'

'Step back,' Jonakar whispered to Giria. 'We are too close; I think our presence distracts him.'

She obeyed. Lias began to speak again.

'There is a house . . . ah, no; more than that; there are many buildings . . . a woman, dressed in white. I have seen her face before . . . ah, *yes!*'

Jonakar was concentrating only on Lias, and in the dimly-lit room, no one else was close enough to Giria to see her sudden tensing. She took another step backwards, further from Lias . . .

'Their destination is So . . .' Lias stopped suddenly. He gasped. 'Is the Ma . . .'

The scrying-mirror exploded in a blast of black light and glass shards that detonated outwards from its heart. Jonakar was hurled off his feet, cannoning into Giria; they crashed to the floor, carrying several of the Keepers with them, and screams and cries rang out as the room was plunged into darkness.

'Jonakar!' Jonakar raised his head groggily to find Giria struggling to pull him free from a tangle of people. 'Oh gods, are you hurt?'

Jonakar could feel blood trickling down his face where flying shards had cut him, but that wasn't what concerned him. 'Lias!' he cried in alarm. 'He was right in front of the mirror!'

Giria stood upright and called out, 'Someone, please, bring a light! We must try to be calm until we can see who is injured!'

At the sound of one clear voice the cries and frantic

milling abated. Several shadowy figures were gathered where Lias had been; someone came running with a candle, and the lamps were re-lit.

They showed an ugly scene. Several of the Keepers were unconscious, while many others had been cut, badly in some cases, by the hurtling glass. Lias lay on the floor. He had taken the full brunt of the explosion, and one glance was enough to confirm his followers' worst fears.

Jonakar had gathered his wits; with Giria at his heels he pushed through the group gathered around the old man and crouched down beside him. Lias's face was unrecognisable; black, charred, as though it had been thrust into a fire. All his hair had been burned away, and his body was twitching violently in spasms of shock and pain.

'He needs a physician!' But even as he said it Jonakar knew that Lias was beyond the help of medicine or anything else. He reached out, then hesitated, afraid to touch Lias for fear of worsening his pain. As his hand hovered above the ruined face, Lias groaned, and his eyes, filmed with agony, strained open.

'Hhh . . .' His voice was so feeble that Jonakar could hardly hear. 'I s-saw . . . the sixth . . . Shar is going to S-Southern Ch – *ah!*'

Giria grasped Jonakar's arm. 'Oh, Jonakar, he is in such pain! Don't let him try to talk!'

'No, wait! He was trying to say, "Southern Chaun" And he talked of a woman dressed in white. The Matriarch – it must be!'

Lias struggled to speak again. 'Sh-she will . . . she

185

means to . . .' A spasm racked him, then suddenly he saw Giria. His eyes widened, his hands clawed convulsively and he hissed through clenched teeth, 'Danger!'

'Lias!' Jonakar cried. 'Is there danger to Giria, too?'

'Nhh . . .' The last of Lias's strength was failing. But with a tremendous effort he gasped out two final words.

'Malia . . . knows.'

His head fell back and the life fled from his eyes. Jonakar uttered a soft moan and covered his own face with both hands. Then suddenly a new voice quavered up.

'Sweet gods – look at the painting!'

Shaken out of his grief, Jonakar's head jerked up and he saw the other Keepers staring at the painting of Aeoris; or at where the painting had been. For the picture had gone, and all that remained at the frame's edges were a few tatters of burned, black canvas.

A woman's voice rose up in a terrified wail. 'What have we done? Is Lord Aeoris angry?'

'No.' Jonakar rose slowly to his feet. His face was strained and grim. 'This is nothing to do with the gods. This is something else – something evil!'

Silence fell and faces turned towards him. Jonakar swallowed, and continued, 'There is a dark power at work here. It has killed our leader . . . but before he died, he saw what it was, and where it means to strike next.'

'He said, "Malia knows",' Giria whispered. 'Isn't she the Sister who . . . who was involved with Thel . . .?'

'Yes. And I understand that she is serving her

186

imprisonment in Southern Chaun. At the Matriarch's cot.'

Giria paled. 'That is where Lias said Shar was going! And he saw a vision of the Matriarch herself . . .' Suddenly she looked very frightened. 'Those two others with Shar . . . who could they be? Friends, or – or—'

'I don't know,' Jonakar replied.

'But we must find out! My daughter is in danger!' Eyes wild, she suddenly gripped his hand. 'Jonakar, I must go to Southern Chaun! I must find Shar, warn her, help her – please, oh, please, let me take a horse and leave at once!'

Jonakar was horrified by the thought. Lias's vision had warned them that Giria, too, was in peril. He couldn't let her make such a journey alone. But as he opened his mouth to say so, he realised that nothing anyone could say or do would stop her going. Shar was her child – how could she be expected to consider her own safety?

He thought quickly, then said, 'Of course you must go, I understand. But you must have an escort.'

'I don't need—' Giria began, but he interrupted.

'You *must*, Giria! We'll send three of our people with you, to ensure your safety.'

'I can't let you do that for me!'

'You can, my dear, and you will. Come.' He looked sadly at his leader, whose body was now surrounded by mourning Keepers. 'If we can help you, at least Lias's death won't have been in vain. Hurry, now, and prepare what you need for the journey. And may our Lord Aeoris protect you on the way!'

★ ★ ★

Aeoris of Order's golden eyes burned hot, and a gargantuan thunderstorm roared across the shimmering skies of his realm, darkening the beautiful garden and silencing the birdsong. The storm lasted only a few moments; Aeoris had ferocious self-discipline, and within seconds he had brought his fury under control. As shadows vanished and the light returned to its normal, steady level, he turned his mind away from the mortal world and looked instead to another dimension. Then he spoke. His voice was far more baleful than the storm had been.

'Yandros. I would speak with you!'

There was no obvious response, but Aeoris knew that he had been heard. He turned, made a gesture with one hand, and the garden dissolved into grey, infinite nothingness, in which Aeoris stood on what looked like a vast spider's web of silver threads, radiating away and away into the impossible distance. This was neutral territory, outside the domains of Order or Chaos. A little time passed. Then a second figure appeared; golden-haired, his strange, feline eyes constantly changing colour.

Yandros of Chaos made a mocking bow and said, 'Cousin. You seem a little out of sorts.'

Aeoris curbed the reply he wanted to make. 'I've no time for games, Yandros. My followers have been attacked, and their leader is dead. I want the answer to one question: did you and your brood have any part in it?'

Yandros looked genuinely surprised. 'The Keepers of Light, attacked?' Then his eyes turned a very dangerous crimson. 'Don't insult me, Aeoris. I have better things to do than waste time and effort on your pitiful little mortal devotees.'

It was the answer Aeoris had expected, and he believed it. 'Then,' he said, 'some other power is at work, which owes no allegiance to either of us.' A pause. 'I want to know what that power is.'

'For once we have something in common,' said Yandros.

'So it seems. What did you brother discover on his visit to the Star Peninsula?'

'Ah.' Yandros smiled thinly. 'So you know about that, do you? I should have guessed that you would pry where you weren't invited.'

Aeoris's face darkened with anger. 'And what invitation did *you* have? You forget the terms of our pact!'

'Oh, nonsense!' Yandros waved a dismissive hand. 'In truth, Aeoris, Tarod discovered nothing, so I doubt if we know any more of this matter than you do. Although . . .' He paused. 'I *do* have my suspicions.'

So did Aeoris, but he wasn't about to reveal them. Instead, he frowned and said, 'Then I'll give you a piece of advice, and I strongly recommend that you take it. Don't interfere. This is a mortal matter, and not your concern.'

'Nor yours.' Yandros's eyes were purple now, and there was lightning in them.

'That,' said Aeoris sternly, 'depends on you. Meddle any further, and it *will* be my concern.'

Yandros considered that. 'So if this proves to be what

189

I think we both suspect—'

'I'm not interested. And I won't warn you a second time. If you make any move behind my back, I will take it as a breach of our pact. And you know what that could lead to.'

For several moments Yandros didn't reply. His face was very still and his expression impossible to read. At last, quietly and calmly, he said, 'War between us? That would not be advisable, Aeoris.'

'I agree. So I suggest that you tread very carefully from now on.' Aeoris's lips curled in a smile that had no warmth in it. 'I'll wish you good day, *cousin*. And I will be watching.'

He turned on his heel, and his figure faded into the grey infinity.

FIFTEEN

Neryon, Pellis and their armed escort arrived in Wester Reach in the small hours of the following morning. They had ridden without sleep for a day and a half, changing horses at hamlets on the route but stopping only long enough to snatch a little food and replenish their water-bottles before travelling on again. Exhausted, they took rooms incognito at a tavern and were asleep as soon as their heads touched the rough pillows.

The sun was just rising when they woke, and after a few enquiries Neryon discovered where the Keepers of Light could be found. He and Pellis arrived at the mission house to find the Keepers making preparations for Lias's funeral. Jonakar, who was now effectively the group's new leader, was astounded to find the High Initiate on his doorstep, and hastily took the visitors to a room where they could talk in private. As concisely as he could he related all that had happened since Shar's disappearance, including the details of Lias's vision and what had followed. Neryon's face grew grave as he listened, and when Jonakar had told all he knew, he said, 'So Giria – if that is who she is – left yesterday, for Southern Chaun?'

'Yes, sir. I sent three of our people with her. We're none of us trained swordsmen, but they should be able to protect her in case of trouble.'

'Mmm.' Neryon tried to sound more optimistic than he felt. 'I hope so, for all their sakes. Although with luck we might catch up with them on the road.'

'You'll be going after them?' Jonakar said eagerly. 'I'm relieved to hear it, sir. And if there's anything more we can do to help—'

'You've done more than enough already, Jonakar. More than anyone could have asked – and it had cost you dearly. I'm very sorry.'

'Thank you.' Jonakar inclined his head, then added a little diffidently, 'High Initiate . . . do *you* know the nature of the power that killed Lias? There was one thing he said before he died; just one word, but it has preyed on my mind . . . He said something about the "Sixth".'

Pellis drew in a sharp breath and Neryon felt himself tense. Jonakar saw their reactions and his expression became sombre. 'The Sixth Plane,' he said softly, hollowly. 'Then my fears are true . . .'

Neryon gazed steadily back at him. 'We can't be sure of anything yet, Jonakar. It's possible that your fears aren't justified; at least not in that way.'

Jonakar shivered and looked towards the window. 'When I think of Shar, travelling with two strangers who might mean her harm – and now Giria, even with our people to care for her—'

'I think we may rest assured that we know who Shar's companions are,' said Neryon. 'Kitto is her close friend, and according to our information the other is likely to be Reyni Trevire.'

'The young musician?'

'We believe so. You know him, Jonakar; do you think he can be trusted?'

'I would say certainly.' Jonakar was obviously relieved.

'Then that's something in Shar's favour. Though if this *is* what we fear, she's going to need more help than Reyni and Kitto can give her. Giria, too.' Neryon hesitated, frowning, then decided to be blunt. 'Jonakar, I must ask you this. You believe, I know, that Giria genuinely is who she claims to be. I ask you now to think hard, and to tell me if there is anything – anything at *all* – that might give the lie to that claim.'

Jonakar considered. Then at last he replied, 'No, High Initiate. We tested her ourselves, and though we don't pretend to have the powers of the Circle, I think we *do* have enough skill to judge truth from falsehood.' He smiled wryly, sadly. 'As Lias discovered to his cost.'

'Of course,' Neryon said. 'Forgive me; I meant no insult.'

'None is taken, I assure you. But I think you can safely assume that the woman who came to us *is* Shar's mother.'

Neryon and Pellis left the mission a short while later. As they walked back towards their lodging Pellis said, 'Our bodyguards should be awake and refreshed by now. We could leave for Southern Chaun at once.'

The High Initiate glanced at her. 'You're not too tired to get into the saddle again?'

She shook her head. 'I want to catch up with Shar . . . before anything else does.'

She echoed Neryon's own feelings, and he said, 'I'll

send word of our intentions to the castle; a messenger-bird should get there by noon. The Circle Council will alert the Matriarch and that will save us time. I'd like to think we'll be the first to arrive at her cot, but somehow I doubt that it's possible.'

'If what the Keepers' leader saw is accurate,' said Pellis uneasily, 'then I fear that there may be some developments with Sister Malia before we can get there. If anything happens, will the Matriarch be able to control it?'

'She'll do all she can,' Neryon replied.

'I know.' Pellis hunched further into her coat. 'I only pray that it will be enough.'

The Matriarch, Ulmara Trin, had just sat down to supper in her sitting-room when one of the senior Sisters came running to tell her that the first of their expected visitors had arrived.

Ulmara left her meal at once and hurried to the cot's central courtyard. By the fluttering light of torches a solitary rider was being helped down from her horse; she saw the white-robed figure coming towards her and said,

'Matriarch? Oh, Matriarch, I'm so glad to be here! I am—'

Ulmara interrupted. 'I know who you are, Adept Giria – we had word that you were coming.' She and Giria had never met, but under these circumstances there was no room for formality, and she clasped Giria's hands with emphatic relief. 'Thank the gods that you've arrived safely! But where's your escort?'

Giria shook her head. 'I have no escort. There wasn't time—'

'You've ridden here *alone* from Wester Reach?' Ulmara interrupted, shocked. 'Great Aeoris and Yandros, do you realise the *risk* you were taking? In the light of the news from the castle—'

Giria's head came up sharply. 'The castle?'

'Yes, yes; I received a letter just a few hours ago, explaining the situation. Your daughter—'

'Is Shar here?' Giria asked frantically.

'Not yet; and of course we don't know when or where her boat will reach the coast. The High Initiate is also on his way here, though you must have had a good start over him.'

Giria nodded. In the shadows cast by the unsteady torchlight Ulmara couldn't see her expression.

'Now,' the Matriarch went on, 'there's a great deal to tell you, and I don't doubt you, too, have a lot to relate. But first of all we must attend to the basics of food and comfort. Come with me; your horse will be looked after.'

She shepherded Giria across the courtyard and into the main building. As they walked towards the refectory, a sound echoed from somewhere overhead. It was a woman's high-pitched scream.

Giria stopped in her tracks. 'What was that?'

The Matriarch's face set into a hard line, and instead of answering the question she called to a senior Sister who had just passed them. 'Missak! Check on Sister Malia. Don't go alone; take someone with you.'

Sister Missak replied, 'Yes, Matriarch,' and hurried away. Giria was staring at Ulmara. 'Malia?' she said. There was a very strange look on Giria's face, which the Matriarch interpreted as distaste and fear. *Little wonder*, she thought, and said aloud, 'She can do nothing to harm you now. But there have been some new developments which you should know about. Come; I'll explain everything while you eat.'

Giria looked at the ceiling, as though trying to see through it to the rooms above. For a moment she seemed about to speak. Then she changed her mind and followed the Matriarch along the corridor.

Shar and her companions had reached Southern Chaun as the sun was setting. The voyage took less time than Reyni had anticipated, and for all his and Kitto's private fears it had also been uneventful. They had enough money left between them to pay for overnight lodging and food at a harbour inn, and the fee for their overland journey to the Matriarch's cot. A carrier's cart was due to leave on the following morning, and by nightfall they would be at their destination.

They had a meal together at their lodging. Shar was very quiet, and Reyni's attempts to make light conversation soon flagged, so they ate mostly in silence. Kitto couldn't stop thinking about Thel Starnor. During the voyage from the Brig Shar had told them all about the encounter with her uncle, and Kitto shivered as he thought of what would have happened if he and Reyni hadn't arrived when they did. There was no doubt in his mind that what Thel had revealed when he'd tried to kill Shar was true. The entities of the Sixth Plane wanted revenge on her, and they had possessed Thel in order to use him against her.

Now, the creatures meant to try again. And this time, Sister Malia was to be their instrument.

Kitto found himself wishing to all the gods that he hadn't agreed to come to Southern Chaun. They should have gone straight back to the castle, told the High Initiate everything and asked him for help. This quest of Shar's wasn't just reckless, it was downright *crazy*. In the boat he had tried, once, to make Shar see sense, but she had refused to listen. It was this business about her mother that was at the root of it, Kitto thought unhappily. Now that Shar believed she *was* alive, she also believed her claim that there was an unknown enemy among the Circle. The only person Shar now trusted at the Star Peninsula was Hestor; but Hestor had neither the power nor the authority to do anything, so she had resolved to take matters into her own hands. Shar meant to face Sister Malia and the alien horror that was working through her. And she wanted vengeance of her own.

Their meals were only half finished but no one wanted any more. Shar was the first to go up the inn stairs to her room, and Reyni and Kitto followed her example a few minutes later. Kitto was asleep within minutes. And he dreamed uneasily of Hestor, and of a small white candle that neither of them had dared to light . . .

'She's been like this ever since Giria arrived,' Sister Missak told the Matriarch as they stood together at the door of Malia's room the following afternoon. 'Just sitting there, muttering to herself, then suddenly breaking into bouts of manic laughter.'

The Matriarch nodded. 'And what she mutters makes no sense?'

'No, Matriarch; not as far as we can tell. It all seems to be gibberish.'

Ulmara continued to watch for a few moments more, then nodded to Missak and they both withdrew. Malia didn't look round as the door closed; as far as it was possible to tell, she had been completely unaware of her visitors.

As the two women went back down the stairs Missak said, 'I ought to tell you, Matriarch, that Giria asked to see Malia.'

'Did she?' Ulmara frowned. 'When?'

'After the midday meal. I refused, of course. I hope that was right?'

'It was, Missak. Why, I wonder, did Giria make such a request?'

'I can't imagine. She didn't say.'

'Well, whatever her reasons, I want to ensure that she and Malia are kept apart until the High Initiate arrives and takes charge. In the light of the warning from the castle, it's possible that Malia has been trying to exert some influence. Have her watched more closely from now on, Missak. I don't want to take any chances.'

'Yes, Matriarch,' said Missak.

Outside, the fine weather had broken and it was

raining in a steady, soaking drizzle. Not good travelling weather, Ulmara thought. She hoped that it wouldn't delay the High Initiate for too long.

As they reached the ground floor, a young Sister came running along the hall.

'Matriarch!' The Sister's face was flushed with excitement. 'A carrier's cart has just set down three passengers at the gate, and one of them is a girl with auburn hair!'

Missak's eyes widened. 'Shar Tillmer . . .' she said.

'It must be! Thank the gods, she's arrived safely!' And the Matriarch set off towards the courtyard with Missak hurrying in her wake.

Since early morning Shar, Kitto and Reyni had sat among parcels and sacks and casks as the carrier's cart trundled steadily through the orchards and vineyards of Southern Chaun. When the rain began they had pulled a tarpaulin over themselves, but it was an inadequate shelter and within an hour they were soaked through. Chilled and tired and all but hypnotised by the unchanging landscape, Shar couldn't begin to express her relief when at last the white walls of the cot came in sight, and as she climbed stiffly down from the cart she thought of nothing beyond dry clothes and a warm fire.

Then the gate burst open, and in a daze she was swept into a flurry of white-robed figures, talking and exclaiming and asking questions. All three of them were hastened through the gate and into a courtyard surrounded by low, pleasant buildings in whose windows lights burned like welcoming beacons, then the Matriarch was there, taking over from the agitated Sisters and shepherding everyone to shelter.

They had nearly reached the door when another figure appeared. She paused on the threshold. Then, tremulously, she called, 'Shar . . .?'

Shar stopped at the sound of her voice. She looked, saw Giria framed in the doorway . . . and the tension within her shattered under a huge wave of emotion and joy.

'Mother!' she cried. 'Oh, *Mother!*'

She ran from the Matriarch's side and flung herself into Giria's open arms, sobbing as if her heart would break.

'I'm so sorry I doubted you,' Shar said. 'I should have known. I should have *realised.*'

'My dear, I understand.' Tears trembled on Giria's lashes and she smiled through them. 'If I had been in your place I wouldn't have dared to trust either, not without proof. But everything's all right now.'

The Sisters had given them adjoining rooms in the cot's guest wing, and they sat together now on Giria's bed. The curtains were closed against the rainy night and the room was warm with fire- and lamp-light. Tactfully, the Matriarch had given instructions that they were not to be disturbed for a while.

'It's grotesque that it was Thel who showed me the truth,' Shar said. 'I never imagined I'd owe him a debt like that.'

Giria laughed hollowly. 'Neither did I. When I think of what he did . . . all the years I spent . . .' She collected herself. 'But that's over now.' Her mouth hardened a little. 'I'm glad he's dead. *Glad* that — that monstrosity has destroyed him. But Shar, you know we're not out of danger yet. The Sixth-Plane entity still has one channel left that it can work through.'

'Yes.' Shar frowned. 'Sister Malia.' She had heard the rest of the story now; about Malia's dreams and fits, and of Lias's vision before he was attacked and killed. 'I wish the High Initiate would get here. The Matriarch says he must have left Wester Reach the morning after you did — surely he should have arrived by now?'

'He could be delayed for any number of reasons,' Giria pointed out. 'A lame horse, an incident on the road; even the weather might have held him up.' But then her expression changed and she took hold of Shar's hands. 'All the same, I have to admit that I'm beginning to worry. You're right; Neryon *should* have reached the cot by this time.'

'You don't think—' Shar's fingers tightened convulsively in hers.

'I don't know. And we mustn't start imagining the worst. However . . . I don't believe we can afford to take chances. You know what happened to Thel; how the entity controlled and used him. I have little doubt that it has the same power over Malia, and is only awaiting the right moment to manifest itself.' She paused. 'With your arrival, it now has both its intended victims under the same roof. I suspect it would prefer to strike before the

High Initiate is present to help us combat it.'

An icy sensation settled in the pit of Shar's stomach as she realised the sense of Giria's words. Her mouth suddenly dry, she said, 'The Sisters have some ability—'

'Not enough to fight a being like that,' replied Giria. 'No, Shar; I think we must take steps to protect ourselves, and the best way to do that is to remove you from Malia's reach until Neryon and his party arrive. The entity can't harm you directly; Thel revealed that. But it can – and I believe will – use Malia to try and trick you into playing into its hands. If that happens . . .' She didn't need to say the rest.

Shar said nervously, 'What should I do?'

'I have an idea,' Giria leaned forward, her face eager. 'A little way from this cot, just beyond the orchards, is a small tower that the Matriarch uses for her private retreats. If she agrees, I think you and I should go there to wait for Neryon. And in the tower we can take other precautions for our safety.' She smiled a little wryly. 'We're both adepts of the Circle, after all, even if I've not had the chance to use my skills for a very long time.'

Both adepts of the Circle; she, and her mother . . . the thought lifted Shar's spirits and she felt a surge of inner warmth.

'Do you think the Matriarch will agree?' she said.

Giria stood up. 'The only way to find out is to ask her. Come with me; we'll talk to her, now. Then if she says yes, we can make our preparations and leave straight away.' She drew a deep breath. 'It won't be for long, Shar. Neryon will be here soon, I'm certain of it.'

'I pray you're right,' Shar said fervently. She too rose to her feet. 'But in the meantime . . . Yes, Mother. Let's go and find the Matriarch.'

The Matriarch approved of Giria's idea. She too was worried by the High Initiate's failure to arrive; not only because she was concerned for his safety, but also because she feared trouble with Malia, and was not sure that she and her Sisters could cope. Kitto, though, was less happy. If anyone was to protect Shar he wanted it to be him, and he tried hard to persuade her that he should join her in the tower. But Shar refused, for two reasons. Firstly, there would be magical work to do, to protect the tower from any dark influence, and Kitto's presence might hinder that. And secondly, she wanted some time alone with her mother. Kitto couldn't argue with that, and gave way. But as he watched Shar and Giria setting off for the tower, accompanied by an escort of two Sisters caped against the drizzle, he felt more than a twinge of unease.

Someone else was also watching the departure from an upstairs window, and as the cot gate closed behind the party there was a sudden tumult on the upper floor. Three Sisters heard Malia's shrieks, and ran to her room to find the door shaking on its hinges with the force of her fists beating on it. They couldn't make out the words she was screaming, but she sounded as if she was in agony, and hastily they unlocked the door and opened it.

Malia burst out of the room like a wild-eyed dervish, taking the Sisters unawares. She was past them before they could grab her, and as she rushed towards the stairs her voice rose in a screech that rang through the cot.

'*Kill her! KILL HER!!*'

She plunged down the stairs with the Sisters in pursuit. The furore brought others running, including the Matriarch who had been in her study, but Malia eluded them and, still screaming, headed for the outside door.

They finally seized her in the courtyard. She fought like a wild animal, but their numbers were too great for her. Five Sisters, red-faced with exertion, carried her back into the building; someone had sent for the cot's senior healer and she came hurrying with her medical bag.

Malia was gasping, still trying to scream but now without the breath to do so. As the healer quickly prepared a herbal powder, the Matriarch looked down, a mixture of sorrow and anger on her face.

'Giria's fear was all too well-founded, it seems,' she said.

At the sound of her voice Malia suddenly fell silent, and her head jerked round until she was looking directly into Ulmara's eyes. Her own eyes looked completely demented; then her mouth jerked violently, spittle running down her chin, and she hissed ferociously, '*Going to kill her!*'

The Matriarch's expression hardened with disgust. 'You're going to do no such thing, you foul abomination! We know your plan, and Shar is out of your reach!'

'*No!*' Malia screeched. '*Kill her – Death! DEATH!*'

Ulmara turned away. 'Dose her,' she said to the healer.

'And make sure that it's strong – I don't want her to wake until morning.'

'Yes, Matriarch.' Tight-lipped, the healer nodded to the other Sisters to hold their patient still, and the sleeping potion was forced between Malia's lips. She moaned as she swallowed it, as though she understood what was being done to her but hadn't the strength left to resist. The draught took effect quickly; within a few minutes she was relaxing, and within a few more her eyes closed.

'Take her to her bed,' said the Matriarch sombrely. 'Lock the door, and set someone to keep watch outside it through the night.' She glanced uneasily towards the window. 'Thank the gods that Giria thought to take Shar away. If they'd not gone to the tower, and Malia had found them . . .' She shuddered. 'They will be safe now, though. I think we can be sure of that.'

SIXTEEN

Neryon, Pellis and their escort reached the cot the following morning. Their horses were seen approaching, and by the time they clattered through the gate a relieved and thankful throng was waiting to greet them.

'High Initiate.' Ulmara made the formal bow of the Sisterhood, then, forgetting formality, kissed him on both cheeks. 'My dear Neryon, we'd almost given you up for lost!'

'I'm sorry, Ulmara; we should have sent word.' Neryon looked weary and dishevelled; wet, too, for the rain had only stopped an hour ago. 'We would have been here yesterday, but there was an incident at a village on the way and we couldn't avoid becoming involved.'

'What of the others, Matriarch?' Pellis asked anxiously. 'Are they here?'

'All here and all safe,' Ulmara assured. 'They all have a great deal to tell you.' She exchanged a glance with Sister Missak. 'As have we.'

Malia was still asleep in her room. She had woken soon after dawn, but as soon as she woke she had started screaming again, so the Sisters had given her a further sleeping dose. Otherwise the time had been uneventful.

Kitto and Reyni were hovering in the entrance hall when Neryon and Pellis walked in. Pellis kissed Kitto, much to his surprise, and Neryon gave him a dry smile. 'Well, boy, it seems we owe you a debt – despite the fact that you didn't have the sense to confide in us in the first place!'

Kitto coloured to the roots of his hair. 'I'm sorry, sir . . . but . . .'

Neryon waved a hand. 'Let it rest, Kitto. You've helped Shar; that's what matters.' He looked at Reyni. 'As have you, I understand; and at no gain to yourself. It was a very selfless act – thank you.'

Reyni blinked, then smiled hesitantly. 'It was a pleasure, High Initiate.'

Neryon looked around at the gathering. 'Where are Shar and her mother?' he asked.

The Matriarch told him of Giria's suggestion, and also of Malia's fit the previous night, and he nodded. 'I think Giria acted wisely. Now, though . . . if Malia is still unconscious, we have time to make preparations before she wakes. Perhaps you'd send word to the tower, and let Shar and Giria know that they can return?'

'Of course.' Then the Matriarch paused. 'You said you were delayed by an incident at a village, Neryon? It wasn't anything to do with this?'

The High Initiate shook his head. 'No; though it was unpleasant enough in its own way. Three bodies were found on the road outside the village; mangled beyond recognition. They'd not been there long by the look of them, and the villagers were in a ferment, because it looked like a brigand attack and they haven't had any real trouble of that kind in living memory.'

'The gods give rest to their souls.' Ulmara made the splay-fingered sign of reverence. 'Were they from the locality?'

'It seems not, for no one has gone missing. But when we arrived, the local elders saw our Circle badges and asked us for help. The village doesn't have a militia, and they're nowhere near a messenger-bird post, so we arranged for word to be sent to the Province Margrave, and then performed a cleansing and protecting ritual.' Neryon sighed. 'It was little enough to do for them. They were badly frightened.'

'That's understandable.' Ulmara shivered. 'And it makes me realise how lucky Giria was. When I think of her, riding alone from Wester Reach, my blood turns quite—'

'Alone?' Neryon interrupted sharply.

She looked at him in puzzlement. 'Yes. She had no escort. I told her that it was foolish of her and anything could have—'

'Wait, Ulmara, wait,' Neryon interrupted again. 'Giria did have an escort. The Keepers of Light's leader told me so. He picked them himself, and saw them on their way.'

The atmosphere was suddenly charged with tension. Pellis was very still. The Matriarch and the High Initiate looked at each other. Then Ulmara said in a small, uneasy voice,

'How many went with her?'

Neryon's face had paled. 'Three . . .'

For perhaps five seconds the tension held, and with it absolute silence. Then, like a man snapped out of a trance,

Neryon turned towards the door and snapped, 'Where is the tower?'

They ran through the orchard – even the Matriarch picking up her skirts with no thought for dignity. The tower was a small, modest structure just beyond the last of the trees; built of white stone like the cot, and with a flight of stairs at ground level that led up to a single, round room. The door was locked, but Ulmara had brought her own key; her hands shook as she turned it, and the door swung open.

Neryon was the first inside, Pellis and Ulmara on his heels and Kitto, not caring about propriety, barging after them. Their feet scuffed on the stone stairs; below, a gaggle of Sisters watched anxiously as they reached the door that led to the tower's one room.

The door opened. The room beyond was neat, tidy . . .

And empty.

By the fourth morning after his mother and the High Initiate had left for Wester Reach, Hestor's frustration was becoming unbearable. From the moment of their departure he had been helplessly thwarted, longing to take some action but powerless to do anything at all. To make matters worse, his efforts to get any information had been immovably and sternly rebuffed. Gant Birn Sangen, the senior adept whom Neryon had placed in temporary charge of the Circle, knew all about Hestor's suspension and had taken a dim view of his plea to be told what the High Initiate intended to do. That was not the business of a junior initiate, Adept Gant said severely. And Hestor would do well to bear in mind that unless he learned his place he wouldn't even *be* an initiate for much longer. Knowing Gant as a stickler for rules, Hestor gave up his efforts. If he was to learn anything, he would have to find another way.

As part of his suspension he was also excluded from the initiates' study classes, which added to his discomfort by leaving him idle for much of the time. Not that he could have concentrated on studying under the circumstances, but at least it would have been better than screaming boredom. So at last, out of sheer desperation, he offered to help with cellar-clearing. There was a huge cellar network in the castle's foundations; the upper levels were used for storing dry foodstuffs, but the lower ones, which tended to be damp, were either filled with disused items or empty but for grime and spiders and rats. Records of the low cellars' contents were lost – if they had ever existed, which was unlikely – and no one knew for certain what was there. So every now and then a section was tackled, useful items catalogued and the unwanted rubbish cleared out. People joked that the castle would probably fall down before the task was completed, but the efforts continued sporadically, and for those who wanted to make themselves useful there was always something to do. It was dirty work, and tedious, but Hestor reasoned that it would at least keep him occupied. And some physical activity might stop the feeling that he was going mad with frustration.

So, as the High Initiate and Pellis were arriving at the

Matriarch's cot, Hestor was deep underground, in his oldest clothes, helping two servants and two third-rank initiates to investigate a mound of old furniture that had been crammed anyhow into a small room.

'Great gods,' Broen, one of the adepts, said with feeling, as he and Hestor wrestled with two chairs whose legs seemed to be hopelessly entangled. 'This detritus must have been here for at least ten years!'

'More – if you – ask me,' the other adept put in breathlessly, as he tried to pull a table free from the pile. '*And* most of it's beyond repair. Why anyone – bothered to – keep it at all is – beyond me!'

The chairs came apart at last, and the back and two legs of one fell off with a dismal clatter. 'Firewood,' Broen said. 'It's not fit for anything else. Hestor, if you'll just – hey, cat, look out! How did *he* get in there?'

One of the castle cats had appeared from the middle of the furniture heap and jumped down to the floor, where it shook its head and pawed cobwebs from its whiskers. Under a layer of dust, Hestor saw that the animal's fur was white . . .

Suddenly he heard himself say, 'Oh, leave him. He's not doing any harm – might even catch a rat or two while he's here.'

The cat eyed him, then turned and wriggled back into the heap, leaving Hestor wondering why he had said what he had. It was as if something had put the words into his head and *made* him utter them . . .

A scratching and scrabbling came from the depths of the stacked furniture; then a muffled yowling.

'Oh, no; sounds like the wretched creature's got itself stuck!' Broen tried to peer into the tangle. 'I can't see it . . . Cat, cat! Can't pick up its thoughts, either. That's odd; I usually sense *something* from them.'

For reasons which he didn't begin to comprehend, Hestor's heart was thumping. 'If we move that chest—' he began.

'Yes . . . All right, I can manage.' There was a scraping, a groan – and suddenly the heap collapsed. The cat shot from its hiding place and out of the door, and Broen swore as he jumped clear amid a crash of falling furniture.

'Well!' Hands on hips, he surveyed the mess. 'If there was anything intact a minute ago, it won't be now!'

Hestor's nose wrinkled. 'What's that smell?' he asked.

Broen sniffed, then pulled a face. 'We rot . . . Good gods, it's hardly surprising; look at the state of those pieces that were right at the back!' He waved a hand against the stink. 'These foundations must be sopping! Yes, look; the mortar's completely decayed in that corner.'

Hestor was starting to feel sick, and it wasn't just the smell. 'We'd better tell the head steward,' he said. 'Something's obviously wrong.'

'Too true!' Broen had climbed over the furniture and was probing at the wall with his belt-knife. 'See; the mortar's just crumbling away. Stones are loose, too – *Uff!* It's a miracle we didn't smell this from the great hall!'

As he spoke these last words a piece of the stonework sagged and collapsed altogether, exposing a gaping hole. An appalling stench rushed over them all like a wave;

they stumbled back, gagging – and Broen's voice rose in horrified shock.

'*Yandros and Aeoris!*'

Hand clamped over his mouth and nose, Hestor looked at the hole and saw what had fallen out of it. *Bones.* They were brown and stained, and in their midst lay a skull, which was all too horribly recognisable as human. Nausea churned in Hestor's stomach; he wanted to turn away but he was mesmerised.

Then he saw something glinting. Broen had seen it too; steeling himself, he bent down to look more closely, and, fighting sickness, Hestor forced himself to look, too.

There were two small objects lying among the awful remains. One was a woman's locket on a slender chain.

The other was the gold badge of a Circle adept.

The locket was the final proof; though even without it the conclusion would have been inevitable, for there had been no other mysterious disappearances among the adepts for at least fifty years. This woman, Physician Eln Chandor declared, had not been dead that long; twenty years or less was more likely. Then, when the locket was opened, there could be no further doubt. Inside was a miniature portrait of a man whom the physician recognised at once: Adept Solas Tillmer Starnor, the husband of Giria.

They had found Shar's mother.

Hestor watched numbly as Eln started to wrap the remains in a blanket for removal to the infirmary. 'By the look of this skull,' the physician said, 'she was killed by a

213

blow to the head. Someone had better inform Adept Gant. We'll have to go through the formality of an inquiry, even though the circumstances are obvious, and in the High Initiate's absence—' He stopped. 'Oh, great gods . . .'

'Sir?' Hestor looked at him, startled . . . and suddenly felt an awful, intuitive foreboding. There was a horrified expression on Eln's face as, without a further word to anyone, the physician swung round and headed for the door.

'Sir, what is it?' Hestor started after him. 'Has something—'

'Not now, boy!' Eln snapped curtly. 'Go back – tell no one to touch anything until I return!'

'But—'

'*Do as I say!*' There was such ferocity in Eln's tone that Hestor dared not disobey. But the foreboding feeling sprang into alarm. What had Eln suddenly recalled? What did he know, that had some bearing on this?

'Broen!' Returning at a run to the cellar he grabbed the other adept's arm. 'What was that about? Do you know?'

Broen shrugged. 'Your guess is as good as mine.' Then he hesitated. 'Unless it had something to do with the High Initiate's letter.'

'Letter? What letter?' Hestor had to stop himself from physically shaking Broen to get the information, but Broen only shrugged and said,

'The one that came the other day from Wester Reach. I don't know what was in it, but someone said it

214

concerned Shar and her mother, and soon after it arrived Gant was busy sending messages off to the Matriarch in Southern Chaun. Beyond that, though – Hestor? Where are you going?'

Hestor was already at the door. 'I've got to see Adept Gant!' he called back by way of explanation; then, remembering belatedly, 'Eln says no one's to touch anything!'

His running footsteps thudded away down the passage.

Hestor all but cannoned into Gant and Physician Eln in the castle's entrance hall. Eln started to say angrily, 'Hestor, I thought I told you to—' but Hestor cut across him.

'Sir, please!' He addressed Gant breathlessly. 'What did the High Initiate's letter say?'

Gant's face darkened. 'How do you know about that letter?'

'*Please*, Adept, it's desperately important!' Hestor implored. 'If our discovery in the cellar means that Shar might be in danger—'

Gant didn't let him get any further. 'Whatever it means, it's no concern of yours, Hestor! It's a matter for the senior adepts and the Circle Council, and at this moment you are holding up urgent business – move aside and let me pass!'

'Wait, Gant,' Physician Eln said suddenly. 'Hestor may have marred his record, but this obviously isn't a frivolous question – and we've had reason to be grateful for his impulsive actions in the past.' He gave Hestor a very searching look. 'All right, I'll tell you this much. The

High Initiate has said that there's evidence to prove that the woman in Wester Reach really is Shar's mother. Thanks to your find, though, we know she's not. But whoever or whatever she is, she had enough skill – or power – to have deceived a large number of people – Neryon included.'

Hestor had paled. 'Whoever . . . or whatever?' he echoed.

'Precisely. Under the circumstances, the High Initiate and your mother must be warned at once.' Eln's mouth pursed. 'We believe that they, and Shar, could be in great danger.'

Hestor's ugly feeling of portent abruptly flared into something far, far stronger. He didn't merely fear danger – he was certain of it.

Mouth dry, he asked, 'Where are they, sir? Still in Wester Reach?'

'No. They've gone on to Southern Chaun, and we understand that Shar and the false Giria are also on their way there.'

Southern Chaun . . . *Sister Malia*, Hestor thought. Suddenly everything began to slot into place.

'Now; we have a lot to do, and no time to waste,' Eln said. He saw Hestor's stricken expression and, misinterpreting it, smiled tightly. 'Don't fear for your mother. We're sending word by the fastest messenger-bird; it'll reach them before sunset.' His eyes hardened a little. 'We can do no more, Hestor. And neither can you.'

The two men strode on their way, leaving Hestor staring after them and knowing, with an awful intuition, that whatever message Gant sent, it would arrive too late. The senior adepts were always so slow, so careful, so *ponderous* . . . he seethed with frustration and fear. *We can do no more*, Physician Eln had said.

Then Hestor thought: *But I can.*

The idea of it brought him out in a cold sweat. How many times had he and Kitto debated this, only to shirk it through uncertainty? Had they been cowards? he asked himself. Should they have acted before? Should he act now, as his instinct was urging him to do? *Dared* he?

A sharp sound made him start and swing round. The white cat was poised on the main stairs, about half way up. Its tail was lashing and its ears lay flat against its head; green-gold eyes glared so furiously at Hestor that he recoiled. The cat yowled once, then streaked away up the staircase; turning at the top and heading in the direction of Hestor's room.

Hestor had his answer, and he raced for the stairs in the cat's wake.

Hestor hurtled into his room, door slamming behind him. The white cat was on his bed, its back arched and tail bristling now, and with it was Shar's own cat, Amber. The two of them set up a wailing chorus as Hestor rummaged feverishly in his linen chest and snatched the candle from its hiding place. It felt ice-cold to the touch and he almost dropped it three times before finally getting it fixed in the small sconce from his bedside table. As he hunted for flint and tinder he thought frantically that he should surely make some ritual of this; incense, trappings, something to mark the magnitude of what he was about to do. Just to light it, without ceremony, seemed like sacrilege—

But there was no time for trappings or ritual or anything else. He had the flint and tinder; with a shaking hand he struck a spark and, hoping that the gods would understand, lit the candle.

The flame burned emerald green; the same colour, Hestor remembered with an inward jolt, as Tarod of Chaos's eyes. Nothing else happened. There was no clap of thunder or shriek of a Warp exploding across the sky. Only the two cats abruptly fell silent, and the silence seemed to crush down on the room like something alive.

Hestor held his breath, waiting . . .

In the realm of Chaos, Tarod looked at his great brother, who stood cloaked in the colours of a furious storm, his eyes burning white-hot.

'If Aeoris meant the threat he made to you,' Tarod said, 'then this will be like throwing a direct challenge in his face.'

'I know.' Yandros's voice had a very dangerous edge.

'*Did* he mean it?'

'Who can say? Aeoris struts and postures; he always has. But he bears grudges, too, and I know full well that he's only looking for a chance to strike back at us for our intervention when the High Initiate's life was threatened.'

'In which case he *will* retaliate in some way. If for no other reason than to save face.'

'Mmm.' Yandros considered for a few moments. Then

his eyes turned to the colour of sapphires and he turned to look directly at his brother.

'Damn Aeoris,' he said. 'We'll answer the call.'

He smiled, and with slow, keen amusement Tarod returned the smile. A moment later, Yandros was alone.

Hestor couldn't hold the air in his lungs any longer and had counted thirty more of his own heartbeats since he started to breathe again; yet still there was no response, no sign. The candle was burning unnaturally fast; half of it was already gone. Amber and the white cat were motionless, staring at it, but Hestor felt his spirits sinking fast. Had he made a mistake somehow? Was there something else he should have done, or said, or—

Suddenly he couldn't stand to wait in the room any longer. If he didn't *do* something, he would explode. He ran for the door, not knowing where he might go but desperate to break the unbearable tension inside him.

He grasped the latch, wrenched the door open. And his heart gave a colossal thump of shock as he came face to face with Tarod of Chaos on the threshold.

SEVENTEEN

'There's nothing.' Neryon's voice was racked with tension and his face looked stark. 'Just a darkness, a void – I can't sense anything at all!'

Pellis's gaze flicked rapidly around the room as though searching for answers, though they had already combed the tower from top to bottom. The only clue they had come across was now clasped in her hand; the key that Giria had taken when she and Shar left. It had a sinister implication, for the door had been locked when they arrived, suggesting that Giria and Shar had not left the tower by any physical means.

Neryon shook himself, throwing off the last of his trance-state, and stepped out of the circle he had hastily created on the floor. He hadn't had much faith in the attempt to trace Shar by magical means but it had been worth the attempt, for they had little else to help them. Now he looked at his companions; Pellis and the Matriarch tight-lipped and silent, Kitto deadly pale and shivering, and said, 'There's only one person who might provide us with some answers.'

'Malia . . .' The Matriarch wished that she hadn't ordered Malia to be drugged again. But there would be a way to wake her. There *had* to be.

'In the light of this, we can't be sure how much Malia

truly knows, or even if she's involved willingly,' the High Initiate continued. 'But we've got to try everything we can.'

They left the tower and hurried back through the orchard towards the cot, where the Matriarch summoned the healer, Sister Lellin, and asked her if Malia could be roused from her herb-induced sleep.

'I don't know, Matriarch.' Sister Lellin looked dubious. 'There is an antidote to the potion, but it doesn't always work. And to force her out of unconsciousness could be dangerous for her.'

Ulmara glanced at the High Initiate, who said, 'I think we must take the chance, Sister. We simply daren't wait until she wakes of her own accord.'

As Sister Lellin headed for her infirmary to mix the draught, Kitto addressed Neryon. 'Sir . . . there's so much I don't understand!' He swallowed. '*Does* Giria – or whoever she is – want to harm Shar? Or are they both in danger?'

Neryon sighed. 'I don't know, Kitto; not yet.' He hesitated. 'It's still possible that she really is Shar's mother, but that she has been possessed just as Thel was – and maybe even because of Thel.' He drew the boy aside a little way. 'Now Thel is dead and Malia has been put into a drugged sleep, they're both useless to the Sixth-Plane entities. I suspect that the powers that were controlling them have sought another outlet, and thus turned their attention to Giria.'

Kitto looked back at him with frightened eyes. 'Can she fight it, sir? Will she have the strength to resist?'

Neryon's face was grave. 'Who can say? She's a trained Circle adept, but that in itself is unlikely to be enough. However, if she truly is Shar's mother, then she will have one great weapon in her fight, and that is her love for Shar. Thel and Malia *wanted* to do evil, but the real Giria does not. The entity might find that she is a great deal harder to control than it expects – and that could be the saving of both her and Shar.'

Kitto nodded. 'I pray it is, sir.'

'So do I,' said the High Initiate fervently.

When Shar woke, the last thing she remembered was finishing the glass of wine her mother had given her. It must have been very strong, she thought – either that, or she was so tired that sheer exhaustion had overtaken her without any warning and she had fallen asleep where she sat.

She rubbed at her eyes and struggled more upright in the chair. She felt strangely hot. It was still night, and the room was lit only by what she assumed was a faint moonglow filtering in at the windows. The candles must have burned out, and Giria hadn't lit any more. Perhaps she was asleep . . .

But she wasn't, for when her vision adjusted to the dark a little Shar saw Giria standing at the northward window. Her figure was a silhouette; she was motionless, gazing out, and didn't seem to be aware that Shar had stirred.

It *was* hot in here. Peculiar, for the rain had cooled the air considerably, and when they first arrived the tower had felt cold. Had they lit a fire? Shar couldn't recall. And suddenly she started to feel ill at ease.

Then Giria turned round from the window. 'Shar.' Strangely, she seemed to see Shar perfectly despite the gloom. 'You're awake; good.'

'What hour is it?' Shar asked.

'Oh, it's late. Very late.'

'Past first moonset?'

Giria laughed softly and didn't answer the question. 'Would you like more wine?' she asked.

She was feeling queasy, Shar realised, and shook her head. 'No, thank you. But . . . could we have some light?'

'Of course.' Giria moved to a table – her skirt made a slightly odd *hushing* sound. There was no sound of flint and tinder but suddenly a candle was alight, burning up with a sulphurous yellow flame that looked faintly unhealthy. Patterns of light and shadows appeared.

And there was something wrong with Giria's face.

Shar blinked rapidly and rubbed her eyes again, and when she focused on her mother once more everything had returned to normal. Just for a moment, though, it had seemed that Giria had no features; no eyes, nose or mouth, but only blank darkness where they should have been.

Trying to forget the image, and the unpleasant mental jolt it had given her, she said, 'There's been no word from the cot?'

'No,' said Giria. 'Oh, no.' She laughed again, still softly, then moved back to the window. 'Come and look, Shar. Come and see what's outside.'

'See what's . . .?' But the words died on Shar's tongue, and the unease in her began to turn into crawling apprehension. Something was wrong. This wasn't like reality; it was more like a dream. Yet she was awake; she knew she was awake. What had happened?

She rose and walked slowly, cautiously towards the window. Giria stepped aside as she reached it; Shar looked out – and bile rose to her throat in a violent surge.

There was no moon, no orchard, no nightscape at all beyond the window. Instead, what confronted her was a thick, alien darkness, like dense fog or foetid, polluted water. It was moving, rolling sluggishly as though disturbed by some unnameable force deep within it; a faint glow oozed from its surface, but the glow was poisonous and colourless. And somewhere in that coagulating foulness was a single, gigantic form, pulsating with baneful intelligence. With hatred. With *hunger*.

Shar's memory smashed back to one hideous night, in the cellar of the house where Thel had once held her captive. He had performed a ritual that opened the way between the mortal world and the elemental planes. He had forced Shar to look into the Sixth Plane, and to see the true horror of what dwelt there. Now, alone in the tower with Giria, she was looking on that horror again.

She heard a whimpering sound, realised that it came from her own lips – and Giria laughed again. This time the laughter didn't stop; it grew stronger, deeper, more ugly, and the swirling murk outside seemed to pulse in rhythm with it. Fighting panic, Shar turned to look at what she had thought was her mother. Giria gazed back at her. Her face hadn't changed. But her hair had turned into something else, something that writhed with a squirming life of its own. And in the depths of her eyes two crimson pinpoints glared like burning embers.

'Nnh – Nnh—' Shar was trying to say *No*, but all that came out was a dreadful, inarticulate noise. Limbs shaking, body jerking, she started to back away. The door; if she could reach the door—

The laughter cut off abruptly and the thing that had been Giria smiled. 'There is no door.' Her voice had undergone a shocking change. It was not human. 'No door, Shar Tillmer – and even if there were, what would you find waiting for you outside? This is merely a semblance of the tower. It is not real. Nothing is real here, for I have taken you out of the world you know, to another.'

Shar found her voice at last. 'You can't h-h—'

'I can't have done? Oh, but I can. You drank the wine, Shar. You accepted my gift, and thus you allowed the link between us to be formed again, as it was once before. I am far wiser than Thel, you see. Far more *powerful* than Thel. But then you have known that from the beginning. For you, the Dark-Caller, know us, and what we can do. You know what we crave. And at last we have what we crave – for you have given it to us!'

Now, her face was changing. Giria's features were dissolving like a mask being washed away, and beneath the mask was a misshapen travesty of a human being. A cloying stench of evil filled the room – or whatever this place truly was – as the swirling darkness filled the world

225

outside. And against her will Shar felt something stirring in her own mind. The link, forged in her by Thel and now reawakened by this entity's deception. The horrifying legacy of the Dark-Caller . . .

The creature extended a hand towards her; it had scaly, broken talons where Giria's fingers had been, and one hooked in a dreadful mockery of a beckoning movement.

'Come, Shar Tillmer. Come with me. You cannot refuse us now.'

Fighting with all her strength and will against blind panic, Shar stammered out, 'Come . . . where . . .?'

'To where *we* rule,' the entity hissed. 'To where *we* will claim our vengeance. You cannot resist the call. Listen to what lurks in your mind, and *come!*'

Pain flared agonisingly in Shar's skull. She clapped both hands to her head, tearing at her hair, battling not to *listen* to the appalling lure that tried to drag her forward to where the monstrosity waited.

'*Come!*' the creature hissed again. '*See what lies ahead. See where you shall go!*'

The floor quaked under Shar's feet and the dimensions of the room seemed to twist in on themselves. A section of the wall distorted, flowed outwards and away, and in mesmerised horror Shar found herself staring into a black vortex, like a bottomless well. Far, far in its depths, at a horrifyingly impossible distance, something waited; something that moved, that breathed, that *hungered* . . .

'Come, Shar. Come, Shar. Come, Shar.'

The command was hypnotic; she couldn't defy it.

Slowly, like a sleepwalker, she started to move towards the vortex's yawning black chasm.

For all Sister Lellin's efforts, Malia could not be woken. The healer tried everything she knew, but in vain: since the last draught had been administered, Malia had slipped into a coma.

Lellin distraughtly blamed herself, convinced that she had made some dreadful mistake in her dosages, but Neryon and Pellis were certain that the herbs had nothing to do with this. Even Eln Chandor's skills couldn't have brought Malia round. Something else was at work here.

'There's only one thing to be done,' the High Initiate said, looking down at Malia's motionless, waxy-faced figure in the bed. 'I'd like her carried to the tower. Then, with your permission, Ulmara, Pellis and I must try to wake her by sorcery. There's no other hope.'

The Matriarch nodded. 'Of course.'

Minutes later a litter was borne away from the cot with Malia, still unconscious, inside it. Neryon and Pellis would follow, when they had prepared for the ritual they planned to perform. They were in the Matriarch's study, gathering together the items they would need, when a livid flash lit the room. The gloom jumped momentarily into startling brilliance, and Pellis looked out of the window, expecting to see storm clouds and hear a rumble of thunder.

The dull sky was unchanged and the thunder didn't come. But there were two people in the courtyard outside. For a second or two Pellis couldn't believe what she was seeing – then, incredulously, she called, 'Hestor?'

'*What?*' Neryon swung round, staring.

'It *is* Hestor! And there's someone with him; a stranger; I don't—' Pellis stopped, and her face turned ashen.

Neryon was beside her at the window in two strides. He looked down, saw Hestor at the side of a tall, gaunt man dressed in black and with a mane of black hair that cascaded over his shoulders. As if sensing Neryon, the man looked in their direction, and Neryon saw his eyes.

'Great g—' The oath choked off as Neryon realised that it would have been all too accurate. For another moment he was motionless, stunned. Then as though some invisible force had shaken him into life, he ran from the room and along the corridor towards the main entrance.

Hestor felt as though he had been pitched headlong into a Warp storm and hurled out on the other side, with half his mind belonging to someone else. He had started to blurt out his story to Tarod, but after three breathless sentences the Chaos lord had heard enough. Without any ceremony he had propelled Hestor out of his room, out of the castle, across the courtyard and through the great black gates to the sward beyond. Hestor had heard him speak one word, in a language he didn't recognise but which brought gooseflesh to his skin. Then without any warning the world vanished and there was an explosion of noise and light and dizzying motion, as though he were being hurled in seven different directions at once. It lasted only seconds – though seconds were more than enough – before, with a blinding, lightning-like flash, he found himself standing with Tarod in the courtyard of the Matriarch's cot.

He was still feeling giddy when Neryon and his mother came running to meet them, with the Matriarch close behind. Some confused minutes followed; the Matriarch could hardly believe that one of Chaos's own lords had arrived in her domain, and there was a flurry of words, questions, obeisances – until Tarod cut through the commotion.

'There's no time for formality.' His voice was authoritative and silenced everyone instantly. 'We have more urgent business. Where is Shar?'

Neryon told him what had happened, adding his own speculation about Giria. 'If the Sixth-Plane entities have possessed her as they did Thel,' he said, 'then—'

'They haven't,' Tarod interrupted.

'My lord?' Neryon's face tensed.

'That creature is not Shar's mother.' Tarod glanced briefly at Hestor. 'Giria Tillmer Starnor – or what little remains of her – was found this morning, walled up in one of the castle cellars.' His gaze flicked to Pellis, who had put a clenched fist to her mouth in shock, and he added more gently, 'I'm sorry.'

For all that the life or death of one mortal could mean nothing to him, Pellis had the impression that he genuinely meant it. 'Th . . . thank you, my lord,' she whispered.

'So,' Tarod went on, 'the question remains: if this

creature is not Giria, what is she?'

'We hoped to interrogate Sister Malia,' said Neryon. 'But she's fallen into an unnatural sleep and the Sisters are unable to wake her. Pellis and I were about to try more drastic methods when—'

'Where is she?' Tarod's eyes had narrowed to cat-like slits.

'She's just been carried to the tower where Shar vanished, my lord. If we're to break through the barrier around her, it seems the most favourable place for the rite.'

Tarod nodded. 'I'll see her for myself.' He glanced at the Matriarch. 'With your permission, madam?'

Ulmara blanched. 'Of course, my lord, whatever you say.'

Neryon led Tarod towards the cot gate, the others following at a cautious distance. Hestor would have gone too, but as he started after them a voice called to him. He turned, and saw Kitto running in his direction.

'Kitto! Am I glad to see you safe!' He thumped the other boy's shoulders as they collided in the middle of the courtyard.

Kitto was breathless. 'You lit the candle!' Awe and relief mingled in his voice as he stared after Tarod.

'Yes.' Tersely, Hestor told him of the discovery in the castle cellars, adding, 'The white cat showed us where to look. You were right about that animal, Kitto.'

'Righter than you know,' Kitto said with feeling, remembering his own experience in the mountains. But that story could wait – what he wanted now was answers.

'Hestor, what happened after you lit the candle?' he asked avidly. 'What did Lord Tarod say, and what's he going to do?'

Hestor opened his mouth to reply, but before he could speak the sound of footsteps made both of them turn.

Reyni was coming towards them. He stopped when he saw Hestor, and Kitto, watching Hestor's face and remembering his attitude towards the young musician, said quickly, 'Hestor. Reyni's been a good friend to Shar and me. If it wasn't for him, none of us would be here now.'

Hestor's eyes narrowed, but Kitto's words went home, and abruptly his resentment dissolved. 'Then he's a friend of mine, too,' he said, and held out his hand to Reyni, who clasped wrists with a hesitant smile.

'We've all got a lot to tell each other,' Kitto said. 'About the storm and the Brig . . . and then there's Hestor's story; you don't know anything about that yet—'

'I've got something to tell you, too,' Reyni said tautly. 'Something *you* don't know.'

They both looked at him. His face had lost some of its colour and had a peculiar expression. 'I think,' he said, 'that before we go any further, I'd better admit the truth about me. And about someone else . . .'

The Sisters who had carried Malia to the tower had placed the litter in the upstairs room and were now by the outer door, waiting for the High Initiate and any further instructions. At Tarod's order the Matriarch shepherded them away, together with everyone else save

231

for Neryon and Pellis. Whatever was about to happen here, the Chaos lord wanted no spectators and no distractions.

The three who remained climbed the stairs, and Tarod entered the tower room first. Neryon followed – and almost collided with the Chaos lord as he stopped dead on the threshold. For a fraction of a second a black aura flickered into life around him, and the flash of his fury blazed into Neryon's and Pellis's minds like fire.

Then Tarod said in a savagely lethal voice, '*What are you doing here?*'

He stalked into the room, and the others, looking uneasily past him, were confronted with the extraordinary sight of a stranger sitting in a chair beside the litter where Malia lay. Malia herself slept on, oblivious, but the stranger rose as Tarod came in, and raked him with a look of contempt. He was as tall as the Chaos lord, but his hair was pure white, and held back from his stern face by a golden circlet. His clothes were white, too, in sharp contrast to Tarod's unadorned black. And his eyes . . .

Pellis made a small, shocked noise and put a clenched fist to her mouth, while Neryon could only stare, mesmerised. For the stranger's eyes had no iris or pupil, but were featureless golden orbs.

He said, 'I think you know the answer to your question, cousin.' Then he looked directly at the two humans who stood transfixed on the threshold. 'My name is Ailind. I am brother to Aeoris of Order – and I am here to see to it that Chaos's interference in your mortal affairs ceases, here and now!'

EIGHTEEN

The two gods faced each other like cats bristling before a fight, and Ailind said, 'I have a message for you, from Aeoris. He says—'

'If Aeoris has anything to say,' Tarod snapped, 'he may say it in person!'

'He has already done so. To Yandros.' Ailind smiled haughtily. 'But perhaps Yandros didn't take the trouble to inform you?'

'Oh, *that*.' Tarod laughed; a short, sharp bark of a sound. 'Do you and Aeoris really expect us to worry about your trivial points of principle in the present circumstances? I had more regard for your intelligence!'

Ailind's eyes flared hotly. 'And I had more regard for yours, *cousin*. You've had our warning; if you choose to disregard it, then—'

'My lords!' To his own astonishment as well to everyone else's, Neryon found the courage to speak. Tarod and Ailind both turned furious gazes on him; he quailed but, aware that he couldn't back out now, continued nonetheless. 'Please, my lords, I don't understand! I'm deeply conscious of the honour you have both done us in coming to us in a time of trouble, but . . .' He swallowed. 'Shar Tillmer is in very great danger, and if we are to save her, there's no *time* for disagreement.'

233

Tarod turned away and Ailind's mouth tightened austerely as he stared at Neryon.

'High Initiate,' he said, 'My presence here has nothing to do with Shar Tillmer. The simple fact is this: Chaos has broken – again – the terms of Equilibrium, which forbid intervention in mortal affairs.'

'Unless mortals ask us to intervene,' Tarod put in drily.

Ailind rounded on him. 'This time, you were not asked! Yandros took it upon himself to send you to the castle to speak secretly with the young initiate Hestor Ennas—'

'With *Hestor?*' Neryon interrupted before he could stop himself. 'And he kept it from me—'

'Yes, Neryon; because I swore him to secrecy and he's more afraid of me than he is of you.' Tarod glanced at the High Initiate and there was a darkly humorous glint in his eyes. 'As he should be. But that isn't the point.' One hand made a sweeping gesture towards the litter and Malia. 'This is what should concern us – *all* of us. If your suspicions are right, then not only is Shar Tillmer in peril, as you say, but we ourselves are faced with a potentially dangerous situation.' He looked at the lord of Order. 'Listen to me, Ailind. There's no love lost between us, but there have been times, albeit rare, when we've cooperated to save both our realms from a common threat. I think we're faced with another such threat now.'

Ailind hesitated, but before he could argue the matter Tarod continued. 'The Sixth-Plane creatures want revenge on Shar – but that's not their sole motive. They don't only hate her; they loathe all humanity with an intensity that mortals couldn't even imagine, and if they succeed in destroying her, it won't end there. They'll use the foothold they've gained in the human world for an onslaught of malevolence – and if the Circle can't stop them, then, invited or not, we must.'

Ailind's unearthly eyes were like banked fires now. 'You're suggesting that we work together?'

'I'm saying that we have no other choice. Unless you want to risk this world's ruin.' Tarod glanced quickly at Neryon and Pellis. 'And if we can save Shar's life into the bargain, that too is in both our interests, for she'll have reason to be grateful to Chaos and Order alike.'

The edges of Ailind's mouth curled cynically. 'Your tactics are as unsubtle as ever,' he said, 'but for once there's some merit in your argument. Very well. Leaving aside Shar Tillmer – she's irrelevant – we'll deal with this between us.'

For a moment they held each other's gazes, then Tarod gave a curt nod. It was the sign of a truce, and Neryon felt relief surge through him. 'My lords,' he ventured, 'Time is not on our side . . .'

Tarod nodded again and looked down at Malia. 'She appears to be in some kind of trance,' he said, 'and it has nothing to do with the good Sisters' herbs.'

Ailind touched Malia's eyelids. 'There's the taint of the Sixth Plane here. They have her in a thrall which won't be easy to break.' His hand moved, the fingers splayed now and hovering above Malia's face. She stirred and moaned but she didn't wake, and with just a trace of lingering resentment Ailind glanced at Tarod. 'Perhaps if we combine our energies . . .'

Tarod moved to his side. There was silence for a few seconds, then both gods stepped back. Ailind was frowning, Tarod looked annoyed, and the High Initiate asked tentatively, 'Is something wrong, sirs?'

The Chaos lord sighed. 'Her mind is locked away beyond reach. The entity has created a wall between her and the real world. We could wake her easily enough, but it would be of no use; she'd be nothing more than a witless shell. If we're to form a link with the entity, we must first form one with the real Malia.'

'We need to goad her memory in an area that the entity can't control,' Ailind said. 'Something from her past, before she became corrupted by this evil.' Again he stretched out a hand over Malia's face, and this time Tarod did the same. Cold light shimmered around their fingers; the watching humans felt a jolt, like a discharge of psychic power—

Malia's body jerked in the bed. Her head turned rapidly from side to side and she began to mutter.

'*Sing . . . sing . . . sing . . .*'

'What's she saying?' Pellis whispered to Neryon.

'*Sing me your little song,*' Malia muttered. '*Sing it for me now . . . good child, good child . . .*'

Neryon and Pellis exchanged bewildered looks, but Tarod and Ailind were concentrating intently on Malia now. Ailind said, 'Ah, yes . . .' and there was a note of triumph in his voice. Then Tarod drew back quickly.

'That's the key – the one thing that still holds her to her own self!' He swung round to face Neryon. 'The musician, Reyni Trevire – is he here at the cot?'

'Yes, my lord. He came with Shar and Kitto—'

'Fetch him. And a musical instrument; the Sisters must have some. Tell him to choose; something that he played as a boy. *Hurry!*'

Pellis said, 'I'll go,' and ran from the room.

Hestor, Kitto and Reyni were together in the cot's entrance hall when Pellis found them. Her errand was too urgent for any greeting and she only said, 'You're Reyni? Lord Tarod wants you, in the tower, and you're to bring a musical instrument; something you played in your childhood.'

Reyni froze. 'An instrument? But—'

'I don't know why, and there's no time to speculate,' Pellis interrupted. 'Hurry, *please!*'

Reyni still seemed paralysed, but Kitto nudged him hard and hissed, 'Don't argue!' The young musician swallowed. Then he ran towards the cot's music room. In the minute it took him to return, Pellis swiftly told Hestor and Kitto what had happened at the tower. Hestor was stunned.

'A lord of Order – and he and Lord Tarod are working together?' He looked aghast. 'Mother, this must be far worse than we knew! Can they succeed? Can they find Shar?'

Reyni was coming back, and though Pellis wanted to reassure Hestor, there simply wasn't time to spare – and in truth she didn't know the answer herself. Reyni was carrying a small, round-bodied lute, and she hurried him away at once. Hestor and Kitto watched them go out of the gate. They exchanged a look.

'No one's *ordered* us to wait here,' Hestor said.

There was a moment's pause. Then, as one, they raced across the courtyard.

Hestor and Kitto climbed the tower stairs and peered cautiously in at the room's open door. No one noticed them; Kitto stared in trepidation at Ailind, but Hestor was watching Reyni. The musician, under Tarod's direction, was moving hesitantly towards the litter, his face looking unhealthily pallid. Malia was still muttering, but as Reyni drew closer she suddenly stopped. Then, at a nod from Tarod, Ailind made a gesture over her – and her eyes snapped open.

Those eyes were empty. There was no intelligence or recognition in them; they simply stared blankly out at the room without a spark of comprehension. Reyni gazed back with pity and horror. Then Tarod said softly, 'Speak.'

In a voice that shook noticeably Reyni said: 'Hello, Aunt Malia.'

'*Aunt?*' The High Initiate drew in a sharp breath, but a quick warning look from Tarod silenced him. Then Tarod said, 'She doesn't know you, Reyni. But a part of her – her *true* self – remembers your music from years ago. Sing for her now, as you used to when you were a child.'

Reyni lifted the lute. He stroked a chord; then, falteringly at first but gradually gaining strength and confidence, started to sing a children's song with an odd

238

little lilt to it. Malia moaned and he wavered, but Tarod whispered, 'Don't stop! Call her back – make her remember!'

Reyni sang on . . . and a grey haze, like mist, began to materialise above Malia's head. It grew denser, and a face took form in it. It was Malia's face – but unlike the real Malia, this spectre was aware of her surroundings.

'Please . . .' The ghostly lips moved and a distant, ethereal voice echoed through the room. 'Help me . . . Help me . . .'

'He's reached her.' Ailind said.

'Yes – and she's frightened. Reyni, keep singing!' Tarod leaned towards the spectre. 'Malia. Do you know who we are?'

The ghostly figure looked from him to Ailind. 'My lords . . .' she breathed.

'Listen to me, Malia. We can and will help you, but only if you do as we command.'

'Yes . . . oh, yes. The evil holds me and it hurts me . . . I am afraid . . . I want release . . .'

'Then you must listen, and obey,' Ailind told her. 'Show us where the power that controls you has gone. Open the way for us to reach it.'

A look of dread came to the spectre's face, and the mist pulsated violently. 'No! It will punish me – I cannot, I dare not!'

'You must!' Ailind repeated, implacable. 'Or there will be no release for you. Obey, Malia! Open the way!'

'I *cannot!*' The figure in the haze was writhing as though in agony. Reyni, who had stopped singing, cried,

'My lords, have pity on her!' and would have tried to interpose, but Neryon grasped his arm, dragging him forcibly back. Ailind and Tarod ignored them both.

'Submit to us, Malia!' Tarod's voice was as baleful as Ailind's, making Kitto shiver as he listened. 'You have no choice – forge the link between this world and the domain of your masters!'

'No!' Terror filled the ghostly voice and Malia's protests rose to ear-splitting shrillness. 'Oh no, please, *no!*'

'*YES!*' Tarod thundered. He raised his left arm, Ailind his right, and twin tongues of crimson and gold fire cracked from their fingertips and whiplashed across the room. They coiled around the spectral figure; her cry was eclipsed by a hiss like red-hot iron being plunged into water – and on the litter, the real Malia jolted like a puppet jerked by huge, invisible strings. She sat up, her eyes bulging madly. Then her head went back, her mouth opened – and from her throat came a sound that could have wakened the dead. It was a howling, a summoning, such as no human voice should have been able to utter, and it went on and on, louder and wilder, an eldritch call to something far beyond the mortal world. Reyni, horrified, staggered back and collided with Hestor in the doorway; Kitto had clapped his hands over his ears, and Pellis and the High Initiate ran to the litter, grasping Malia's arms and supporting her as it seemed her body must break with the strain. The noise swelled, Malia's mouth stretched wider and wider – then suddenly the tower room seemed to invert, and everything was engulfed by a vast, soundless concussion. In one moment the entire world turned dementedly in on itself, then incredible light and incredible darkness and something else far beyond either detonated from the heart of the mayhem. Hestor had an instant to protect himself from it, and that was nothing like enough. The tidal wave of power hit him. And every sense blanked out.

She was no longer Shar Tillmer but someone – some*thing* – else. She had no will of her own any more; all that remained was a pulsing, hating hunger that beat into her mind like drums. Her own hunger, or the hunger of the Sixth Plane? She didn't know, but it made no difference now. They were one and the same, as the words, the persuasive words, kept telling her. *Dark-Caller. Linked with us and bound to us. Too late to turn back. Dark-Caller. Remember how you called to the dark once before, on the night of the eclipse? The dark is answering you again. The dark will always answer. You cannot escape from the dark.*

Over and over again the words whispered, one voice and yet many together. Shar knew she must listen to what they said. Somewhere in the depths of her soul another tiny voice was screaming at her to resist, but it was growing fainter. There was only the vortex, opening before her to welcome her into its embrace. And, waiting at the month of the vortex, the entity that had controlled Thel and controlled Malia and now controlled her, too. The thing which, for a little while, she had truly believed was her mother. She still couldn't bring herself to look at its face, for it was hideous beyond bearing. But she watched its beckoning claw, and she moved at its command, slowly, dreamily, towards her doom . . .

The blackout must have lasted mere seconds, for when Hestor groggily opened his eyes nearly everything was as it had been before the soundless explosion happened. Tarod and Ailind had not moved. Reyni stood beside him, dazed, the lute hanging limply from his hand. The only differences were that the spectre of Malia had gone and the real Malia, silent now, had collapsed back on the litter, with Pellis and Neryon crouched over her. And Kitto was clinging to Hestor's arm as though he were a long-lost brother newly found. Nothing else had changed.

Or so Hestor thought, until suddenly his mind clicked into focus. For the daylight had gone, and there was someone else in the room.

He gasped incredulously, '*Shar?*'

Tarod's head snapped round. 'Be silent, Hestor!' The warning slammed sharply home and Hestor froze. Kitto, too, had seen now, and his clutching fingers tightened violently as he strove to bite back an incoherent oath.

Shar *was* in the tower – and yet she was not. There was a fog across Hestor's vision; something horribly wrong with the room's dimensions, so that each time he tried to see clearly, all the proportions slipped out of kilter. It was like looking into a pool of murky water . . . and abruptly he realised why.

Shar wasn't truly here; at least, not if *here* meant the mortal world. What they were seeing was a mirror image of the room in the tower; a shadowy replica that shifted in and out like a dark dream. There was a borderline between the two dimensions; Hestor could see it, just a step from where Tarod and Ailind stood tense and motionless. And from beyond it, in a slow, pulsing vibration, came a sense of evil that turned his blood to water.

The barrier between worlds had been breached, and he was gazing into the deadly hinterland of the Sixth Plane.

Shar stood with her back to them. She seemed unaware of the change – but something else was not. There was a portal beyond the room's dark mirror image; a yawning cave of blackness that swirled with an ominous, oily motion. And from the threshold of the portal, a figure glared at the intruders from the mortal world. For a fleeting moment it had the appearance of a human woman . . . then suddenly and shockingly it changed. Hestor's stomach gave a massive lurch and sickness rose in his throat; for this *thing* was a foul, misshapen travesty; hideous and mutated and malignant. As it saw them its blood-red eyes lit with rage, then it opened its distorted mouth, and a psychic stench assailed Hestor's senses as it snarled. On the litter Malia writhed, and Tarod glanced quickly at Pellis and Neryon.

'Shield her, as best you can! She has defied the entity – it may try to kill her, as it did Thel Starnor.'

The Sixth-Plane horror heard him and a mocking, cackling peal of laughter resonated horribly through the tower.

'Fools!' Its voice was as repulsive as its form. '*We* have

243

no more need of such minions! *We* have what we want now! *We* have Shar Tillmer, and you are too late to save her!'

Rage surged in Hestor, and despite Tarod's warning he couldn't control it. 'No!' he cried out. 'Shar! Shar, get *away* from it!'

Ailind turned on him furiously – but Tarod intervened, silencing the lord of Order before he could vent his wrath. Shar had heard. She tensed, then turned, and her eyes – which were dazed and dull – widened as she saw the scene behind her. Her mouth trembled; she tried to say, 'Hestor . . .' But the word wouldn't come, and the Sixth-Plane entity laughed again.

'Too late!' it repeated. 'Too late, and too weak!'

Tarod raised his left arm, fingers outstretched. 'Release her!'

The being hissed scornfully. 'You cannot command *us*. Not Chaos, not Order, not mortals – we are beyond your control!' With an awful, undulating movement it turned towards Shar. 'Come, Shar. See what lies ahead for you. Listen to the dark in your mind. You have no will to resist . . .'

It slithered backwards, and its form began to merge into the portal that was the true entrance to its domain. The portal pulsed, and as the merging was completed the blackness within it came to life, pulsing and throbbing like a huge, abominable heart. From its depths the contorted voice lured again, but this time it was many voices in one, like an unholy choir.

'*Come, Shar . . . Come, Shar . . .*'

Shar whimpered. One foot slid forward, falteringly, and she began to move towards the waiting chasm of darkness.

'Shar, don't!' Hestor called desperately. But she paid no heed. She would not look at him. She was taking another inexorable step, and Hestor's control snapped. Yelling Shar's name at the top of his voice, he flung himself towards the dark otherworld. He would save Shar, he would drag her bodily away, he didn't *care* what happened to him—

His desperate bid was shattered as a flick of power from Tarod's mind sent him ricocheting back as though he had smashed into a stone wall.

'Don't be a fool, boy!' Tarod's green eyes flared lethally as he stared down at Hestor. 'Do you want that monstrosity to destroy you as well?'

Hestor could hear his own pulse rushing in his ears, almost but not quite drowning the sharp, rapid muttering of his mother and the High Initiate as they worked, trance-like, to maintain the psychic shield they had built around Malia. The clash of rhythms made him feel irrationally panicky and he forced the reaction away as he scrambled to his feet. 'But we've got to do something!' he implored. 'Lord Tarod, lord Ailind, please, *please*, help her!'

'We can't help her, Hestor,' Tarod said less ferociously. 'She must help herself. She is the only one, now, who can fight this power!'

Aghast, Hestor protested, 'But before – on the night of the eclipse – Lord Yandros stopped what was happening! He saved the High Initiate—'

'Only because Shar had opened the way! She resisted the power of the entities that tried to control her, and she called on Yandros to finish what she had begun. Without that, he could have done nothing.'

'And we,' Ailind added grimly, 'can do nothing now, unless Shar should will it!'

'*Come, Shar . . . Come, Shar . . .*' Still the baneful call whispered through the room, and Hestor said frantically, 'But she won't, she can't! It's taken her over, it's dragging her into its own world!' He flung a wild glance towards Shar. She was still moving, though with an eerie sluggishness, as if time was running more slowly in the otherworld. There was still a chance – but hope was shrinking with every second. And the pulsing darkness waited.

Hestor's mind was racing turbulently. 'When I called to her, she heard me,' he said urgently. 'For a moment she almost turned back. If I can get through to her again – or if something can—' He hurled a look of frenzied appeal around the room at large. Neryon and Pellis worked on, oblivious to him, while Kitto and Reyni stood as rigid as statues in a tableau, and the rage of frustration boiled over in Hestor at their helplessness, their *uselessness*. There had to be something someone could do!

Then like a starburst it came to him. 'Reyni!' His eyes widened and he lunged forward, grabbing the musician's hand and almost pulling him off balance. 'The ballad! Shar's ballad that you sang at the Quarter-Day feast! Sing it for her again, now!'

Startlingly, his plea was echoed by a moan from Malia on her litter. 'Yes!' Hestor cried. 'Yes, don't you see? It worked for Malia, it freed her from that monstrosity's hold! It might work for Shar, too!'

Like someone locked in a nightmare Reyni looked bewilderedly at Tarod and Ailind. 'My lords . . .?'

Ailind said savagely, 'We're clutching at straws!'

'I agree.' Tarod's eyes had narrowed to slits. 'But what is there to be lost?'

'*Try*, Reyni. Please!' Hestor begged, and now Kitto was adding his own voice. 'You've got to!'

Whey-faced, Reyni looked from the two gods to Malia. Her mouth was moving spasmodically; though she was still unconscious she seemed to be trying to speak. Neryon and Pellis had stopped chanting; their trance broken, they watched her uneasily.

Then Malia whispered, '*Sing me your little song . . . Good child, good child . . .*'

A small, choked sound came from Reyni's throat. He moved forward, holding the lute in a shaking hand. Tarod and Ailind moved aside, and Reyni took up a stance before the unsteady border between worlds. Shar was two paces from the portal now, and the darkness was beginning to stir excitedly, as what dwelt within it anticipated the moment when, finally, she would step into its embrace.

'*Come, Shar . . . Come, Shar . . .*' Hestor felt as through the evil, whispering call was crawling through his skin and lodging in his bones. Reyni shivered at the sound of it; for a few seconds he seemed mesmerised as he stared into the dark otherworld. Then Tarod said gently, 'She has no other hope, musician.'

Reyni raised the lute, gripped it. He began to play . . .

NINETEEN

The sound of the music reached Shar as though through a dense, muffling fog that dimmed it to a ghostly echo. At first it didn't really register in her mind; it was just a noise without any meaning. But after a few moments its familiarity began to tug at the edge of her numbed brain – and so did something else.

Hestor. Someone's name. Someone she knew? She couldn't remember, for it seemed to her that she had had no life before the moment when the call of the Sixth Plane began to rise in her. *Hestor.* Calling to her in another way; shouting to her, a warning—

But then there was the other voice. '*Come, Shar...Come, Shar...*' It was a litany in her head now, and the vortex was before her, waiting to welcome her. Somewhere deep down, a tiny spark of terror was struggling to survive, but she ignored it. She couldn't ignore the music, though. It seemed to be louder, as if whatever made the sound was coming closer. Shar smiled. If it did come closer, then the beings of the Sixth Plane would ensnare it. They would ensnare everything and everyone that came within their reach; like Thel and Malia and her mother–

A sensation as if something had stabbed through her skull made her jolt. *Her mother – Giria – but she was not*

249

Giria, she never had been Giria. She . . . it . . . was—

'*Come, Shar . . . Come, Shar . . .*' The calling, luring voice swelled in her ears, and suddenly she realised what it was and what it meant to do to her. Revenge – for defeating it and thwarting its evil intent; for depriving it of its foothold in the world that it had longed, and tried once before, to devour. For the second time she was trying to rob it of the victims it craved. But this time, there was no one to help her. The entity had turned the tables. *She* was the victim now, trapped by the power within her that had enabled Thel to forge the first link with the elemental planes. That power was rebounding, turning back on her; she should control it, she *should*, but her will and her strength were gone, and the evil was reaching out to her, too compelling to resist. It was the greatest hazard of the Dark-Caller's gift – and it had snared her at last.

'*Come, Shar . . . Come to us . . . To us . . .*' The evil was calling, calling – yet the music was still there, too. It held her by a fragile thread to her own world, and if she could only bring it through the wall of darkness in her mind, she could draw strength from it, the strength she needed to fight.

Then from the heart of the vortex came a new sound; a grim, deep rumbling. The ground beneath Shar's feet heaved, and in the depths of the churning blackness she saw something forming, shifting hugely and relentlessly towards her. A peal of appalling laughter rang out like the howl of a cursed soul, and across dimensions, out of the monstrous demon-world of the Sixth Plane, the horror came overflowing like a boiling cauldron.

'*Hestor!*' It was the only name she had, the only word she could cling to in the wild sea of her mind, and Shar screamed it like a banshee with the last failing shreds of her will. '*Hestor, oh, help me!*'

'*SHAR!*' This time even the gods couldn't react fast enough to stop Hestor. He had no conscious knowledge of what he was doing; all he felt was a colossal internal jolt as though someone had pounded his chest with a sledgehammer, and the insanity of it counted for nothing as the impetus drove him on. He rushed at the barrier between dimensions – behind him he heard a clamour of horrified voices; then came a pulse of incredible heat, a suffocating sensation as though he was plunging through thick oil, and he reeled over the threshold, into the elemental world.

'Shar!' He lunged towards her, but suddenly proportion and perspective went mad and everything turned to dizzying confusion. Shar's swaying figure was a ghost, dancing and flickering in five different places at once; and the walls were toppling in yet never reaching him, and one instant the floor was stone and the next it was glass and the next it wasn't even there at all – Hestor could hear Shar screaming defiance but he didn't know whether she was defying him or the entity or something else entirely, for her voice was shredded into shrill echoes that rang and clashed from every direction. Desperately he grabbed for what he thought was the real Shar's arm, but his hands closed on nothing, and as he spun round, searching, six phantoms of himself spun with him.

'*Shar!*' Hestor tried desperately to ignore the mockeries of his own voice that shouted back, *SharSharShar.* '*Where are you?*'

A subterranean roar answered him and the vortex – that alone had kept its monstrous form and position amid this mayhem – seethed with hungry energy. Black tentacles writhed outwards, hunting towards Hestor like deadly, uncoiling snakes, and the evil flooding from the darkness swelled to an intensity that assaulted his mind in battering waves. Hestor staggered backwards under the psychic onslaught; then one flailing arm struck something solid and suddenly Shar was there – this time it wasn't an illusion – and they tangled together, careening across the room.

'*No!*' Shar shrieked. '*Let me go, let me go!*' Her fists beat at him and he tried to dodge the blows, shouting, '*Shar, it's me, it's Hestor!*' But she didn't understand, she was panicking, and he couldn't stop her because the entity was flooding her with unhuman strength as it dragged her will back towards its control.

'Shar! *Shar!*' But it was useless – he couldn't get through to her and frenziedly he twisted his head around and yelled to where the barrier was, where it *should* be.

'For all the gods' sakes, someone *do something!*'

In the mortal world, Pellis screamed her son's name and fought wildly against Neryon's ferocious hold that kept her from plunging vainly after him. Tarod, too, had tried to break through to the other dimension, but the barrier repulsed him; neither he nor Ailind could enter the elemental worlds, and nor could their influences reach into it. In this, the humans were beyond their help. Reyni sang on – no one had told him to stop, and he didn't know what else to do – and Kitto shouted the ballad along with him, trying to make Shar hear.

'My lords!' the High Initiate called frantically to Tarod and Ailind. 'There must be some way—'

Tarod's voice cut ferociously across his. 'We have no link with Shar! Without that link, we are powerless!'

Ailind's head jerked round at his words, and the lord of Order's eyes blazed like furnaces. 'The link—' In two strides he was at the litter. One hand gestured; there was a *crack* of energy and a network of trapped lightning blazed like a spider's web around Malia's inert figure. In a voice that carried deadly authority Ailind commanded, 'Malia! *Awake!*'

Malia uttered a cry and her eyes snapped open. As she was snatched into consciousness there was a violent pulsation in the otherworld, and the backlash of it seemed to punch through the tower as though the creatures of the Sixth Plane had momentarily broken the barricades that kept the two dimensions apart. Malia screamed again. Something grotesquely alien glared from her eyes; Ailind pounced towards her, but Tarod was faster. His hands clamped against Malia's cheeks and his emerald gaze burned into her and through her as he locked his mind into the link between worlds.

'Shar!' he roared. 'Daughter of Storms and Caller of the Dark! Remember your birthright! *Remember!*'

On the brink of the devouring vortex, where she

struggled against Hestor's frenetic efforts to drag her back, Shar recoiled as Tarod's cry slammed into her mind. The vortex howled, the foul darkness agitating wildly – the barrier broke apart and Hestor felt a huge, malignant charge scourge past him as the entity, distracted from its prey, struck blindly and instinctively at the cause of the intrusion into its domain.

That one moment was enough. Summoning all his strength, all his will, Hestor locked Shar's arms in a tight hold and wrenched her backwards, clear of the vortex. They collapsed and fell – crashing to a floor that warped and bucked and flowed molten under them – and he screamed in her ear, 'Hear, Shar! Hear the gods, and use what they have given you! Command this power – command it!'

A massive shock went through Shar. Her eyes widened as the entity lost its thrall over her, and she realised what she had so nearly done. *Thel, Malia, Giria* – but that creature had never been Giria; it was her enemy, it had deceived her, it had stolen her mother's semblance and used it to trap her; and the trap had almost sprung—

A tidal wave of loathing that matched anything the Sixth-Plane entity could conjure fired to life in Shar's soul. She felt her will gathering, felt the dark quailing before it, and with all the strength she possessed she summoned that will out of the depths of herself, channeling it in a single, searing thrust of power.

The shriek resounded from her throat and from Malia's in a shattering duet. Reacting with pure reflex, Hestor protected his head with one upflung arm, the other clutching Shar to him as he tried to shield her with his body.

An instant later the titanic concussion came. Black light blasted Hestor's eyes, then the world turned upside-down and light, sound, air, every atom of *everything* or so it seemed to him, imploded towards the vortex. Amid the rioting tumult he glimpsed hideous faces screaming in pain and fury, saw tentacles torn apart and tumbling helplessly, and he clung with all his strength to Shar, fighting the pull of the huge wind that ripped past and over them as the power of the dark was sucked back into the churning murk that had spawned it.

Then . . .

Hestor could hear someone breathing, and someone else crying. They were the only sounds to break an otherwise complete silence. After a few seconds he realised that the labouring breaths were his own; very cautiously he raised his head . . .

The vortex, the otherworld, and the evil they had contained, were gone. There was just the room in the Matriarch's tower, with daylight filtering in. And when he peered through the disordered tangle of his hair Hestor saw Shar lying on the floor beside him. She had covered her face with her hands, and feebly he said, 'Shar . . . Shar, don't cry . . .'

His voice was squeaky and shaking, not like his own voice at all. Shar's hands slid away and she blinked.

'I'm not crying . . .' she said unsteadily. 'I think it's . . . your mother . . .' Then her eyes rolled up in their sockets and she fainted.

'Hestor.' Tarod was standing beside him; he reached down and gratefully Hestor took his offered arm. He wondered how many people had ever been helped to their feet by a god, and the thought made him want to giggle, though he didn't know why.

'You'd better sit down,' Tarod said, as calmly as though this were a social occasion. 'Neryon; if there's a chair . . .?'

'But Shar—' Hestor mumbled as he was led to a seat.

'Don't worry; we're looking after her.' Kitto was there, crouching down beside Shar and touching her face gently. His gaze met Hestor's in a quick, meaningful glance and he added, 'Seven Hells, that was—'

'Thank you, Kitto, that's enough,' Tarod warned him.

Kitto gulped. 'Sorry, my lord.' He looked at Shar again, anxiously. 'Will she be all right?'

The Chaos lord's green eyes scanned Shar briefly, then he nodded. 'She's unharmed. She'll suffer nothing worse than shock.'

'And,' said Ailind from where he stood near the litter, 'she has shown us in no uncertain terms the true strength of her powers.' He looked at Tarod and one edge of his mouth twitched faintly. 'You should take a little more care with your protégée, cousin. You nearly lost her this time.'

Tarod raised his dark eyebrows. 'That's matter for the Circle, my friend. We don't interfere in human affairs, remember?'

A faint sound that might have been suppressed laughter came from Ailind's throat. But then his expression changed.

'In truth,' he said, 'None of us can take the real credit for what has been done here.' He gestured towards the litter. 'But for Sister Malia, we – and Shar – would have failed.'

Hestor, who now had Pellis sitting beside him and holding tightly to his hands, looked at the litter. Reyni was crouching by it, he realised, and when he looked at the musician's face he knew immediately that Malia could never be thanked in person. One by one the others gathered round, and for some moments there was silence in the tower room. Malia's face was peaceful, its lines smoothed away, its colour pale but not sickly. She looked as if she was merely asleep. But she was not.

At last the High Initiate said, very quietly, 'I'm sorry, Reyni.'

Reyni looked up. His eyes glittered, but he smiled and shook his head. 'I can't grieve too deeply, sir. She chose her path in the first place; she betrayed everyone . . .' The words tailed off and he sighed. 'I hated her for that.'

'Was that why you were so eager to help Shar?' Neryon asked gently. 'To make up for what your aunt had done?'

'I suppose it was, yes.'

'It wasn't your responsibility, Reyni,' Tarod told him. 'Nonetheless, we all have good reason to thank you. And if it's any comfort, Malia has redeemed herself.'

Reyni nodded again. 'Is she . . . at peace, my lord?'

He was thinking of the malignant entity, and how it had possessed Malia and Thel. 'Yes,' Tarod told him. 'Neither the creatures of the Sixth Plane nor any others can touch her now.'

'And the thing that masqueraded as Giria,' the High Initiate ventured. 'Was it — she — ever human?'

'No, it was not,' said Tarod. 'It was a manifestation of the Sixth Plane, and it found its channel into this world — and its knowledge of the real Giria — through Thel. He didn't call to it, for he had no more sorcerous power; the Circle saw to that. But *it* could still reach out to *him.*'

'For, unlike Malia, Thel never came to regret the evil he did,' Ailind added.

Or at least, Kitto thought, remembering the one plea for help Thel had made before the entity destroyed him, *he only regretted it for a moment.* But he kept the thought to himself and instead murmured, 'Shar doesn't know yet. About what was found at the castle.'

'I'll tell her,' Hestor said quietly.

Kitto looked at him. '*We* will. When she's strong enough.'

Pellis rose to her feet and spoke for the first time, addressing Tarod and Ailind.

'My lords, no one has yet said this, so if I may be the first . . . Thank you. For my son's sake, for mine, for all of us.' She faltered, near tears again. 'Despite Equilibrium and the pact, it seems that we mortals *do* need your intervention sometimes. It's a weakness, I know, but—' She spread her hands helplessly, unable to say any more.

Tarod laughed softly. 'Perhaps,' he said, 'the pact should be interpreted a little more leniently than it has been in the past.' He glanced shrewdly at Ailind. 'Yandros would doubtless agree. And Aeoris?'

Ailind smiled thinly. 'Possibly. If it's in Order's interests, of course.'

'Of course.' Tarod turned to Pellis again. 'Mortals aren't perfect, Adept Pellis – any more than gods are. However, when all work together as we have done here, then I think the best qualities of both sides can be found.' He raised his head and looked around the tower room. Everything had returned to normal; even the daylight was brightening as the sun tried to break through the rain clouds; and when his mind probed deeper dimensions he knew that, at last, there was no taint of darkness left.

'Take Shar to the cot,' he said kindly. 'There will be a great deal to tell her when she wakes. And we,' again he looked at Ailind, 'will have a great deal to tell when we, too, return to our proper places.'

Their gazes met, and a flicker of understanding passed between them. Then Ailind said, 'And who knows, cousin – the tale might be the foundation-stone for something that none of us could ever have predicted.'

Tarod's eyes narrowed, and he seemed to look through the boundaries of the mortal dimension and into another world entirely. 'Yes. Indeed it might.'

From the castle battlements there was an incredible view, with the rugged northern coastline sweeping majestically away on either side and, ahead, the glittering vastness of the sea that reached unbroken to the horizon. Shar leaned on the black stones, feeling the wind in her face and knowing that, at last, she would not cry again.

They had all come home (that word, *home*, was comforting) from Southern Chaun some days ago, as soon as Sister Lellin had pronounced her fit enough to travel. At the castle gates Shar had been met by Amber, who came rushing to meet her with yowls and purrs of welcome that touched her heart to its core. There had been more crying then. And today she had shed her final tears as, in a moving ceremony on the beach below the castle stack, the bones of her mother had been given to the sea and her soul commended to the gods' peace.

The gods . . . both Lord Tarod and Lord Ailind had spoken privately with Shar before they departed for their own realms. She would never reveal what they had said to another living soul; not even to Hestor and Kitto, though she believed they understood, for the lords of Chaos and Order had talked to them, too.

And now . . . well, she thought, her world was almost back to normal. Soon after they returned to the castle, the High Initiate and Physician Eln had asked her if she would like them to perform a ritual for her that would enable her to forget, or at least put away, the experiences of recent days. Shar had thanked them, but said no. She didn't want to forget anything. Somehow, it seemed only right that she should remember.

She wondered how Reyni was, back at his home in Prospect. There would be another ballad for her soon; his own this time. He had promised to send it, and Hestor and Kitto had said they would sing it for her, even if their combined voices did sound – as one of the castle's own musicians had despairingly told them – like crows with a sorrow. The thought made Shar smile, then laugh just a little. That was better. It seemed a long time since she had laughed; she had some catching up to do.

She moved from the seaward side of the wall and looked down into the sunlit courtyard. There were a number of people about, and among them she saw Hestor, heading towards a tutorial class for which, as usual, he was late. His gold initiate's badge glinted in the bright light; looking up, he saw her and waved, then made an 'In a hurry!' gesture and sprinted on. Smiling again, Shar walked towards the roof trapdoor and the stairs that spiralled back down into the castle. At the top of the flight she stopped and looked back. Behind her, the massive bulk of the north spire towered giddyingly into the sky, and in its shadow something small and white moved. It was the cat. Not a mortal animal, she knew it for certain now, but a small servant of the Chaos lords, sent to watch over her. It had been a true friend.

The cat paused, and for a moment its emerald eyes met hers in a look that seemed to convey something old and wise beyond her understanding. Then suddenly, as though it knew she had no more need of its protection, the little creature was no longer there.